DARIUS
THE GREAT
IS NOT OKAY

ADIB KHORRAM

DIAL BOOKS

Dial Books
An imprint of Penguin Random House LLC
375 Hudson Street
New York, NY 10014

Library of Congress Cataloging-in-Publication Data

Names: Khorram, Adib.
Title: Darius the Great is not okay / Adib Khorram.
Description: New York, NY : Dial Books, [2018] | Summary:
Clinically depressed Darius Kellner, a high school sophomore, travels to
Iran to meet his grandparents, but it is their next-door neighbor, Sohrab,
who changes his life.
Identifiers: LCCN 2018009825 | ISBN 9780525552963 (hardback) | ISBN
9780525552987 (ebook)
Subjects: | CYAC: Friendship—Fiction. | Grandparents—Fiction. | Depression,
Mental—Fiction. | Iranian Americans—Fiction. | Americans—Iran—Fiction.
| Iran—Fiction.
Classification: LCC PZ7.1.K5362 Dar 2018 | DDC [Fic]—dc23 LC record
available at https://lccn.loc.gov/2018009825
Printed in the United States of America
ISBN 9780525552963

1 3 5 7 9 10 8 6 4 2

Design by Mina Chung • Text set in Chaparral Pro

FOR MY FAMILY,

FOR ALWAYS KEEPING THE KETTLE ON.

THE CHIEFEST AND
GREATEST OF CALAMITIES

Steam belched and hissed. Sweat trickled down the back of my neck.

Smaug the Terrible was furious with me.

"What does it mean, 'filter error'?" I asked.

"Here." Mr. Apatan wiggled the hose where it fed into Smaug's gleaming chrome back. The blinking red error light went dark. "Better?"

"I think so."

Smaug gurgled happily and began boiling once again.

"Good. Were you pushing buttons?"

"No," I said. "Just to check the temperature."

"You don't have to check it, Darius. It always stays at two-twelve."

"Right."

There was no use arguing with Charles Apatan, Manager of the Tea Haven at the Shoppes at Fairview Court. He was convinced, despite all the articles I printed out for him—he refused to read web pages—that each and every tea should be steeped at a full boil, whether it was a robust Yunnan or a fragile gyokuro.

Not that Tea Haven ever got such fine teas. Everything we sold was *enriched with antioxidants* or *enhanced with natural super-fruit extracts* or *formulated for health and beauty*.

Smaug, the Irrepressibly Finicky, was our industrial-strength water boiler. I named it Smaug my first week on the job, when I got scalded three times in a single shift, but so far the name hadn't stuck with anyone else at Tea Haven.

Mr. Apatan passed me an empty pump-action thermos. "We need more Blueberry Açai Bliss."

I shoveled tea from the bright orange tin into the filter basket, topped it with two scoops of rock sugar, and tucked it under the spigot. Smaug, the Unassailably Pressurized, spat its steaming contents into the thermos. I flinched as boiling water spattered my hands.

Smaug, the Chiefest and Greatest of Calamities, was triumphant once more.

As a people group, Persians are genetically predisposed to like tea. And even though I was only half Persian, I had inherited a full-strength tea-loving gene sequence from my mom.

"You know how Persians make tea?" my mom would ask.

"How?" I would say.

"We put hell in it and we damn it," she would say, and I would laugh because it was funny to hear my mom, who never used colorful metaphors, pretend to curse.

In Farsi, *hel* means "cardamom," which is what makes Persian tea so delicious, and *dam* means "to steep."

When I explained the joke to Mr. Apatan, he was not amused.

"You can't swear at the customers, Darius," he said.

"I wasn't going to. It's Farsi. It's a joke."

"You can't do that."

Charles Apatan was the most literal person I knew.

※ ※ ※

After I replenished our strategically located sample thermoses with fresh tea, I refilled the plastic cups at each station.

I was categorically opposed to plastic sample cups. Everything tasted gross out of plastic, all chemical-y and bland.

It was deeply disgusting.

Not that it made much difference at Tea Haven. The sugar content in our samples was high enough to mask the taste of the plastic cups. Maybe even high enough to dissolve them, given enough time.

The Tea Haven at the Shoppes at Fairview Court was not a bad place to work. Not really. It was a significant upgrade over my last job—spinning the daily special sign at one of those take-it-and-bake-it pizza places—and it would look good on my resume. That way, when I graduated, I could work at an artisanal tea store, instead of one that added the latest superfood extract to whatever dismal fannings the corporate tea blenders could find at the steepest discount.

My dream job was Rose City Teas, this place in the Northwest District that did small-batch, hand-selected teas. There were no artificial flavorings in Rose City's tea. But you had to be eighteen to work there.

I was stuffing the cups into their spring-loaded dispenser when Trent Bolger's hyena laugh rang through the open doorway.

I was completely exposed. The entire front of Tea Haven was composed of giant windows, which, though tinted to reduce sun exposure, still offered a full and enticing view of the wares (and employees) inside.

I silently wished for the sun to bounce off the window,

blinding Trent and cloaking me from what was sure to be an unpleasant encounter. Or, at the very least, for Trent to keep on walking and not recognize me in my work uniform of black shirt and bright blue apron.

It did not work. Trent Bolger rounded the corner and instantly got a sensor lock on me.

He grabbed the doorframe and swung himself into the store, followed by one of his Soulless Minions of Orthodoxy, Chip Cusumano.

"Hey! D's Nuts!"

Trent Bolger never called me Darius. Not if there was a suggestive nickname he could use instead.

Mom always said she named me after Darius the Great, but I think she and Dad were setting themselves up for disappointment, naming me after a historical figure like that. I was many things—D-Hole, D-Wad, D's Nuts—but I was definitely not great.

If anything, I was a great target for Trent Bolger and his Soulless Minions of Orthodoxy. When your name begins with D, the sexual innuendos practically write themselves.

At least Trent was predictable.

Trent Bolger was not technically a bully. Chapel Hill High School—where Trent, Chip, and I were sophomores—had a Zero Tolerance Policy toward bullying.

It also had Zero Tolerance Policies toward fighting, plagiarism, drugs, and alcohol.

And if everyone at Chapel Hill High School tolerated Trent's behavior, that meant he wasn't a bully.

Right?

Trent and I had known each other since kindergarten. We were friends back then, in the way that everyone is friends in kindergarten, before sociopolitical alliances begin to cement, and then, by the time third grade rolls around, you find yourself spending every game of Heads Down, Thumbs Up with your head down and your thumb up, completely ignored by your entire class until you begin to wonder if you've turned invisible.

Trent Bolger was only a Level Two Athlete (Level Three at best). He played something-back on the Chapel Hill High School junior varsity football team (Go Chargers). And he was not particularly good-looking, either. Trent was almost a head shorter than me, with close-cropped black hair, blocky black glasses, and a nose that turned up sharply at the end.

Trent Bolger had the largest nostrils of anyone I had ever seen.

Nonetheless, Trent was disproportionately popular among Chapel Hill High School's sophomore class.

Chip Cusumano was taller, better-looking, and cooler. His hair was long and swoopy on top, with the sides shaved. He had the elegant sort of curved nose you saw in statues and paintings, and his nostrils were perfectly proportioned.

He was also nicer than Trent (to most people if not to me), which of course meant he was far less popular.

Also, his real name was Cyprian, which was an even more unusual name than Darius.

Trent Bolger shared his last name with Fredegar "Fatty" Bolger, a Hobbit from *The Lord of the Rings*. He's the one that stays home in the Shire while Frodo and company go on their adventure.

Fatty Bolger is pretty much the most boring Hobbit ever.

I never called Trent "Fatty" to his face.

It was a Level Five Disaster.

I had avoided letting anyone at Chapel Hill High School know where I worked, specifically to keep that knowledge from falling into the hands of Trent and the Soulless Minions of Orthodoxy.

Chip Cusumano nodded at me from the doorway and began to examine our line of brightly colored steeper mugs. But Trent Bolger headed straight for my station. He was wearing gray swishy shorts and his Chapel Hill High School Wrestling Team sweatshirt.

Trent and Chip both wrestled in the winter. Trent was junior varsity, but Chip had managed a spot on the varsity roster, the only sophomore to do so.

Chip had on his team sweatshirt too, but he wore it with his usual black joggers, the kind with stripes down the sides that taper around the ankles. I never saw Chip in swishy shorts outside of gym class, which I assumed was for the same reason I avoided them.

It was the only thing we had in common.

Trent Bolger stood in front of me, grinning. He knew I couldn't escape him at work.

"Welcome to Tea Haven," I said, which was the Corporate Mandated Greeting. "Would you like to sample one of our fine teas today?"

Technically, I was also supposed to produce a Corporate Mandated Smile, but I was not a miracle worker.

"Do you guys sell tea bags?"

Across the store, Chip smirked and shook his head.

"Uh."

I knew what Trent was trying to do. This was not Chapel Hill High School, and the Tea Haven at the Shoppes at Fairview Court did not have a Zero Tolerance Policy toward bullying.

"No. We only sell mesh strainers and biodegradable sachets."

"That's a shame. I bet you really like tea bags." Trent's grin crept up one side of his face. He only ever smiled with half his mouth. "You just seem like the type of guy who would really enjoy them."

"Um."

"You must get tea-bagged a lot, right?"

"I'm trying to work, Trent," I said. Then, because I had the tingly feeling that Mr. Apatan was somewhere close by, carefully watching and critiquing my customer service, I cleared my throat and asked, "Would you like to try our Orange Blossom Awesome Herbal Tisane?"

I refused to call it tea when it did not contain any actual tea leaves.

"What's it taste like?"

I pulled a sample cup out of the stack, filled it with a pump of Orange Blossom Awesome, and offered it to Trent, using my flat palm as a sort of saucer.

He downed it in one swallow. "Ugh. This tastes like orange juice and balls."

Chip Cusumano laughed into the empty tea tin he was examining. It was one of our new spring-patterned ones, with cherry blossoms on it.

"Did you brew it right, Darius?" Mr. Apatan asked behind me.

Mr. Apatan was even shorter than Fatty Bolger, but somehow he managed to take up more space as he stepped between us to fill a sample cup of his own.

Fatty winked at me. "Catch you later. D-Bag."

D-Bag.

My newest suggestive nickname.

It was only a matter of time.

Trent nodded at Chip, who grinned and waved innocently at me, as if he hadn't just played accomplice to my humiliation. They jostled each other out the door, laughing.

"Thank you for visiting Tea Haven," I said. "Come again soon."

The Corporate Mandated Farewell.

"Did he just call you *tea bag*?" Mr. Apatan asked.

"No."

"Did you tell him about our mesh baskets?"

I nodded.

"Hmm." He slurped his sample. "Well, this is right. Good job, Darius."

"Thanks."

I had done nothing worthy of praise. Anyone could brew Orange Blossom Awesome.

That was the whole point and purpose of Tea Haven.

"Was that a friend of yours from school?"

Clearly the nuances of my interaction with Fatty Bolger, the World's Most Boring Hobbit, were lost on Charles Apatan.

"Next time, have him try the Blueberry Bliss."

"Okay."

TRUCK NUTS

The bike rack for the Shoppes at Fairview Court was located at the far end of the shopping center, right outside one of those clothing stores that catered to Soulless Minions of Orthodoxy like Fatty Bolger and Chip Cusumano. The kind that had pictures of shirtless guys with abdomens that could only be expressed in integers.

Five different kinds of overpowering cologne waged war in my sinuses as I passed the store. When I made it out into the parking lot, the sun was still up, barely, but the mercury lights had come on. The air smelled dry and vacant after weeks of rain.

I had been riding my bike from Chapel Hill High School to the Tea Haven at the Shoppes at Fairview Court ever since I got the job. It was easier than getting a ride from either of my parents.

But when I got to the bike rack, my bicycle was gone.

Upon closer inspection, that was not technically true—only part of my bike was gone. The frame was there, but the wheels were missing. The bike slumped against the post, held on by my lock.

The seat was missing too, and whoever had taken it had left some sort of blue blob in its place.

Well, it was not a blue blob. It was a pair of blue rubber testicles.

I had never seen blue rubber testicles before, but I knew right away where they had come from.

Like I said, there was no Zero Tolerance Policy toward bullying at the Shoppes at Fairview Court. There was one toward stealing, but apparently that didn't cover bicycle seats.

My backpack sagged on my shoulders.

I had to call my dad.

"Darius? Is everything okay?"

Dad always said that. Not *Hi, Darius*, but *Is everything okay?*

"Hey. Can you come pick me up from work?"

"Did something happen?"

It was humiliating, telling my father about the blue rubber testicles, especially because I knew he would laugh.

"Really? You mean like truck nuts?"

"What are truck nuts?"

"People hook them on the hitch of their truck, so it looks like the truck has testicles."

The back of my neck prickled.

In the course of our phone call, my father and I had used the word *testicles* more than was healthy for any father-son relationship.

"All right, I'll be there in a bit. Did you get the goldfish?"

"Um."

Dad breathed a Level Five Disappointed Sigh.

My ears burned. "I'll go grab them now."

"Hey, son."

Dad got out of his car and helped me load my wheel-less, seat-less bike into the trunk of his Audi.

Stephen Kellner loved his Audi.

"Hi, Dad."

"What happened to the truck nuts?"

"I threw them away."

I did not need the reminder.

Dad pressed the button to close the trunk and got back in. I tossed my backpack onto the backseat and then slumped in the passenger seat with the goldfish suspended in their plastic prison between my legs.

"I almost didn't believe you."

"I know."

It had taken him thirty minutes to come get me.

We only lived a ten-minute drive away.

"Sorry about your bike. Does security know who did it?"

I buckled my seat belt. "No. But I'm sure it was Trent Bolger."

Dad put the Audi in drive and took off down the parking lot.

Stephen Kellner liked to drive much too fast, because his Audi had lots of horsepower and he could do that kind of thing: Accelerate to escape velocity, slam the brakes when he had to (in order to avoid running over a toddler holding his brand-new Build-a-Bear), and then accelerate again.

Thankfully, the Audi had all sorts of flashing lights and sensors, so it could sound Red Alert when a collision was imminent.

Dad kept his eyes on the road. "What makes you think it was Trent?"

I wasn't sure I wanted to tell my father the entire humiliating saga.

"Darius?"

Stephen Kellner never took no for an answer.

I told him about Trent and Chip, but only in the broadest strokes. I avoided mentioning Trent's references to tea-bagging.

I did not want to talk to Stephen Kellner about testicles ever again.

"That's it?" Dad shook his head. "How do you know it was them, then?"

I knew, but that never mattered to Stephen Kellner, Devil's Advocate.

"Never mind, Dad."

"You know, if you just stood up for yourself, they'd leave you alone."

I sucked on the tassels of my hoodie.

Stephen Kellner didn't understand anything about the sociopolitical dynamics of Chapel Hill High School.

As we turned onto the freeway, he said, "You need a haircut."

I scratched the back of my head. "It's not that long." My hair barely touched my shoulders, though part of that was how it curled away at the ends.

That didn't matter, though. Stephen Kellner had very short, very straight, very blond hair, and he had very blue eyes too.

My father was pretty much the Übermensch.

I did not inherit any of Dad's good looks.

Well, people said I had his "strong jawline," whatever that meant. But really, I mostly looked like Mom, with black, loosely curled hair and brown eyes.

Standard Persian.

Some people said Dad had Aryan looks, which always made him uncomfortable. The word *Aryan* used to mean noble—it's an old Sanskrit word, and Mom says it's actually the root word for Iran—but it means something different now.

Sometimes I thought about how I was half Aryan and half *Aryan*, but I guess that made me kind of uncomfortable too.

Sometimes I thought about how strange it was that a word could change its meaning so drastically.

Sometimes I thought about how I didn't really feel like Stephen Kellner's son at all.

THE DISTINGUISHED PICARD CRESCENT

Despite what boring Hobbits like Fatty Bolger might have thought, I did not go home and have falafel for dinner.

First of all, falafel is not really a Persian food. Its mysterious origins are lost to a prior age of this world. Whether it came from Egypt or Israel or somewhere else entirely, one thing is certain: Falafel is not Persian.

Second, I did not like falafel because I was categorically opposed to beans. Except jelly beans.

I changed out of my Tea Haven shirt and joined my family at the dinner table. Mom had made spaghetti and meat sauce—perhaps the least Persian food ever, though she did add a bit of turmeric to the sauce, which gave a slight orange cast to the oil in it.

Mom only ever cooked Persian food on the weekends, because pretty much every Persian menu was a complicated affair involving several hours of stewing, and she didn't have the time to devote to a stew when she was overwhelmed with a Level Six Coding Emergency.

Mom was a UX designer at a firm in downtown Portland, which sounded incredibly cool. Except I didn't really understand what it was that Mom actually did.

Dad was a partner in an architecture firm that mostly designed museums and concert halls and other "centerpieces for urban living."

Most nights, we ate dinner at a round, marble-topped table in the corner of the kitchen, all four of us arranged in a little circle: Mom across from Dad, and me across from my little sister, Laleh, who was in second grade.

While I twirled spaghetti around my fork, Laleh launched into a detailed description of her day, including a complete play-by-play of the game of Heads Down, Thumbs Up they played after lunch, in which Laleh was "it" three different times.

She was only in second grade, with an even more Persian name than mine, and yet she was way more popular than I was.

I didn't get it.

"Park never guessed it was me," Laleh said. "He never guesses right."

"It's because you have such a good poker face," I said.

"Probably."

I loved my little sister. Really.

It was impossible not to.

It wasn't the kind of thing I could ever say to anyone. Not out loud, at least. I mean, guys are not supposed to love their little sisters. We can look out for them. We can intimidate whatever dates they bring home, although I hoped that was still a few years away for Laleh. But we can't say we love them. We can't admit to having tea parties or playing dolls with them, because that's unmanly.

But I did play dolls with Laleh. And I had tea parties with her (though I insisted we serve real tea, not imaginary tea, and certainly not anything from Tea Haven). And I was not ashamed of it.

I just didn't tell anyone about it.

That's normal.

Right?

At last, Laleh's story ran out of steam, and she began scooping spaghetti into her mouth with her spoon. My sister always cut her spaghetti up instead of twirling it, which I felt defeated the point and purpose of spaghetti.

I used the lull in conversation to reach across the table for more pasta, but Dad pressed the salad bowl into my hands instead.

There was no point arguing with Stephen Kellner about dietary indiscretions.

"Thanks," I mumbled.

Salad was inferior to spaghetti in every possible way.

After dinner, Dad washed the dishes and I dried them while I waited for my electric kettle to reach 180° Fahrenheit, which is what I liked for steeping my genmaicha.

Genmaicha is a Japanese green tea with toasted rice in it. Sometimes the toasted rice pops like popcorn, leaving little white fluffy clouds in the tea. It's grassy and nutty and delicious, kind of like pistachios. And it's the same greenish yellow color as pistachios too.

No one else in my family drank genmaicha. No one ever drank anything besides Persian tea. Mom and Dad would sniff and sip sometimes, if I made a cup of something and begged them to taste it, but that was it.

My parents didn't know genmaicha had toasted rice in it, mostly because I didn't want Mom to know. Persians have very strong feelings about the proper applications of rice. No True Persian ever popped theirs.

When the dishes were done, Dad and I settled in for our nightly tradition. We sank into the tan suede couch shoulder to shoulder—the only time we ever sat like this—and Dad cued up our next episode of *Star Trek: The Next Generation*.

Every night, Dad and I watched exactly one episode of *Star Trek*. We watched them in broadcast order, starting with *The Original Series*, though things got complicated after the fifth season of *The Next Generation*, since its sixth season overlapped *Deep Space Nine*.

I had long since seen every episode of each series, even *The Animated Series*. Probably more than once, though watching with Dad stretched back to when I was little, and my memory was a bit hazy. But that didn't matter.

One episode a night, every night.

That was our thing.

It felt good to have a thing with Dad, when I could have him to myself for forty-seven minutes, and he could act like he enjoyed my company for the span of one episode.

Tonight, it was "Who Watches the Watchers?" which is an episode from the third season where a pre-warp culture starts to worship Captain Picard as a deity called The Picard.

I could understand their impulse.

Captain Picard was, without doubt, the best captain from *Star Trek*. He was smart; he loved "Tea. Earl Grey. Hot."; and he had the best voice ever: deep and resonant and British.

My own voice was far too squeaky to ever captain a starship.

Not only that, but he was bald and still managed to be confident, which was good, because I had seen pictures of the men on my mom's side of the family, and they all shared the distinguished Picard Crescent.

I didn't take after Stephen Kellner, Teutonic Übermensch, in many ways, but I hoped I would keep a full head of hair like his, even if mine was black and curly. And needed a haircut, according to Übermensch standards.

Sometimes I thought about getting the sides faded, or maybe growing my hair out and doing a man-bun.

That would drive Stephen Kellner crazy.

Captain Picard was delivering his first monologue of the episode when the *doot-doot* klaxon of Mom's computer rang through the house. She was getting a video call. Dad paused the show for a second and glanced up the stairs.

"Uh-oh," he said. "We're being hailed." Dad smiled at me, and I smiled back. Dad and I never smiled at each other—not really—but we were still in our magic forty-seven-minute window where the normal rules didn't apply.

Dad preemptively turned up the volume on the TV. Sure enough, after a second, Mom started yelling in Farsi at her computer.

"Jamsheed!" Mom shouted. I could hear her even over the musical swell right before the act break.

For some reason, whenever she was talking over the computer, Mom had to make sure the sound of her voice reached low Earth orbit.

"Chetori toh?" she bellowed. That's Farsi for "How are you," but only if you are familiar with the person you are speaking to, or older than them. Farsi has different ways of talking to people, depending on the formality of the situation and your relationship to the person you're addressing.

The thing about Farsi is, it's a very deep language: deeply specific, deeply poetic, deeply context-sensitive.

For instance, take my Mom's oldest brother, Jamsheed.

Dayi is the word for uncle. But not just uncle, a specific uncle: your mother's brother. And it's not only the word for uncle— it's also the relationship between you and your uncle. So I could call Dayi Jamsheed my dayi, but he could call me dayi also, as a term of endearment.

My knowledge of Farsi consisted of four primary vectors: (1) familial relations; (2) food words, because Mom always called the Persian food she cooked by its proper name; (3) tea words, because, well, I'm me; and (4) politeness phrases, the sort you learn in middle school foreign language classes, though no middle school in Portland has ever offered Farsi as an option.

The truth was, my Farsi was abysmal. I never really learned growing up.

"I didn't think you'd ever use it," Mom told me when I asked her why, which didn't make any sense, because Mom had Persian friends here in the States, plus all her family back in Iran.

Unlike me, Laleh did speak Farsi, pretty much fluently. When she was a baby, Mom talked to her in Farsi, and had all her friends do the same. Laleh grew up with the ear for it— the uvular fricatives and alveolar trills that I could never get quite right.

When she was a baby, I tried to talk to Laleh in Farsi too. But I never really got the hang of it, and Mom's friends kept correcting me, so after a while I kind of gave up. After that, me and Dad talked to Laleh exclusively in English.

It always seemed like Farsi was this special thing between Mom and Laleh, like *Star Trek* was between Dad and me.

That left the two of us in the dark whenever we were at gatherings with Mom's friends. That was the only time Dad and I were on the same team: when we were stuck with Farsi-speakers and left with each other for company. But even when that happened, we just ended up standing around in a Level Seven Awkward Silence.

Stephen Kellner and I were experts at High Level Awkward Silences.

Laleh flounced onto the couch on Dad's other side and tucked her feet underneath her butt, disturbing the gravitational fields on the couch so Dad leaned away from me and toward her. Dad paused the show. Laleh never watched *Star Trek* with us. It was me and Dad's thing.

"What's up, Laleh?" Dad asked.

"Mom's talking to Dayi Jamsheed," she said. "He's at Mamou and Babou's house right now."

Mamou and Babou were Mom's parents. Their real names were Fariba and Ardeshir, but we always called them Mamou and Babou.

Mamou and *babou* mean mother and father in Dari, which is the dialect my grandparents spoke growing up Zoroastrian in Yazd.

"Stephen! Laleh! Darius!" Mom's voice carried from upstairs. "Come say hello!"

Laleh sprang from the couch and ran back upstairs.

I looked at Dad, who shrugged, and we both followed my sister up to the office.

MOBY THE WHALE

My grandmother loomed large on the monitor, her head tiny and her torso enormous.

I only ever saw my grandparents from an up-the-nose perspective.

She was talking to Laleh in rapid-fire Farsi, something about school, I thought, because Laleh kept switching from Farsi to English for words like *cafeteria* and *Heads Down, Thumbs Up*.

Mamou's picture kept freezing and unfreezing, occasionally turning into chunky blocks as the bandwidth fluctuated.

It was like a garbled transmission from a starship in distress.

"Maman," Mom said, "Darius and Stephen want to say hello."

Maman is another Farsi word that means both a person and a relationship—in this case, mother. But it could also mean grandmother, even though technically that would be *mamanbozorg*.

I was pretty sure *maman* was borrowed from French, but Mom would neither confirm nor deny.

Dad and I knelt on the floor to squeeze our faces into the camera shot, while Laleh sat on Mom's lap in her rolling office chair.

"Eh! Hi, maman! Hi, Stephen! How are you?"

"Hi, Mamou," Dad said.

"Hi," I said.

"I miss you, maman. How is your school? How is work?"

"Um." I never knew how to talk to Mamou, even though I was happy to see her.

23

It was like I had this well inside me, but every time I saw Mamou, it got blocked up. I didn't know how to let my feelings out.

"School is okay. Work is good. Um."

"How is Babou?" Dad asked.

"You know, he is okay," Mamou said. She glanced at Mom and said, "Jamsheed took him to the doctor today."

As she said it, my uncle Jamsheed appeared over her shoulder. His bald head looked even tinier. "Eh! Hi, Darioush! Hi, Laleh! Chetori toh?"

"Khoobam, merci," Laleh said, and before I knew it, she had launched into her third retelling of her latest game of Heads Down, Thumbs Up.

Dad smiled and waved and stood up. My knees were getting sore, so I did the same, and edged toward the door.

Mom nodded along with Laleh and laughed at all the right spots while I followed Dad back down to the living room.

It wasn't like I didn't want to talk to Mamou.

I always wanted to talk to her.

But it was hard. It didn't feel like she was half a world away, it felt like she was half a universe away—like she was coming to me from some alternate reality.

It was like Laleh belonged to that reality, but I was just a guest.

I suppose Dad was a guest too.

At least we had that in common.

Dad and I sat all the way through the ending credits—that was

very sharp memory of Dad yelling at me to stop cry-
could examine my hand, and how I wouldn't let him
cause I was afraid he was going to make it worse.

d I didn't play with the door anymore after that.

d down Dad's bottle and set it on the counter, then
he lid off my own and shook out my pills.

d I both took medication for depression.

from *Star Trek*—and not speaking Farsi—depression
ty much the only thing we had in common. We took
medications, but we did see the same doctor, which
t was kind of weird. I guess I was paranoid Dr. Howell
lk about me to my dad, even though I knew he wasn't
d to do that kind of thing. And Dr. Howell was always
with me, so I tried not to worry so much.

k my pills and gulped down the whole glass of water. Dad
ext to me, watching, like he was worried I was going to
He had this look on his face, the same disappointed look
when I told him about how Fatty Bolger had replaced my
s seat with blue truck nuts.

vas ashamed of me.

vas ashamed of us.

rmensches aren't supposed to need medication.

swallowed his pills dry; his prominent Teutonic Adam's
bobbed up and down as he did it. And then he turned
and said, "So, you heard that Babou went to the doctor
?"

looked down. A Level Three Awkward Silence began to
ce around us, like interstellar hydrogen pulled together
vity to form a new nebula.

part of the tradition too—and then Dad went upstairs to check
on Mom.

Laleh had wandered back down during the last few minutes
of the show, but she stood by the Haft-Seen, watching the goldfish swim in their bowl.

Dad makes us turn our end table into a Haft-Seen on March
1 every year. And every year, Mom tells him that's too early.
And every year, Dad says it's to get us in the Nowruz spirit,
even though Nowruz—the Persian New Year—isn't until the
first day of spring.

Most Haft-Seens have vinegar and sumac and sprouts and
apples and pudding and dried olives and garlic on them—all
things that start with the sound of *S* in Farsi. Some people add
other things that don't begin with *S* to theirs too: symbols of
renewal and prosperity, like mirrors and bowls of coins. And
some families—like ours—have goldfish too. Mom said it
had something to do with the zodiac and Pisces, but then she
admitted that if it weren't for Laleh, who loved taking care of
the goldfish, she wouldn't include them at all.

Sometimes I thought Dad liked Nowruz more than the rest
of us combined.

Maybe it let him feel a little bit Persian.

Maybe it did.

So our Haft-Seen was loaded with everything tradition
allowed, plus a framed photo of Dad in the corner. Laleh insisted
we had to add it, because *Stephen* begins with the sound of *S*.

It was hard to argue with my sister's logic.

"Darius?"

"Yeah?"

"This goldfish only has one eyeball!"

I knelt next to Laleh as she pointed at the fish in question.

"Look!"

It was true. The largest fish, a leviathan nearly the size of Laleh's hand, only had its right eye. The left side of its head—face—(do fish have faces?)—was all smooth, unbroken orange scales.

"You're right," I said. "I didn't notice that."

"I'm going to name him Ahab."

Since Laleh was in charge of feeding the fish, she had also taken upon herself the solemn duty of naming them.

"Captain Ahab had one leg, not one eye," I pointed out. "But it's a good literary reference."

Laleh looked up at me, her eyes big and round. I was kind of jealous of Laleh's eyes. They were huge and blue, just like Dad's. Everyone always said how beautiful Laleh's eyes were.

No one ever told me I had beautiful brown eyes, except Mom, which didn't count because (a) I had inherited them from her, and (b) she was my mom, so she had to say that kind of thing. Just like she had to call me handsome when that wasn't true at all.

"Are you making fun of me?"

"No," I said. "I promise. Ahab is a good name. And I'm proud of you for knowing it. It's from a very famous book."

"Moby the Whale!"

"Right."

I could not bring myself to say *Moby-Dick* in front of my little sister.

"What about the others?"

"He's Simon." She pointed to the
funkel. And that's Bob."

I wondered how Laleh was certai

I wondered how people identified

I decided I didn't want to know.

"Those are all good names. I like tl
Laleh on the head. She squirmed but
away. Just like I had to pretend I did
with my little sister, Laleh had to pre
from her big brother, but she wasn't ve

I took my empty cup of genmaicha to
and dried it by hand. Then I filled a
from the fridge and went to the cabin
one's medicine. I sorted through the
found my own.

"Mind grabbing mine?" Dad asked fr

"Sure."

Dad stepped into the kitchen and slid
this heavy wooden door, on a track so
right behind the oven. I didn't know a
door like that.

When I was little, and Dad had just
Trek, I liked to call it the Turbolift Door.
time, and Dad played too, calling out deck
puter to take us to like we were really on l

Then I accidentally slid the door shut
hard, and ended up sobbing for ten minu
that the door had betrayed me.

I had a
ing so he
hold it be

Dad a

I pull
popped t

Dad a

Aside
was pre
differen

I though
would t
suppose
honest

I too
stood
choke.
he had
bicycle

He

He

Übe

Dad
apple
to me
today'

He

coales

by gr

"Yeah. Um." I swallowed. "For his tumor?"

I still felt weird saying the word out loud.

Tumor.

Babou had a brain tumor.

Dad glanced at the turbolift door, which was still closed, and then back to me. "His latest tests didn't look good."

"Oh." I had never met Babou in person, only over a computer screen. And he never really talked to me. He spoke English well enough, and what few words I could extract from him were accented but articulate.

He just didn't have much to say to me.

I guess I didn't have much to say to him either.

"He's not going to get better, Darius. I'm sorry."

I twisted my glass between my hands.

I was sorry too. But not as sorry as I should have been. And I felt kind of terrible for it.

The thing is, my grandfather's presence in my life had been purely photonic up to that point. I didn't know how to be sad about him dying.

Like I said, the well inside me was blocked.

"What happens now?"

"Your mom and I talked it over," Dad said. "We're going to Iran."

SLINGSHOT MANEUVERS

It wasn't like we could drop everything and leave the next day. Mom and Dad knew it might happen. But we still had to get plane tickets and visas and everything.

So it was a couple weeks later when I sat down at the lunch table and announced, "We're leaving tomorrow."

I immediately executed Evasive Pattern Beta, a swift dodge to the left. My lunch companion, Javaneh Esfahani, tended to spray Dr Pepper out her nostrils if I surprised her at the lunch table.

Javaneh sneezed twice—she always sneezed twice after spraying Dr Pepper out of her nose—and wiped her face with one of the cafeteria-issue brown paper towels. She tucked a lock of hair blown loose by her violent sinus eruptions back into her headscarf.

Javaneh always wore her headscarf at Chapel Hill High School, which I thought was very brave. The sociopolitical landscape of Chapel Hill High School was treacherous enough without giving people an excuse to pick on you.

Javaneh Esfahani was a lioness.

She blinked at me. "Tomorrow? That's fast. You're serious?"

"Yeah. We got our visas and everything."

"Wow."

I mopped up the carbonated explosion on the table while Javaneh sipped her Dr Pepper through a straw.

Javaneh Esfahani claimed she was physiologically incapable

of burping, so she always used a straw to drink her Dr Pepper from the can. To be honest, I wasn't sure that was really a thing—being physiologically incapable of burping—but Javaneh was the closest thing I had to a friend at Chapel Hill High School, so I didn't want to risk alienating her by prying too deeply.

Javaneh had the smooth, olive-toned look of a True Persian, arched eyebrows and all. I was kind of jealous of her—Mom had inherited Mamou's pale coloring, which meant I didn't even get a half dose of Persian melanin—but then again, Javaneh was constantly getting asked where she was from, something I mostly avoided until people learned my first name.

She grabbed a tater tot. "I've always wanted to see Iran. But my parents don't want to risk it."

"Yeah. My mom didn't either, but . . ."

"I can't believe you're really going. You're going to be there for Nowruz!" Javaneh shook her head. "But won't you miss Chaharshanbeh Suri?"

"They were the cheapest tickets," I said. "Besides. We might fly over a fire. That counts, right?"

Chaharshanbeh Suri is the Tuesday night before Nowruz. Which is weird since *Chaharshanbeh* technically means Wednesday. But I guess it sort of means the night before Wednesday. Either way, the traditional way to celebrate Chaharshanbeh Suri is with fire jumping.

(And a mountain of Persian food. There are no Persian celebrations that do not involve enough Persian food to feed the entire Willamette Valley.)

Mom and Dad always took us to the Chaharshanbeh Suri celebration at Oaks Park, where all the True Persians and Fractional Persians and Persians-by-Marriage—regardless of faith—gathered every year for a huge nighttime picnic and bonfire approved by the Fire Marshall of the City of Portland.

Stephen Kellner, with his long legs and Teutonic jumping strength, was an excellent fire jumper.

I was not a fan.

According to family legend, when I was two years old, Dad tried to hold me in his arms as he jumped over the fire, but I wailed and cried so much, he and Mom had to abandon the celebration of Chaharshanbeh Suri and take me home.

Dad didn't try it again. Not until Laleh came along. When Dad held her in his arms and jumped over the fire, she squealed and laughed and clapped and demanded to go again.

My sister was a lot braver than me.

Truth be told, I was not that sad to miss Chaharshanbeh Suri. I was much more comfortable flying over a bonfire at 32,000 feet than I was jumping over one, even if it did deprive Stephen Kellner of another excellent opportunity to be disappointed in me.

After lunch, I headed to the nurse's office. Because of Chapel Hill High School's strict Zero Tolerance Policy toward drugs, the school nurse had to dispense all medications for Chapel Hill High School students.

Mrs. Killinger handed me the little crinkly paper cup with my pill in it. It was the kind used in every mental institution in every movie and television show ever.

Except *Star Trek*, of course, because they used hyposprays to deliver medication directly through the skin in compressed air streams.

There were slightly larger crinkly paper cups for water, which I poured from the drinking fountain in the corner of Mrs. Killinger's office. I couldn't bend over a drinking fountain and take medication that way; I either choked or accidentally spit my pills all over the basin. And I couldn't dry-swallow my pills like Stephen Kellner either; the one time I tried, I got a Prozac lodged in the back of my throat and spent five minutes trying to hack it back up, while it slowly dissolved into skunky powder in my esophagus.

That was before Dr. Howell switched me off Prozac, which gave me mood swings so extreme, they were more like Mood Slingshot Maneuvers, powerful enough to fling me around the sun and accelerate me into a time warp.

I was only on Prozac for three months before Dr. Howell switched me, but it was pretty much the worst three months in the Search for the Right Medication.

Dad never really talked about his own diagnosis for depression. It was lost to the histories of a prior age of this world. All he ever said was that it happened when he was in college, and that his medication had kept him healthy for years, and that I shouldn't worry about it. It wasn't a big deal.

By the time I was diagnosed, and Dr. Howell was trying to find some combination of medications to treat me properly, Stephen Kellner had been managing his depression so long that he couldn't remember what it was like. Or maybe he'd never had

Mood Slingshot Maneuvers in the first place. Maybe his medication had recalibrated his brain right away, and he was back to being a high-functioning Übermensch in no time.

My own brain was much harder to recalibrate. Prozac was the third medication Dr. Howell tried me on, back when I was in eighth grade. And I was on it for six weeks before I experienced my first Slingshot Maneuver, when I freaked out at a kid in my Boy Scouts troop named Vance Henderson, who had made a joke about Mom's accent.

I'd been dealing with jokes like that my entire life—well, ever since I started school, anyway—so it was nothing new. But that time it set me off like a high-yield quantum torpedo.

It was the only time in my life I have ever hit anyone.

I felt very sorry for myself afterward.

And then I felt angry. I really hated Boy Scouts. I hated camping and I hated the other boys, who were all on their way to becoming Soulless Minions of Orthodoxy.

And then I felt ashamed.

I made a lot of Mood Slingshot Maneuvers that afternoon.

But I wasn't ashamed of standing up for Mom, even if it did mean hitting Vance Henderson. Even if it did mean leaving a perfect red palm-print on his face.

Dad was so disappointed.

A NON-PASSIVE FAILURE

Chapel Hill High School had two gymnasiums, supposedly called the Main Gym and the Little Gym, but most of us called them the Boys' Gym and the Girls' Gym, because the boys were always in the larger Main Gym.

This, despite Chapel Hill High School's Zero Tolerance Policy toward sexism.

I was halfway down the stairs to gym when I heard him: Chip Cusumano.

I kept my head down and took the stairs faster, swinging myself around the rail as I reached the landing.

"Hey," he called from behind. "Hey! Darius!"

I ignored him and went faster.

"Wait!" Chip shouted again, his voice echoing off the concrete walls of the stairwell. I had just hit the last landing when he tugged on my backpack.

"Let go."

"Just—"

"Leave me alone, Chip." I jerked forward to loosen his grip.

Instead, my backpack experienced a non-passive failure, splitting across the seam holding the main pocket together. My books and papers spilled down the stairs, but at least my tablet stayed Velcroed in.

"Oh."

"Really, Chip?" I knelt and grabbed for my papers before someone could kick them away. "Thanks. Thanks a lot."

"Sorry." Chip handed me a book from a few steps down. He had this goofy grin on his face as he shook the hair out of his eyes. "I was just gonna tell you your backpack was open."

"Wasn't my bike enough?"

"Hey. That was just a joke."

"Me not having a bike anymore is a joke to you?"

"What are you talking about? Your tires were right in the bushes."

I glared at him.

How was I supposed to know that?

"You never found them?"

"Leave me alone, Chip."

The warning bell rang: One minute to make it to class.

"Come on, man. Let me help."

"Go away." There was no way I was going to trust Cyprian Cusumano to help me.

He shrugged and stood. "Okay. I'll tell Coach Fortes you'll be late."

I got all my papers into a mostly straight pile and sandwiched them between my econ and geometry books.

My backpack was totally unsalvageable: With the seam blown out, the straps had failed as well. The only usable part was the pouch in front holding my pencils.

The tardy bell rang. I knotted the two loose straps together so I could sling the derelict hulk of my backpack over my shoulder like a satchel, gathered my stuff up, and hurried to gym.

Coach Fortes shook his head when he saw my pile of books and the remains of my backpack. "Cusumano told me," he said.

Why do gym teachers always call guys by their last names?

"Sorry, Coach."

Why do guys always call their gym teachers Coach and leave off their name?

"It's fine. Go get dressed."

We were doing our Net Sports Unit, which meant two weeks of Badminton, two weeks of Ping-Pong/Table Tennis, and the grande finale: two weeks of Volleyball.

I was terrible at Net Sports. I wasn't that good at any form of sportsball, really, although I used to play soccer when I was a kid. I did better at the ones where I could at least run around, because I was not bad at running. I had a lot of stamina and I was pretty fast, which surprised people since I was kind of overweight.

Well. Not kind of. I was overweight, period, which is why Stephen Kellner was always handing me the salad bowl.

As if salad would counteract the weight gain from my meds.

As if lack of discipline was the root of all my problems.

As if all the worry about my weight didn't make me feel worse than I already did.

I pulled on my gym clothes—black swishy shorts and a red Chapel Hill Chargers T-shirt—and ran out to join warm-ups. I caught the tail end of sit-ups, and then we had to run laps for five minutes.

Chip Cusumano caught up with me on our third lap. "Hey, D," he said.

Now that he was at Chapel Hill High School, with an enforced Zero Tolerance Policy toward bullying, he couldn't add the -Bag.

I ran faster, and Chip kept pace with me, but at least he wasn't smiling anymore. "I was just gonna tell you your zipper was open. I didn't mean to split your backpack."

"Whatever. At least you can't hide truck nuts in it."

"And I'm sorry about your bike. Really."

I almost believed him.

Almost.

Unlike the rest of the Net Sports Unit, which was haphazardly arranged, we had assigned teams for volleyball. Coach Fortes set us up to play tournament-style. There were no eliminations, but the team with the best record would get extra credit.

I did not understand the point and purpose of assigning extra credit to the winners when they were—statistically speaking—the most likely to be athletic types and therefore the least likely to need the extra credit.

Me being me, I was stuck on a team with Fatty Bolger, which gave him even more opportunities to joke about balls flying at my face.

Like I said. At least he was predictable.

Trent served first—he always served first—and we bump-set-spiked back and forth, while I tried to stay out of Trent's way, because he was a very intense volleyball player. He was especially intense since we were playing against Chip's team. Despite being best friends, Chip and Trent battled like Emotionally Compromised Vulcans when they were on opposing teams.

I didn't get that at all. If I'd had a best friend—Javaneh was my closest friend, but we weren't anything approaching best friends—we would have always been on the same team. Not in the sense of a Net Sports team, but in the sense that I'd be happy for them if they won, and they'd be happy for me if I won.

Fatty elbowed me out of the way to set the ball for Craig, who was in front of us, to spike.

"Get with the program, Kellner!" Coach Fortes shouted.

I was with the program. It's just that Fatty Bolger seemed to be operating a different version of it.

So the next time the ball came at me, I planted myself right under it, locked my elbows and bumped it.

But instead of going upward, the ball shot straight forward, right into the back of Craig's head.

I was terrible at Net Sports.

Craig looked back at me as he scooped up the ball.

"Sorry."

Craig shrugged and tossed the ball under the net to Chip, who was serving next.

"Watch where you're aiming," Trent said. "Terrorist."

This was not the first time I had been called a terrorist. It didn't happen often—no teacher let it slide if they heard it—but school was school, and I was a kid with Middle Eastern heritage, even though I was born and raised in Portland.

It didn't bother me that much.

Not really.

I mean, *D-Bag* was a lot worse.

Terrorist was so ridiculous that I could shrug it off.

Mom always said those kinds of jokes didn't bother her, because Persians couldn't be terrorists. No Persian can get up early enough in the morning to bomb anything.

I knew she said it because it really did bother her. But it was easier if we could make fun of ourselves about it. That way, when boring Hobbits like Fatty Bolger said things, it didn't matter. We had already made the joke ourselves.

I guess it actually did bother me.

Just a little bit.

INTERMIX RATIO

"**H**ey, son. What happened to your backpack?"

I stuck my homework in the Audi's backseat and got in front. "Structural integrity field collapse."

Dad laughed at my *Star Trek* reference, and also because he was finally getting his wish: He had been after me to get a new backpack all semester. "Better at school than in the airport."

"Chip Cusumano wouldn't have been at the airport to rip it open." I explained how it all happened, and Dad started shaking his head about halfway through the story.

"All you have to do is stand up to him."

"I did. He didn't listen."

"He's only doing it because he can tell he's getting to you."

I wondered if that's why Dad treated me the way he did. Because he could tell he was getting to me.

Ever since my bicycle had been removed from active service, I had been taking the bus to school in the morning, and Dad had picked me up in the afternoon to drop me off at Tea Haven. His work schedule was a lot more flexible than Mom's.

I think Dad and I got along as well as we did—which wasn't that well, but still—because I didn't see him that often, with school and then work in the evenings. And when I did see him, it was usually for dinner, when Mom or Laleh were around to provide a buffer, or for *Star Trek*, which was sacrosanct.

The extra time in the car was throwing off our carefully calibrated intermix ratio.

I really did like riding in Dad's Audi, though.

I just couldn't tell him that.

Dad shrugged and waited for an opening to pull away from the curb. "It'll be fine," he said. "We'll get you a new one when we get back. And I'm sure it was just a misunderstanding with Chip."

Stephen Kellner clearly didn't understand my social standing at Chapel Hill High School. He'd never had to deal with the Fatty Bolgers and Cyprian Cusumanos of the world.

Stephen Kellner was a Paragon of Teutonic Masculinity.

"I made us appointments to get haircuts." He turned right out of the parking lot, toward the Shoppes at Fairview Court.

I didn't have to work that night—Mr. Apatan had given me the last week off, to get ready for our trip—but that's where Dad usually got his hair cut.

"Um," I said. "I'm fine."

"You need a haircut." Dad waved his hand up and down in my direction. "This is out of control."

"I like it like this. It's not even that long."

"It's nearly as long as your sister's. What kind of example are you setting for her?"

"No it's not." I mean, maybe it was technically, because my head was larger than Laleh's, but proportionally my hair was still shorter.

"You could at least get it trimmed."

"It's my hair, Dad," I said. "Why is it such a big deal to you, anyway?"

"Because it's ridiculous. Did you ever think that you wouldn't get picked on so much if you weren't so . . ."

Dad worked his jaw back and forth.

"So what, Dad?"

But he didn't answer.

What could he possibly say?

I waited in the car while Dad stomped out and got his hair cut.

I couldn't stand to be in the same place as him. I don't think he could stand to be in the same place as me either.

When we got home, he stormed upstairs to his office without another word. I dropped my decommissioned backpack on the kitchen table and filled the kettle from the pitcher of filtered water I kept on the counter. I always used filtered water—it tasted way better than tap water—though Stephen Kellner liked to complain about the redundancy of keeping a pitcher of filtered water when the refrigerator already had a water filter built in.

Stephen Kellner complained about everything I liked.

In Russia, people use a samovar—a smaller version of Smaug the Voluminous—to heat a bunch of water, and then mix it with über-strong tea from a smaller pot. Persians have adopted that method too, except most Persians use a large kettle and a smaller pot you can stack on top, like a double boiler.

So, when the water boiled, I filled our teapot—a stainless steel one that came in a gift set with the kettle—with three scoops of our Persian tea blend and one sachet of Rose City Earl Grey tea. Mom called it her secret ingredient: It had enough bergamot in it to scent a teapot twice as large as ours, so whenever she had Persian guests they always complimented her on how fragrant her tea was.

43

I pulled down the cardamom jar, pulled out five pods, and stuck them beneath the jar.

Whack, whack, whack!

Maybe I was a little more enthusiastic about smashing hel than usual, after my fight with Dad.

Maybe I was.

I dropped the crushed pods into the pot, filled it with water, and waited for it to finish damming.

Mom picked up Laleh on her way home from work. She went upstairs to pack, while I had tea with Laleh, which was our tradition when I didn't have to work after school.

Laleh always took her tea with three cubes of sugar and one cube of ice, and she always clanged the teaspoon against the sides of her glass teacup as she stirred. Somehow, no matter how hard or how vigorously Laleh stirred, she never slopped tea over the sides of her glass or spilled on herself. I didn't know how she did it.

I still spilled tea on myself at least once a week.

Laleh took a tentative sip, holding her tea with both hands.

"Too hot?"

She smacked her lips. "Nope."

I didn't understand how Laleh could drink lukewarm tea.

"Taste good?"

"Yeah." She took another slurp.

It was nice, sharing tea with Laleh. I didn't get to see her that much on work nights, but like I said, Mr. Apatan had given me the week off. Despite his frustrating literal-mindedness, Mr. Apatan was a pretty cool boss.

"It's your first time going home?" he had asked.

"Uh." I thought it was interesting, how he had called it *home*.

I wondered why he called it that. What made him call Iran home, when he knew I was born and raised in Portland.

"It's my first time to Iran."

"It's so important, you know? To see where you came from." Mr. Apatan was born in Manila, and he still went to visit once a year. "You have a lot of family there?"

"Yeah. My mom has two brothers. And her parents."

"Good." Mr. Apatan had peered at me over the top of his glasses. "Have a good trip, Darius."

"Thanks."

Mom ordered pizza for dinner, to avoid having a big mess to clean up before we left. It was a thin crust, half pepperoni, half pineapple.

Laleh loved pineapple on her pizza.

Normally, I was thrilled to get pizza—it was pretty much the best dietary indiscretion ever—but I could feel Dad watching me at every bite, flaring his nostrils.

First I had refused to cut my hair, and now I was eating pizza.

And there weren't even any vegetables on it.

Laleh told us how her teacher had googled pictures of Iran to show the class where Laleh was going, which I thought was pretty cool.

"How about your day, Darius?" Mom asked.

"It was okay."

"How were your classes?"

"Um. Econ was okay. Gym was okay." I didn't want to get

into being called a terrorist. "You heard about my backpack."

"What happened to your backpack?" Laleh asked.

"Uh. It broke."

"How?"

"Chip Cusumano broke it when he pulled on it too hard."

"That was rude!"

Dad huffed. Mom glared at him.

"Yeah," I agreed.

"Maybe if you . . ." Dad began, but Mom cut him off.

"We'll get you a new one when we get home. But your dad has a bag you can borrow. Right?"

Dad looked at Mom. It was like they were exchanging telepathic messages.

"Right. Sure."

I wasn't sure I wanted to borrow anything of Stephen Kellner's.

But I didn't have much choice.

We didn't watch *The Next Generation* that night. There wasn't time, with all the packing.

Besides, *Star Trek* was when we acted like we were a real father and son.

Neither of us felt like acting that night.

I was folding up my boxers when Mom hollered that Mamou and Babou were on Skype.

"Mamou, Babou," Mom said. "Darioush is here."

Mom did that sometimes: call me Darioush instead of Darius.

Darioush is the original Persian version of the name Darius.

I had made it my Priority One Goal in life never to let Trent

Bolger, or any of his Soulless Minions of Orthodoxy, learn the Persian pronunciation of my name, which is *Darr-yoosh*.

It was an even more imperative goal, now that I was D-Bag.

The opportunities for rhyming were too gruesome to consider.

I squeezed myself into frame, looming over Mom's shoulder. Mamou and Babou were squeezed next to each other in two seats. Babou sat back a bit, looking at the monitor over the rim of his glasses.

"Hi, maman!" Mamou said. Her smile looked ready to burst through the screen. "I'm so happy to see you soon."

"Me too. Um. Do you need anything from Portland?"

"No, thank you. Just you come."

"Okay. Hi, Babou."

"Hello, baba," my grandfather said. His voice was gravelly, and his accent was heavier than Mamou's. "Soon you will be here."

"Yeah. Um. Yeah."

Babou blinked at me. He didn't smile, not really, but he didn't frown either.

This is how most of my conversations with Babou went.

We didn't know how to talk to each other.

I studied my grandfather in the monitor. He didn't look any different. He had the same severe eyebrows, the mustache that quivered when he spoke, the distinguished Picard Crescent (though his was a bit fluffier, since his hair was curly like mine).

But according to Mom and Dad, he was dying.

I didn't know how to talk about that. About how sad I was. About how bad I felt.

And I didn't know how to tell him I was excited to finally meet him either.

I mean, you can't just tell your own grandfather "Nice to meet you."

I had his blood in me. His and Mamou's. They weren't strangers.

But I was about to meet them for the first time.

My chest started to clench up.

"Um." I swallowed. "I better go finish packing."

Babou cleared his throat. And then he said, "See you soon, Darioush."

OLYMPUS MONS

Here's the thing:

No one should have to wake up at three o'clock in the morning.

My phone was set to play the *Enterprise*'s RED ALERT sound as an alarm, but even with the klaxon going off, I wanted to pull the pillow over my head and go back to sleep.

But waking up at three in the morning wasn't even the worst part. That was waiting for me when I looked in the mirror.

My forehead had become host to an alien parasite: the biggest pimple I'd ever had in my entire life.

It was glowing red and ominous between my eyebrows like the Eye of Sauron, lidless and wreathed in flame. It was so massive, it emitted its own gravitational field.

I was certain that, if I popped it, the implosion would suck me, my family, and our whole house into a singularity we'd never escape.

But I did pop it. I couldn't travel with an alien organism inhabiting my face.

I swear it smelled like natural gas and pu-erh tea when it ruptured, which was weird and gross.

I never drank pu-erh. It was the one category of tea I could never learn to love. It smelled like compost and tasted like week-old sushi, no matter how many kinds I tried or how many steepings I did.

The pimple bled for a long time. I scrubbed at its remains in the shower with my oil-control acne-fighting face wash, and my forehead was still stinging as I got dressed.

Without my backpack, I had to use one of Dad's messenger bags from work as my carry-on, or "personal item."

Like I said, I didn't understand the point and purpose of messenger bags. The one Dad lent me had his company logo on it: a stylized *K* and a stylized *N,* made out of scale rules and T-squares and drafting pencils, even though Kellner & Newton had been entirely digital since before I was born.

I'd packed my suitcase the night before, but I had left the Kellner & Newton Messenger Bag for the morning. That was a mistake.

Stephen Kellner of Kellner & Newton was not very pleasant at 3:30 in the morning. Especially since he was clearly still mad at me.

"Darius." He poked his head in my room. "We've got to go in thirty minutes. Why are you still packing?"

"It's just my carry-on. I'll be ready."

"Don't forget your passport. Or your meds."

I had already checked five different times that my passport was in the front pocket of the Kellner & Newton Messenger Bag. And I'd checked my meds three times.

I said, "I got it, Dad."

It was hard to fit books into the messenger bag. My backpack, of blessed memory, could fit four schoolbooks in it, but the Kellner & Newton Messenger Bag was clearly designed for product placement and not storage capacity. I was only able to squeeze one book in, sandwiched between the packets of homework I planned to do on the plane.

I chose *The Lord of the Rings,* since I hadn't read it in over a year, and it was long enough to last me a good portion of the trip.

I also had to fit in a pyramid tin from Rose City Teas: some loose leaf FTGFOP1 First Flush Darjeeling I bought as a gift for Mamou. It had this sort of fruity, floral scent, but the taste was smooth.

FTGFOP means Finest Tippy Golden Flowering Orange Pekoe, which is the highest grade of tea leaf, and the "1" means the very best of the FTGFOP leaves.

Mr. Apatan got mad if I ever mentioned tea grading at Tea Haven. He said it was "elitist."

I really hoped Mamou would like the tea. Persians are notoriously picky about their tea—like I said, I had to keep the ingredients in genmaicha a secret from my own mother— but I couldn't think of anything else that would make a nice enough gift.

It was hard to shop for someone I barely knew, even if it was my own grandmother.

"Darius!" Dad bellowed from downstairs.

"Coming!"

My sister did not function well at 4:30 in the morning, which is when we pulled into the parking garage at Portland International Airport.

I was grateful—grudgingly—for the Kellner & Newton Messenger Bag, because I was able to sling it in front of me and carry my sister piggyback through the airport until we reached security, while Mom and Dad pulled our luggage. It was windy, and Laleh's fine hair kept blowing into my mouth. It smelled like strawberries, because of her shampoo, but it did not taste like strawberries at all.

"You got her?" Dad asked.

"Yeah. I'm good."

"Okay." Dad glanced at Laleh's sleeping face for a moment and then back at me. "Thanks, Darius."

"Sure."

The woman in front of us at the TSA Security Checkpoint was wearing knee-high combat boots. Who wears knee-high combat boots on an airplane? They were black leather, with steel toes and acid-green laces that ran from ankle to bony kneecap, where they ended in neon bunny ears.

Combat Boot Lady wore a too-large Seattle Seahawks jersey and a pair of sweat shorts, which I felt somehow explained everything.

The combat boots were too large for the gray plastic tubs, so Combat Boot Lady tossed them onto the conveyer belt behind her bin of less than 3.4 ounces of fluids (in a clear plastic bag) and stepped through the backscatter X-ray chamber.

The TSA agent at the scanner yawned and stretched so hard, I thought the buttons would pop off his uniform and fly everywhere. I could smell his coffee breath from the other side of the line.

He scratched his nose and nodded at Combat Boot Lady.

"Laleh." I jiggled her legs up and down where they rested in my elbows. "Time to wake up."

"I'm tired," Laleh said, but she let me put her down. She was still in her pajamas, except for her little white tennis shoes.

My sister had the cleanest white tennis shoes of any eight-year-old ever. I didn't know how she kept them so pristine.

"We can sleep on the plane. But you have to go through the scanner first."

I tossed my Kellner & Newton Messenger Bag on the conveyer belt, double-checked all my pockets, and waited for Laleh to get the all-clear so I could take my turn in the scanner.

I stood with my arms above my head and had to resist saying "Energize!"

I felt like I was on a transporter pad, except no one ever had to hold their hands above their head for three seconds on the *Enterprise*.

I was "randomly selected" for an enhanced screening after that, even though my messenger bag had nothing liquid, gel, or aerosol in it.

"Where are you headed?" asked the officer—a burly guy with dark, angular eyebrows and a round face—as he ran the little brown paper over my hands.

"Um. Yazd. I mean, we're flying into Tehran. But my grandfather lives in Yazd." The officer stared at me, still holding my palm with one of his blue-gloved hands, which made me nervous. "He has a brain tumor."

"Sorry to hear that." The machine beeped. "Good to go."

He threw away the paper swab and looked me over again.

"I didn't realize your people did the dot thing too."

"Um. The dot thing?"

"You know." He tapped his index finger against his forehead, right between his robust eyebrows.

I placed a fingertip in the same spot on my own forehead and felt the scabbed-over ruins of Olympus Mons, which is what I had decided to name the remains of my pimple.

Olympus Mons is the highest peak on Mars. It's a volcano nearly sixteen miles high, and it takes up more square mileage than the entire state of Oregon. Technically, Olympus Mons would have been a better name for the pimple in its un-popped state, since the scab looked more like a crater than a volcano, but it was the best I could do at three in the morning.

"Um." My ears burned. "It was a pimple."

The officer laughed so hard, his face turned red.

It was deeply embarrassing.

TEMPORAL DISPLACEMENT

That morning, we flew from Portland to New York. Our connection to Dubai wasn't until the evening.

I slept all the way to JFK, with my head against the window and my knees pressed up against the seat in front of me. Since New York was three hours ahead of Portland, it was past lunch by the time we landed. We ate a cursory meal in the food court (I had a salad to appease Dad, who was unhappy I had finished off the cold pizza for breakfast), and then Laleh used the rest of our interminable layover to visit every single store and stall in JFK's Terminal 4.

Our flight to Dubai was fourteen hours, and we crossed another eight time zones. I was wide-awake. Laleh had acquired a bag of Sour Patch Kids while she browsed Terminal 4, and the combination of sugar and temporal distortion proved an incendiary one.

She turned around and stuck her face between her and Dad's seats, peppering Mom with questions about Iran, about Yazd, about Mamou and Babou. Where were we going to sleep? What were we going to do? What were we going to eat? When would we arrive? Who was going to get us at the airport?

A knot started forming, right in the middle of my solar plexus.

All those questions were making me nervous, because Laleh wasn't asking the really important questions.

What if they didn't let us in?

What if there was trouble at Customs?

What if it was weird?

What if no one liked us?

Laleh finally tired out at about midnight Portland time, though I had no idea what the local time was, or even what time zone we were in. She turned around and leaned against Dad's shoulder and fell asleep.

Mom played with my hair, twisting the curls around her fingers, as I steeped a sachet of Rose City's Sencha (a Japanese green tea) in the little paper cup of hot water I got from our flight attendant.

I pulled the sachet out and dropped it in the empty cup of water I'd used to take my medicine.

"Hey, Darius. Can I talk to you about something?"

"Sure."

Mom pursed her lips and dropped her hand.

"Mom?"

"Sorry. I don't really know how to explain it. It's . . . I just want you to be prepared. People in Iran don't think about mental health the way we do back home."

"Um."

"So if anyone says anything to you, don't take it personally. Okay, sweetie?"

I blinked. "Okay."

Mom's hand returned to my head. I sipped my tea.

"Hey. Mom?"

"Hm?"

"Are you nervous?"

"A little."

"Because of me and Dad?"

"No. Of course not."

"How come, then?"

Mom smiled, but her eyes were sad. "I should have gone back a lot sooner."

"Oh." The knot in my solar plexus tightened. Mom pushed a loose strand of hair behind my ear as I stared out the window.

I had never flown over an ocean before. It was night out, and looking down at all that black water below, capped white where the moon glinted off the swells, left me feeling like we were the last humans left alive on planet Earth.

"Mom?"

"Yeah?"

"I'm a little nervous too."

It was night again when we landed at Dubai International Airport. We had flown all the way into one day and back out again.

I couldn't remember the last time I had taken my medication. Or brushed my teeth. And my face felt oily enough to generate two or three more Olympus Mons–sized pimples.

My body said it was yesterday, but the clocks said it was tomorrow.

This is why I hate time travel.

"Our flight's in three hours," Mom said as I stood and stretched, bending over Laleh's seat to try and extend my back. "We should grab some dinner."

"Is it dinner?" My body didn't think so. All I could think about was a hot cup of tea. I had been cultivating a headache for the last few hours—the kind of headache that felt like it was going to pop my eyes right out of my skull—and caffeine usually helped.

Laleh was hangry, the first sign of an impending Laleh-pocalypse. She dragged her feet down the jet bridge, holding my hand and staring at the floor desultorily, until we stepped into the terminal and she caught the scent of Subway.

Subway was my sister's favorite restaurant.

The glow cast by the white and yellow letters instantly rejuvenated her. She wrenched her hand out of mine and sprinted straight for it. I chased her, my Kellner & Newton Messenger Bag banging against my legs.

I detested messenger bags.

"Can we have Subway?" Laleh asked.

"We have to ask Mom and Dad."

"Mom? Dad? Can we?" Her voice was getting whinier by the second, the pitch rising higher and higher like a teakettle on the cusp of whistling.

"Sure, sweetie." Mom studied the menu. Even in the United Arab Emirates, Subway was Subway. The menu was pretty much the same as it was in Portland, except for a seafood sub and a chicken tikka masala sub.

Dad shifted his own Kellner & Newton Messenger Bag on his shoulder. His was dark leather with the logo embossed on it—much nicer than my canvas-and-polyester one. "What do you want?"

"Um." My stomach gurgled.

I had eaten two meals on the plane—a sort-of dinner and

a sort-of breakfast—and though neither of them left me that satisfied, I did not want Subway.

I couldn't stand the smell of Subway—not since my old job spinning signs for the pizza place. It had been across the parking lot from a Subway, and ever since, I couldn't smell baking Subway bread without feeling trapped and claustrophobic from the porcupine costume I was forced to wear.

What kind of pizza place has a porcupine for a mascot?

"Um," I said again. "I don't really feel like Subway."

"You can't keep eating Laleh's Sour Patch Kids."

Stephen Kellner was extremely attentive to my dietary indiscretions.

I studied the menu. "Um. The chicken tikka masala sub?"

Dad sighed. "There's nothing with vegetables that sounds good?"

"Stephen," Mom said. She looked at Dad, and they seemed to be exchanging some sort of subspace communiqués. Laleh rocked back and forth on her heels and glanced at the counter. She was dangerously close to full-on Laleh-geddon.

"Never mind. I'm not that hungry anyway."

"Darius," Mom said, but I shook my head.

"It's fine. I have to use the bathroom."

I stayed in the bathroom as long as I could.

I still had some of Laleh's Sour Patch Kids left.

But when I couldn't hide any longer, I found Mom, Dad, and Laleh seated around a brushed-steel table with little blue hourglass-shaped stools. Laleh had demolished her meatball sub, leaving gallons of sauce spread around her mouth: a conquering Klingon warrior drenched in the blood of her enemies. She was licking her fingers clean, ignoring Mom and Dad's conversation.

"You can't keep trying to control him," Mom said. "You have to let him make his own decisions."

"You know how he gets treated," Dad said. "You really want that for him?"

"No. But how is making him ashamed of everything going to fix it?"

"I don't want him to be ashamed," Dad said. "But he's got enough going on with his depression, he doesn't need to be bullied all the time too. He wouldn't be such a target if he fit in more. If he could just, you know, act a little more normal."

Mom glared at Dad as soon as she saw me. "Here," she said, pulling out a seat for me. "You sure you don't want something? We can go somewhere else."

"I'm okay. Thanks."

"You feeling all right?" Mom pressed the back of her hand against my forehead. It was greasy from being on the stuffy plane for so long.

"Yeah. I'm fine. Sorry."

Dad wouldn't look at me. He kept studying his hands, wiping at them with his white Subway-brand napkin, though I doubted they were dirty, since he'd eaten a salad.

Stephen Kellner always ordered salad at Subway.

"I'll be right back. Anybody need anything?"

Mom shook her head. Dad grabbed his empty water cup and took it back for a refill.

Once he was out of earshot, Mom said, "Darius . . ."

"It's fine," I said.

"Don't be mad." She squeezed my hand. "He just . . ."

Laleh chose that moment to let out a huge, resonant burp.

Unlike Javaneh Esfahani, Laleh was perfectly capable of burping.

I laughed, but Mom was appalled.

"Laleh!"

"Sorry," she said, but at least she was smiling again.

Thankfully, the meatball sub had averted the impending Laleh-clysm.

She was still giggling when Dad sat back down. He dipped his napkin in his ice water and handed it to Laleh for her to clean off her mouth, but it was a lost cause.

"Here," Mom said, standing. "Let's go to the bathroom, Laleh. Come on."

A Level Six Awkward Silence descended upon us, despite the bustle of the terminal all around.

Awkward Silences were powerful like that.

"Hey." Dad cleared his throat. "About earlier."

I glanced up at Dad, but he was staring at his hands.

Stephen Kellner had angular, powerful hands. Exactly what you'd expect from an Übermensch.

"Let's try to get along. Okay? I want you to enjoy this trip."

"Okay."

"I'm sorry."

"It's fine."

I mean, it wasn't fine.

I wasn't even sure which part he thought he was apologizing for.

I still had a knot in my solar plexus.

Like I said, Dad and I only got along if we didn't see each other that much, and the trip to Iran had already compromised our intermix ratio.

But then Dad looked at me and said, "Love you, Darius."

And I said, "Love you, Dad."

And that meant we weren't going to talk about it anymore.

I couldn't sleep at all on the flight to Tehran. We were scheduled to arrive at Tehran Imam Khomeini International Airport at 2:35 a.m. local time, which constituted a thirty-minute journey into the future.

I didn't understand. What was the point and purpose of a half-hour temporal displacement?

As the flight attendants wandered the aisles collecting all the tiny plastic bottles of alcohol, the women on the flight started pulling headscarves out of their carry-ons and covering their hair.

Laleh was young enough that she didn't technically have to wear one, but Mom thought it would be a good idea anyway. She handed Dad a light pink scarf over the back of the seat, and Dad wrapped it around Laleh's head. Mom's own headscarf was dark blue, with peacock feather designs embroidered on it.

My heart did its own sort of feathery flutter when the captain said to prepare for arrival, and the plane began to descend.

The smog blanketing Tehran was transformed into dense orange clouds by the lights of the city below, and then we were flying through it and I couldn't see anything else. We were soaring through a golden, glowing void.

"I don't want to fly anymore," Laleh announced. She scratched at her headscarf but refused to let Dad adjust it for her. "My head itches."

"Soon, Laleh," Mom said over the seat. She whispered something to Laleh—something in Farsi, I couldn't catch what—and then leaned back and took my hand.

She wrapped our fingers together and smiled at me.

We were nearly there.

I couldn't quite believe it.

There was only one stall open as we wound our way through Customs. The officer on duty looked like he was experiencing a bit of chronometric distortion himself. He had Level Eight Bags under his eyes, and he yawned every time someone new handed him a passport. Part of me expected the Customs officer to have a turban and a full beard, like all the other Middle Easterners on TV. Which was sad, since I knew it was just a stereotype. I mean, I knew plenty of Middle Easterners myself that didn't fit that image.

The Customs officer was pale, even paler than Mom, with green eyes, auburn hair, and a five o'clock shadow. Or five thirty, given the temporal displacement.

Apparently, green eyes are common in Northern Iran.

I kind of wished I had green, Northern Iranian eyes myself.

The officer glanced at Dad, then at me, and then his eyes skimmed Mom and Laleh before locking back onto Dad. "Passports?" His voice was grainy, like mustard, and his accent wasn't much stronger than Mom's. He flipped through all our passports, holding the picture page up to us to check that we were, in fact, who the United States Department of State claimed we were. "Why did you come to Iran?"

"Tourism," Dad said, because that is what he was supposed to say. But Stephen Kellner was genetically incapable of deception. "And we're visiting my wife's family in Yazd. Her father is ill."

"Do you understand Farsi?"

"No. My wife does."

The Customs officer turned to Mom and asked her a few questions in Farsi, too fast for me to make out any words other than *you* (he used the formal *shomaa*). He nodded and handed back our passports.

"Welcome to Iran."

"Merci," Dad said.

Farsi and French use the exact same word for "thank you." Mom had never been able to adequately explain why.

I tucked my passport back into my borrowed messenger bag and snapped the clasp shut before following Dad. Behind us, Laleh clung to Mom's hand, dragging her feet so her shoes squeaked on the tile floor.

"I'm tired," she reminded us.

"I know, sweetie," Mom said. "You can rest on the way to Yazd."

"My feet hurt."

"I can carry her," I said, but then I had to stop, because another Customs officer stepped right in front of me with his hand up.

"Come with me, please," he said.

"Uh."

My first instinct was to run.

Unlike his predecessor, Customs Officer II did not look sleepy at all. He looked keen and alert. His eyebrows contracted into a sharp arrow above his long nose.

"Um. Okay. Mom?"

Mom called to Dad, who hadn't noticed I'd been stopped. She

tried to follow me, dragging Laleh, who skidded across the tile floor on her rubber soles, but the officer held up his hand, careful not to touch her.

"Only him."

I wondered what I had done that made him single me out.

I wondered what made me such a target.

I wondered what it was he wanted.

Mom said something in Farsi, and the officer answered, but again, it was too fast for me to make anything out. Not that I could have made out much, unless they were talking about food.

Customs Officer II shook his head, took me by the elbow, and led me away.

There is an episode in the sixth season of *Star Trek: The Next Generation* called "Chain of Command."

Actually, it's a two-part episode, so it's "Chain of Command, Parts I & II." In it, Captain Picard gets captured by Cardassians at the end of Part I, and spends most of Part II getting interrogated and tortured. The interrogator, Gul Madred, shines four lights in Captain Picard's face and keeps asking how many there are.

Every time, Captain Picard answers "four," but Gul Madred tries to break him by insisting there are five.

Customs Officer II led me to a small room.

There were four fluorescent lights in the ceiling.

When he sat down behind a large wood-grained desk—the kind where it was obviously not made of wood, but covered with something that looked like it—my heart thundered.

Unlike Customs Officer I, Customs Officer II did have the full and resplendent beard of a True Persian.

"Passport?"

His voice was deep, crisp, and heavy.

I dug through my Kellner & Newton Messenger Bag, wishing again for my old backpack, my fingers fumbling for the passport I had slid inside only a few minutes before.

"Why are you in Iran?"

"Visiting my family," I said. "My grandfather has a brain tumor."

Customs Officer II nodded and wrote something down. He didn't look particularly sorry about my grandfather's brain tumor.

There was a dark window behind his seat—one of those windows that you can see through from only one direction.

I didn't get why they were called two-way mirrors when they were really one-way windows.

"How long are you here for?"

"Um. Leaving April third."

"You have your papers? Airline tickets?"

I swallowed. "My dad has everything."

"Where is your father?"

"Outside." I hoped.

I assumed Mom had stopped him, but it would not be the first time Stephen Kellner had accidentally left me behind.

Mom still liked to tell the story of my first real trip to the grocery store. Apparently I managed to climb out of the shopping cart on my own and start wandering the aisles, and Dad didn't realize I wasn't sitting in the cart until he reached the cash register.

I scratched my ear. Customs Officer II was still writing. I couldn't read Farsi at all, not even food words, but it made me nervous.

There were four lights.

"What is in your bag?"

I was so nervous, I dropped it.

"Sorry. Um. It's my homework. For school. And a book. And my medicine."

He opened and closed his hand, gesturing for me to hand it over. I picked the messenger bag off the floor and passed it to him. He dug through it, pulling out my school papers and *The Lord of the Rings*.

He thumbed through *The Lord of the Rings* for a minute and then tossed it aside, digging deeper until he pulled out my little orange child-proof medicine bottle.

"You have prescription?"

I nodded. "Yeah. Um. At home. It's written on the bottle."

"What is this for?"

"Depression."

"That's all it's for? What are you depressed about?"

My ears burned. I glanced up at the four lights and hoped I wasn't going to be chained to the ceiling and stripped naked.

I hated that question: *What are you depressed about?* Because the answer was *nothing*.

I had nothing to be depressed about. Nothing really bad had ever happened to me.

I felt so inadequate.

Dad told me I couldn't help my brain chemistry any more than I could help having brown eyes. Dr. Howell always told me not to be ashamed.

But moments like this made it hard not to be.

"Nothing," I said. "My brain just makes the wrong chemicals is all."

"Probably your diet," Customs Officer II said. He looked me up and down. "Too many sweets."

I swallowed away the sand in my throat. My ears burned hotter than a matter/antimatter reaction chamber.

Customs Officer II pointed at the Kellner & Newton logo stitched onto the corner of my messenger bag's front flap. "What is this?"

"Um. My dad's company. He and his partner are architects."

Customs Officer II's eyebrows shot up. "Architects?"

"Yes."

And then he smiled, a smile so big and bright, it was like the room really did have five lights.

It was the most stunning (and alarming) transformation I had ever witnessed.

"We have lots of architecture in my country," he said. "You must see the Azadi Tower."

"Um." I had seen pictures of the Azadi Tower, and it was stunning—gleaming white angles intertwining into a tall edifice, with intricate latticework that made me think of *The Lord of the Rings*.

Only Elves could have wrought something so delicate and fantastic.

"And the Tehran Museum."

I didn't know that one.

"And the Shah Cheragh in Shiraz."

That one I had heard of. It was a mosque covered with mirrors on the inside, and the reflected light turned the whole thing into a shimmering jewel box.

"Okay."

"Here." He shoved my papers and medicine back into the Kellner & Newton Messenger Bag. I slung it over my shoulder.

"You can go," he said. "Welcome to Iran."

I wasn't sure what was happening, but I said thank you and backed out of the room.

Part of me wanted to shout, "THERE! ARE! FOUR! LIGHTS!" as I left, the way Captain Picard did when he was finally released, but Customs Officer II seemed to have decided he liked me, and I didn't want to ruin it with a reference he probably wouldn't understand.

Besides.

I didn't want to cause an international incident.

Mom kept a Level Seven Death Grip on my arm the rest of the way through the airport.

I wanted to pull away, to tell Dad about my interrogation and how there really were four lights.

I wanted to tell him about the Azadi Tower and the other places Customs Officer II mentioned.

I wanted to tell him how impressed Customs Officer II was that he was an architect.

But Dad walked ahead of us, fighting a losing battle to keep Laleh upright and walking on a relatively direct heading.

My sister was on the verge of collapse. "I'll take her," I said.

Mom released me so I could take Laleh piggyback, and we walked through the sliding glass doors into the cool Tehran night.

THE DANCING FAN

It was colder than I expected outside. I shivered, even with Laleh warm against my back. I was in a long-sleeved T-shirt and pants—Mom had said that was the best thing to wear through Customs—and I wished I had a hoodie, but they were all in my suitcase.

Tehran didn't smell much different from Portland. I guess I had kind of expected everything to smell like rice. (To be fair, most Persian households, even Fractional ones like ours, smell at least a little bit like basmati rice.) But Tehran's air was regular city air, with a tang of smog to it, and a bit less of Portland's rain-soaked earth smell.

A scream split the night, like the piercing cry of a Nazgûl, and I almost dropped Laleh. "Eyyyyyyyy!"

Mamou—my real, flesh-and-blood grandmother—was screaming and charging toward us. She crashed into Mom and grabbed her by the face, kissed her on both cheeks, left-right-left, and then wrapped her in a hug strong enough to buckle a starship's hull.

Mom laughed and hugged her mother for the first time in seventeen years.

It was the happiest I had ever seen her.

Dayi Jamsheed had driven Mamou to Tehran, and we all piled into his silver SUV for the ride to Yazd. Mom sat up front with him, talking in Farsi and sharing a bag of *tokhmeh,* roasted watermelon seeds, which are the favorite snack of True Persians everywhere. Dad sat in the back with Laleh stretched across his lap—she had finally collapsed, though not before being hugged to within an inch of her life by Mamou and Dayi Jamsheed.

I shared the middle with Mamou.

Fariba Bahrami was a short woman—I had only seen her from the shoulders up before—but when she wrapped her arms around me, it was like she had fifteen years' worth of hugs saved up just for me. She kept her arm draped across my back the whole ride, holding me against her.

I studied her hands. I had never really seen my grandmother's hands before.

Mamou kept her fingernails short and nicely manicured, painted pomegranate red. Her perfume smelled like peaches. And she was so warm. She squeezed and squeezed me, like she was worried I would blow out the window if she didn't hold on tight enough.

Maybe she was trying to fit a lifetime of missed hugs into the one car ride.

Maybe she was.

"Tell me about your school, maman."

"School is okay. I guess."

The sociopolitical climate of Chapel Hill High School seemed a little too complicated to get into with Mamou on a car ride, especially since I didn't want her to know that people called me D-Bag and left bright blue fake testicles on my bicycle.

I never wanted to talk about testicles with my grandmother.

"You have lots of friends? A girlfriend?"

My ears went straight to red alert.

True Persians are heavily invested in the reproductive opportunities of their descendants.

"Um. Not really," I said. The red alert was spreading to my cheeks.

"Not really" was the safest form of "no" I could come up with.

I couldn't stand to disappoint my grandmother.

"Eh? Why?" Mamou had a funny way of curling the ends of her words to make them into questions. "You are so handsome, maman."

I didn't know how she could say that. I was oily and puffy from thirty-two hours of flying, and I still had the caldera of the solar system's largest volcano smoldering between my eyebrows.

Besides. No one ever noticed me. Not the way they noticed Soulless Minions of Orthodoxy like Chip Cusumano, who really was handsome.

I shrugged, but the shrug turned into a yawn. All the temporal dilations we had gone through were catching up with me.

"You're tired, maman."

"I'm okay."

"Why don't you have a sleep? It's still a few hours to Yazd." She pulled me closer still, so I could lean my head on her shoulder, and ran her fingers through the curls of my hair. "I'm so happy you are here."

"Me too." Her hand was warm, but her fingers sent shivers of euphoria through my scalp.

She kissed the crown of my head, over and over again, until it was wet where her tears had trickled down and run into my hair.

I didn't mind, though.

"I love you, maman."

Grandma and Oma, Dad's moms, didn't say that very often. It's not that they didn't love me and Laleh, but they were full of Teutonic reserve, and didn't express affection very often.

Mamou wasn't like that.

For Fariba Bahrami, love was an opportunity, not a burden.

I swallowed away the lump in my throat. "I love you, Mamou."

I only half slept on the drive to Yazd. I was too tired to fall all the way asleep, and even though Mamou was soft and warm, leaning up against her wasn't a terribly comfortable position to sleep in. So I dozed and floated on the clouds of Farsi that blew my way from the front seat of Dayi Jamsheed's SUV.

It reminded me of when I was little, and Mom chanted to me in Farsi every night before bedtime. It's hard to describe Farsi chanting: the way Mom drew her voice out like the notes of a cello as she recited poems by Rumi or Hafez. I didn't know what they meant, but that didn't matter. It was quiet and soothing.

It was Mom's job to put me to sleep, because Dad got me too excited before bedtime. He would sit on my bed and tuck me in, and then he would start telling me a story, leaving gaps for me to fill in with heroes and monsters.

We told the story together.

There's a lot I don't remember from back then, the years before my own Great Depression. Dr. Howell says antidepressants can do that sometimes, dull the memory, plus I was pretty little at the time anyway. But I remember Story Time with Dad, because I remember the night it stopped.

It was about six months before Laleh was born.

Dad came to tuck me in. He kissed me, said "Love you," and turned to leave.

"Dad? Don't I get a story?" I squeaked.

My voice was much squeakier back then, like a cheese curd.

Dad blinked at me. He sighed. "Not tonight, Darius."

And then he left. Just walked out of my bedroom.

I lay there and waited for Mom to come chant to me.

And we didn't tell stories anymore after that.

I didn't get why Dad had stopped. I didn't understand what I had done wrong.

"You didn't do anything wrong," Mom explained. "I can tell you a story."

But it wasn't the same.

Shirin Kellner was an expert chanter but a lackluster story-teller.

And no matter the story she told, the one I told myself, the one I understood deep down, was this:

Stephen Kellner didn't want to tell me stories anymore.

"Wake up, Darioush-jan." Mamou scratched my scalp, which sent goose bumps down my neck. "We're here."

I blinked in the gray morning, sat up, and took my first look at Yazd.

To be honest, even though I had seen plenty of pictures, I still kind of expected Yazd to look like a scene from *Aladdin*: dirt streets lined with palm trees, domed palaces made out of sparkling alabaster, laden camels carrying goods to a bazaar of wooden stalls covered in jewel-colored fabric awnings.

There were no camels anywhere in sight, despite what Fatty

Bolger might have claimed. I didn't even know camel jockey was a legitimate slur until the first time he called me one. Trent Bolger was not particularly creative, but he was thorough, and subtle enough to evade detection by the enforcers of Chapel Hill High School's Zero Tolerance Policy toward racial and ethnic slurs.

The streets of Mamou's neighborhood didn't look so different from the streets back home: dull gray asphalt.

The houses didn't look so different either, except they were made of whitish bricks instead of seamless siding. Some had ornate wooden double doors in front, with elaborate metal knockers. They almost reminded me of Hobbit-hole doors, except they weren't round.

Dayi Jamsheed pulled up in front of a white house that looked more or less like all the others. It was a single story, with a thin strip of yard full of sparse, scrubby grass in front.

There were no cacti anywhere—another oversight on Fatty Bolger's part, because I looked it up, and cacti are actually native to the Americas.

Dayi Jamsheed parked the SUV under the shade of a gigantic walnut tree that hung over the street and thrust its roots beneath the cracking sidewalk.

"Agha Stephen," Dayi Jamsheed said. He pronounced it *esStephen*, which is what a lot of True Persians called Dad. In Farsi you couldn't start a word with two consonants. You had to put a vowel before them (or between them, which is why a few people called Dad "Setephen").

"Wake up, Agha Stephen."

His voice sounded like the crack of a whip, and he was always smiling, eyebrows arched and mischievous. My uncle had two discrete eyebrows—not a single connecting hair between them—which was deeply reassuring, because I had always worried about growing a Persian Unibrow.

Dayi Jamsheed started unloading our stuff from the back. I shook the sleep off my head and slid out of the SUV after Mamou, while Dad tried to rouse Laleh. "Let me help you, Dayi."

"No! You go in. I've got it, Darioush-jan."

We had a lot of suitcases, and Dayi Jamsheed only had two hands. It was clear he needed help, but he was genetically predisposed to refuse it.

It was my first official taarof in Iran.

Taarof is a Farsi word that is difficult to translate. It is the Primary Social Cue for Iranians, encompassing hospitality and respect and politeness all in one.

In theory, taarof means putting others before yourself. In practice, it means when someone comes to your house, you have to offer them food; but since your guest is supposed to taarof, they have to refuse; and then you, the host, must taarof back, insisting that it's really no trouble at all, and that they absolutely must eat; and so on, until one party gets too bewildered and finally gives in.

I never got the hang of taarofing. It's not an American Social Cue. When Mom met Dad's parents for the first time, they offered her a drink, which she politely declined—and that was that.

She really did want something to drink, but she didn't know how to go about asking.

She had yet to learn the proper American Social Cues.

Every Thanksgiving, Dad tells the story again, and every

year, Mom laughs and says she's going to kill him if he tells it one more time.

Maybe joking is the Primary American Social Cue.

"Please," I said. "I want to help."

"It's fine." Like Mamou, Dayi Jamsheed had a funny way of twisting the ends of his words. "You're tired. You are a guest."

Both of those statements were technically true, but truth was irrelevant when it came to taarof.

"Um."

Mom came to my rescue. "Jamsheed." She reached into the SUV to extract Laleh's unconscious body from Dad. My sister was pretty much a rag doll when she was asleep. "Let Darioush help."

Dad unfolded himself from the back of the SUV while Dayi Jamsheed argued with Mom in Farsi. For a beautiful, poetic language, it sounded harsh as Klingon when they fought, especially when Mamou joined in and turned it into a three-way argument.

Laleh still hung in my mom's arms. I didn't know how she could sleep through it.

Dad yawned and swung around doing trunk twists. He blinked at me and cocked his head toward Mom.

I shrugged. "Taarof," I whispered, and Dad nodded.

This was not the first time Dad and I had been stuck spectating at a taarofing match we couldn't understand.

We could have had all the luggage taken inside in the time it took them to allow us to help.

Finally, Mom prevailed, and Dayi Jamsheed handed me Laleh's roller bag. "Thank you, Darioush-jan."

"Sure."

Laleh's suitcase was twice as heavy as mine, because it was also crammed full of the stuff Mom had brought with her from America.

It wasn't just stuff for our family. When Mom announced we were going to Iran, every Persian family in the Willamette Valley started calling her, asking if she could take something to Iran for a relative, or bring something back.

It would be Mamou's job to distribute what Mom had brought after we left. It was all random stuff too: a particular kind of shampoo, or a face cream, or even Tylenol PM, which apparently you couldn't buy in Iran.

I grabbed my own suitcase, slung my Kellner & Newton Messenger Bag around the retractable handle, and followed Mamou up the driveway.

"Where's Babou?"

"In bed." Mamou lowered her voice as she let us inside. "He wanted to come to the airport, but he was too tired. He is sleeping more."

I got this sort of flutter in my stomach.

Meeting Mamou—really meeting her, I mean—but not Babou felt wrong, like ending an episode on a cliffhanger.

I was anxious to meet my grandfather, but I was a little scared too.

That's normal.

Right?

The lights were still off, and the narrow windows didn't let in much of the morning sun. Where they did, thin shafts of light struck the dust motes suspended in the air and lit the photos on the walls.

There were a lot of photos on the walls. Some were framed, singly or in groups, but plenty were tacked in place with tape, or pinned up by clothespins, or tucked into whatever corner would hold them. I wanted to stop and look at them—the Bahrami Family Portrait Gallery—but instead, I kicked off my Vans on the doormat and followed Mamou down the hall that ran the length of the house. She stopped at the last room on the right.

"Is this one okay?"

"Sure."

"It has a washroom." She pointed to a door in the corner.

"Uh." Mom had warned me about Persian bathrooms.

"Are you hungry, maman?"

"No. I don't think so." The truth was, I couldn't tell anymore. Our journey through the space-time continuum, followed by my near brush with State-Sanctioned Torture at the hands of Customs Officer II, had left me feeling disoriented and gross.

"You're sure? It's no problem."

It was my second taarof in Iran, and this time Mom wasn't around to help me.

"Um. I'm sure. I think I'm going to shower if that's okay. And maybe take a nap."

"Okay. There are towels for you in the closet."

"Thanks."

Mamou pulled me down into a hug, kissed me on both cheeks, and then went to help put Laleh to bed.

I left Laleh's suitcase in the hall, pulled my own in after me, and shut the door.

The room was maybe half the size of my bedroom back home: a twin bed with olive-green covers, and matching green curtains covering the small round window above it. A tiny wooden desk stood in the corner, with more photos on the wall above it. I recognized Dayi Jamsheed and Dayi Soheil and their kids, but there were strangers in some of them too. A few were really old black-and-whites from when Mamou was growing up.

One was familiar: a photo of Mamou with her parents. Mamou was my age, with long straight hair that fell all the way down to her chest. She wasn't smiling, but she looked like she wanted to.

Mom had a copy of that photo framed in our living room at home, on the wall closest to the kitchen and the Turbolift Door. It was the only picture of my great-grandparents (on Mamou's side) that we had.

I peeled off my shirt. It was sticky and musty from the day's travel. My face was so greasy, I thought it might slide off right onto the floor. I needed a shower.

More than that, though, I really had to pee.

I stared at the toilet: a perfect porcelain bowl, set in the floor with rose-colored tiles arranged all around in an abstract mosaic.

Mom had warned me about Mamou toilets. In Iran—especially in older homes—you were supposed to squat over the toilet instead of sitting on it. It was considered much more healthy.

I hoped my leg muscles were strong enough, when the time came. As it was, I circled the toilet, studying it like a Klingon Warrior sizing up his enemy. I wasn't sure exactly how I was supposed to use it without making a mess.

But I really did have to pee.

I showered, pulled on some shorts, and got my medicine out, but then I decided I should take it when I got back up, so I could have it with breakfast.

The air in the bedroom was too close. It was not humid, but I could feel every single air molecule as it brushed against my freshly scrubbed face. There was a box fan tucked into the corner, so I dragged it away from the wall and turned it on. It buzzed a little bit, and I had a brief vision of it experiencing a non-passive failure and exploding into a billowing cloud of smoke and motor particles, but then it got up to speed.

The fan would not stay still. It jiggled and jittered across the floor, dancing toward me.

I angled it so it would dance away from me instead. But by the time I'd gotten my pants off and pulled back the sheets, the fan had danced itself around to face me once more, shaking and shimmying inexorably toward my bed.

That fan was evil.

I pulled the Dancing Fan to the middle of the room and then propped my suitcase against it to hold it in place. It rattled ominously and hopped back and forth on its rubber feet. The suitcase blocked some of the airflow, but at least I knew it wouldn't creep up on me while I was sleeping.

I slipped into bed and faced the wall, but I could feel that fan.

It was watching me. Waiting for me to lower my guard.

It was deeply unnerving.

THE HISTORY OF
AMERICAN-IRANIAN RELATIONS

*T*hud.

Tap squeak tap.

I blinked and looked around. I had tossed off my covers while I was asleep, and the Dancing Fan lay facedown, its blades pushing air impotently at the floor.

The bedroom had become stuffy and dry. The back of my neck stuck to Mamou's beige pillowcase when I sat up. My mouth was crusty and gross.

Tap squeak tap. Something rattled the window behind the green curtain. A shadow fell across it, most likely humanoid. I peeled back the curtain and peeked out, blinking against the brightness, but whoever (or whatever) was out there had already vanished.

I pulled on some clothes and tiptoed down the hall.

The house was quiet. Mom, Dad, and Laleh were still asleep after our long journey through the space-time continuum, but I found the kitchen, and a door leading out to the backyard.

I blinked in the sun and waited for my eyes to adjust, sneezing at the brightness. The sun in Yazd was more intense, and it was directly overhead. Every surface glowed.

It was blinding.

I sneezed again.

A deep voice spoke from above, something in Farsi. I blinked and looked up.

Ardeshir Bahrami—my grandfather—had leaned a ladder against the side of the house, right next to the little round window above my bed, and he was halfway up to the roof.

Babou was taller than I expected. He wore khaki dress pants, a white pinstriped button-up shirt, and dress shoes, with the socks bunched around his ankles. And he was climbing a ladder.

He looked healthy to me, even though Mom and Dad said he wasn't. Even though Mamou said he was sleeping more.

He looked fine.

I cleared my throat and pushed my hair off my face. I had serious bed head (it was one of the burdens of having Persian hair), even though I hadn't slept for that long. I thought. Maybe what had felt like a few hours had actually been an entire day.

Maybe it was already tomorrow.

I tried to say hello, but my throat had closed off, and I made a sort of squeaking sound instead.

It felt weird to speak, knowing he could hear me. Knowing I could reach out and touch him—if he ever came down from the roof.

I guess I had pictured our first meeting a bit differently.

Babou hoisted himself onto the roof, teetering for a moment at the top, and I was convinced I was about to witness my grandfather plummet to his death off his own rooftop.

"Sohrab!" he shouted. He was staring out into the garden, past the rows of herbs, toward a shed hidden behind a trellised kiwi tree.

Persian children—even Fractional ones—learn their fruit-bearing trees at an early age.

There was a boy stringing a hose from the shed, un-loop-ing and wrestling the knots and kinks out of it as he went.

I had never seen the boy before. He looked about my age, which meant he couldn't be one of my cousins, because they were all older than me.

I glanced at Babou, who shouted "Sohrab!" again, and then at the boy, who shouted back in Farsi.

"Um."

Babou swayed for a moment and then looked down at me.

His eyebrows lifted.

"Eh! Hello, Darioush. I will be down soon. Go help Sohrab."

Sohrab shouted back and then waved me over. The sun pressed against the back of my neck as I ran out to meet him, the rough stone of the patio giving way to scrubby grass and then back to stone again. It was warm against the soles of my bare feet.

Sohrab was shorter than me, compact and lean. His black hair was cropped close, and he had the most elegant Persian nose of anyone I had ever met. He had brown eyes, just like me, but there was some light hidden behind them.

It made me think maybe brown eyes weren't so boring after all.

"Um," I said. "Hey."

And then I realized that was quite possibly the most inane greeting in the history of American-Iranian relations.

So I said, "I mean, *salaam*."

Salaam means "peace." It's not a Farsi word—it's an Arabic one—but it's the standard greeting for most True Persians.

"Salaam," Sohrab said.

"Um. *Khaylee kami Farsi harf mizanam.*"

I knew just enough Farsi to stutter that I barely knew how to speak Farsi.

Sohrab's eyes crinkled up when he smiled. He almost looked like he was squinting.

"English is okay."

"Oh good. Uh. I'm Darius. Babou's . . . Agha Bahrami's grandson."

"From America." Sohrab nodded and handed me one of the knots he was working on. I held the hose as Sohrab took the end and wove it back through the loops. He had short, proportional fingers. I noticed them because I always thought my own fingers were weirdly long and skeletal.

Sohrab shook the hose to loosen it. I grabbed another knot for him.

"Um."

Sohrab glanced at me and then back at his work.

"Are we related?" I asked.

It was an awkward but legitimate question for one Persian to ask another. I was related—distantly—to several Iranian families in Portland. It was usually through marriage, but I had a third cousin, once removed, in Portland too.

When it comes to keeping track of our family trees, Persians are even more meticulous than Hobbits. Especially Persians living outside of Iran.

Sohrab squinted at me and shrugged. "I live close."

It had never occurred to me that Mamou and Babou could have neighbors.

I mean, I knew there was a whole city around them, but the other residents of Yazd had always been abstract. Even the photographs I had seen were usually devoid of human inhabitants.

Mamou and Babou had always existed in their own cuboid universe: the two of them, and the walls of the computer room around them.

Sohrab pulled the last tangle out of the hose. And then, before I could stop him, he pointed the sprayer toward me and squeezed the handle. I held up my hands and shouted, but the water just dribbled out.

Sohrab laughed. I liked Sohrab's laugh: It was loose and free, like he didn't care who heard it.

When he squeezed my shoulder, his hand was warm, even though he'd been handling the clammy hose. "Sorry, Darioush. It's not on yet."

I tried to glower at Sohrab, but it was impossible, because he was squinting again and I ended up laughing instead.

I decided I liked Sohrab.

Here's the thing:

Every Iranian knows someone named Sohrab. If they don't, they know someone who knows someone named Sohrab. Back in Portland, one of Mom's friends (who we were not related to) had a nephew named Sohrab.

Now I had a Sohrab of my own.

The name Sohrab comes from the story of Rostam and Sohrab in the *Shahnahmeh*, which is basically the *Silmarillion* of Persian fables and legends. It has other stories too, like Feridoun and his three sons, and Zal and the Simurgh (which is the Persian version of a phoenix), and King Jamsheed, but none of them are as famous as the story of Rostam and Sohrab.

Rostam was a legendary Persian fighter who accidentally killed his own son, Sohrab, in battle.

It was deeply tragic.

It was also deeply ingrained in the DNA of every Persian man and boy, which is probably why all Persian boys work so hard to please their fathers.

I wondered if all fathers secretly wanted to kill their sons. Just a little bit.

Maybe that explained Stephen Kellner.

Maybe it did.

"Sohrab! Darioush!"

"Bebakhshid, Agha Bahrami."

That means "I'm sorry." Or "excuse me."

Like I said, Farsi is a deeply context-sensitive language.

I helped Sohrab drag the hose to Babou, who hoisted a few coils up to the roof. Sohrab stood at the base of the ladder with his left foot on the bottom rung.

"Do you like figs, Darioush?"

"Uh." Liking figs was not a Persian trait I had inherited.

All True, Non-Fractional Persians like figs.

But I thought they were weird, because I accidentally read about how figs are pollenated by little wasps that climb inside them, mate, and then die. Ever since then, I couldn't stop thinking that I might be eating dead wasps when I ate a fig.

"Your grandfather grows the best figs in Yazd," Sohrab said. But then he shrugged. "They won't be ready until summer, though."

"Darioush-jan," Babou called from the roof. He waved

his hand back toward the shed. "Turn the water on, please."

"Okay."

The hose leaked a little when I turned it on, so I tightened it as best I could, and then I stood by Sohrab and we watched Babou. He tottered across the roof tiles, spraying his fig trees like it was the safest, sanest procedure in the world.

Sohrab squinted at me. "Relax, Darioush. He does this every week."

That only made me worry more.

My breath hitched when Babou leaned over the edge of the roof to reach the farthest leaves of his fig trees.

I stood on the opposite rung of the ladder and leaned in toward Sohrab.

"Should he really be doing that?"

"Probably not."

"So we just watch him until he's done?"

"Yes."

"Okay."

A HOLODECK VISION

Babou spent a full ten minutes watering the canopy of his fig trees, strolling up and down the roof. He never did fall, though he came pretty close when he leaned over to yell at me to turn the water off. The ground smelled like wet clay where the hose had dripped all over, despite my efforts to tighten it. I wiggled my toes in the cool water.

Sohrab held the ladder for Babou when he finally climbed down. He handed the hose to Sohrab and waved me over as Sohrab wrestled the hose back into the shed.

"Hello, Darioush-jan." He squeezed my shoulders with his strong hands and held me at arm's length. His hands were wet, and his palms were so callused I could feel them through the cotton of my shirt. "Welcome to Yazd."

I kind of thought Babou would pull me into a hug—I was so convinced, in fact, that I started to lean into him. But he kept a grip on me and looked me up and down.

"You are tall. Like your dad. Not like Mamou."

"Yeah. Um." I stood up straighter, because I had been a little hunched in anticipation of the hug that seemed not to be forthcoming. Babou's eyebrows quirked, but he didn't smile.

Not quite.

"Thank you. *Merci*. For having us."

"I am glad you could come." Babou let go and waved toward Sohrab. "That is Sohrab." He pointed at Sohrab, who was fighting the hose. "He lives down the street."

"Yes."

"He is a good boy. Very nice. You should be friends with him."

I had never been ordered to befriend someone before.

I glanced back at Sohrab, who crinkled up his eyes and shook his head.

My ears burned.

"Sohrab. It's fine. Leave it."

"Baleh, Agha Bahrami."

Babou asked Sohrab something in Farsi, but all I caught was *Mamou* and *robe*, which is pomegranate molasses.

Like I said, I could usually recognize food words.

"Of course. Darioush, you want to come?"

"Um. Where?"

"His amou's store," Babou said. "Go with him, baba."

"Okay."

"Come on, Darioush," Sohrab said. "Let's go."

I laced up my Vans while Babou handed Sohrab a few folded bills, and we headed out.

Yazd was blinding in the daylight. I had to blink for a moment and sneeze. Without the shade of Babou's fig trees, the neighborhood was a luminous white, so bright, I was certain I could feel my optic nerves cooking.

Now that it was daytime, and I wasn't quite so sleep deprived, I could appreciate how each house on Mamou's block had its own character. Some were newer and some were older; some had large gardens like Babou's, and some had an extra lane to park a car behind the house. There were khaki houses and beige houses and off-white houses and even some that had been worn to a light tan.

Nearly every car parked on the street (or occasionally up on the curb) was light-colored and angular, makes and models I had never seen before.

I wondered where Iranian cars came from.

I wondered what Stephen Kellner thought of Iranian cars, and how they compared to his Audi.

I wondered if he was still asleep. If he'd wake up and we'd be able to get along, the way he wanted.

Sohrab cleared his throat. "Darioush." He kicked a white stone off the sidewalk. "What do you think of Yazd?"

"Oh." I swallowed. "Um. I haven't seen much yet. But it's neat. You live close by?"

Sohrab waved behind him. "The other way."

"Oh."

Sohrab led me out of Mamou's neighborhood, past more khaki walls and old wooden doors and little shaded gardens, and onto a larger street with a tree-lined median that we would have called a boulevard back home.

I didn't know the Farsi word for *boulevard*.

Stores with brightly colored awnings lined the side opposite us, and the houses on our side got smaller as we walked.

It was weird, seeing real-life Iranians walking down the sidewalks, popping in and out of the stores, carrying plastic bags of groceries or whatever. Most of the women had on headscarves and long-sleeved jackets, but some wore full chadors: big black robes that covered them from head to toe, except the perfect hole where their faces peered out.

I wondered how they didn't overheat, covered in black.

My own dark, Persian hair was baking in the sun. If I cracked an egg over it, I could have shaken scrambled eggs out of my curls.

That would have been gross.

The Yazd in Mom's old photos gave me a holodeck vision of it: crisp and static and perfect. The real Yazd was messy and bustling and noisy. Not loud, but full of the sounds of real people.

"This is your first time to Iran?"

"Huh? Yeah. I think my mom was kind of scared to come. You know, 'cause my dad is American. And we hear lots of stories."

"I think it's not so bad, you know."

I thought of Customs Officer II, who I had imagined stringing me up to the ceiling and interrogating me before he decided to let me go.

"Um. Yeah. It wasn't so bad coming in."

I reached for something else to say, but I came up blank.

Sohrab didn't seem to mind, though. It was a comfortable silence between us. Not awkward at all.

I liked that I could be silent with Sohrab.

That's how I knew we really were going to be friends.

We took another left, past a furniture store and down the street, until Sohrab pointed to the green awning above his uncle's grocery store. After our blinding journey through the sunlit streets of Yazd, it seemed almost dark inside, despite the warm golden walls.

The first thing I noticed was that Sohrab's amou's store looked almost exactly like the Persian grocery store back home: tightly spaced aisles filled with stacks of dried goods and canned goods and bottled goods in the middle, a long refrigerator filled with dairy and meat on one wall, and produce on the others.

I don't know why I expected any different. Or what different would have looked like.

The second thing I noticed was Sohrab's uncle, who stood behind the counter. He was the largest Iranian I had ever seen: taller than Stephen Kellner but heavier too. He seemed to take up half the store, though part of that could have been his wild smile, red and huge as a carved watermelon. His mouth curved up the same way as Sohrab's, with one side a little higher than the other.

I could tell he was a True Persian by the density of his luxurious chest hair, which stuck out of the collar of his shirt.

"Alláh-u-Abhá, Sohrab-jan!" he said. His voice was low, like the drone of a thousand bees. "Chetori toh?"

"Alláh-u-Abhá, amou."

Alláh-u-Abhá is the traditional Bahá'í greeting. It means something like "God is the most glorious."

I hadn't realized Sohrab was Bahá'í.

"This is Darioush. Agha Bahrami's grandson. From America."

Sohrab's uncle turned his smile toward me. I didn't think it was possible, but it got bigger somehow.

"Darioush, this is my amou Ashkan."

"Nice you meet you, Agha . . . um . . ."

"Rezaei," Sohrab said.

"Nice to meet you, Agha Rezaei," I said.

"Nice to meet you, Agha Darioush. Welcome to Yazd."

"Thanks."

"Babou sent us to get some robe for Mamou."

"Sure." Agha Rezaei stepped out from behind the counter and squeezed himself into one of the aisles. He asked Sohrab something in Farsi. Sohrab turned to me.

"Mamou likes more sour or more sweet?"

"Um."

My ears burned.

I didn't know there was more than one kind.

I didn't know what my grandmother liked.

"I'm not sure."

"This one is better," Agha Rezaei said, and pulled down two garnet bottles of robe. He led us back to the counter, talking to Sohrab in Farsi. Unlike Mom, Agha Rezaei didn't pepper his sentences with English words—it was pure Farsi, and a lot harder for me to track. He kept saying "baba," but that was all I could follow. Something about Sohrab's dad.

"Agha Darioush. You want faludeh?"

"Amou makes the best in Yazd," Sohrab said, pointing to the freezer behind the counter.

Faludeh is rosewater sorbet with thin starchy noodles. It sounds weird, but it is actually delicious, especially when you drizzle it with sour cherry syrup and lime juice.

"Are you going to get some?"

"I can't," Sohrab said.

"How come?"

"We are fasting. We are Bahá'í. You know what Bahá'í is?"

"Yeah. Mom has some Bahá'í friends back home. How long are you fasting?"

"Until Nowruz. We do it every year, for the last month."

"Oh."

I couldn't eat in front of someone who couldn't eat with me.

"I'm okay for now. Can we come back after Nowruz? Then we can both have some."

Sohrab squinted at me. "Sure."

We paid for the robe—well, Sohrab paid for it—and said good-bye.

Agha Rezaei promised to have fresh faludeh for us when we came back.

"Maybe I can bring my sister," I said as we headed back to Mamou's, the bottles clinking in their plastic bag at my side.

"Laleh. Right?"

"Yeah."

"How old is she?"

"She's eight. How about you? Any sisters? Brothers?"

"I don't have any," Sohrab said.

"Oh. Do you want one?"

"It would be nice to have a brother. Someone to play football with." Sohrab squinted at me. "Do you play football? Soccer?" He pronounced it *sock-air*, which seemed like a cool way to say it.

"Uh."

I hadn't played on a proper soccer team since I was twelve, but we played it in physical education sometimes, when we weren't doing Net Sports or Whiffle ball or timed mile runs.

"We play most days. You should come. Tomorrow afternoon?"

"Okay."

I wasn't sure why I had agreed. I didn't like soccer/non-American football that much.

Somehow Sohrab made it sound like the best thing ever.

He laughed at me again, but it wasn't a mean laugh. "You don't taarof, do you?"

"Oh. Sorry." I had completely forgotten the Primary Social Cue. "Do you not want me to come?"

Sohrab threw his arm across my shoulder.

"No. You should come and play with us, Darioush."

"Okay."

Sohrab led me back to Mamou's house.

"See you tomorrow? For football?"

"Yeah," I said. "Tomorrow."

"I will come get you. Be ready in the afternoon."

"Okay."

"Okay." Sohrab jogged down the block and waved at me before he turned the corner.

I took the robe to the kitchen, where Babou was pouring himself a cup of tea.

"Uh. Is everyone else still asleep?"

"Yes. You want tea, Darioush-jan?"

"Oh. Yes. Please."

I had forgotten to taarof yet again, but Babou didn't seem to mind. He poured me a cup, then grabbed a cube of sugar and clenched it in his teeth. I had seen lots of Persians drink their tea this way—sipping it through a cube of sugar—but I was categorically opposed to sweetening tea in any way.

I think it was because of Tea Haven.

We sat and drank our tea in total silence, except for the intermittent sound of slurping. Babou seemed content not to talk, and I had no idea what to say to him anyway.

I thought it would be different, seeing my grandfather in real life.

I thought I would know what to say.

But I had spent so long on the other side of a computer monitor from him, watching him like an episode of *Star Trek*.

I didn't know how to actually talk to him.

Babou blinked and smoothed his bushy mustache with his finger. Maybe he was used to watching me like an episode of *Star Trek* too.

It was deeply uncomfortable.

Someone was playing with my hair.

"Darius," Mom said. "Wake up. Time for dinner."

I sat up and banged my knee on the table, rattling the bowl of tokhmeh and knocking over my empty teacup.

"Sorry. I'm awake."

"Come on. Let's eat something and then you can go back to sleep."

"Okay."

Mamou had made ash-e reshteh, which is a sort of Persian noodle soup.

It was not my favorite, but I couldn't tell her that.

We all scooped soup up with our crusty Persian bread, while Babou interviewed Laleh in Farsi. She kept up fairly well, though she switched to English a few times, like for "meatball sub" and "airport."

She seemed to be telling Babou the entire saga of our journey through the space-time continuum.

I didn't know where she got the energy.

I kept nodding off, shaking my head, until Mom finally said, "Darius, why don't you go to bed? It's okay."

"Um."

"It's the time difference, maman," Mamou said. "It's okay. You can go to bed."

This is why I hate time travel.

Mamou led me back to my room.

"Thank you for getting the robe for me, Darioush."

"Oh. It was mostly Sohrab. I just went along."

"Babou says you are going to play football tomorrow."

"Yeah."

"I'm happy for you. I'm glad you made a friend already."

"Yeah," I said. I had made a friend.

And I was actually looking forward to soccer.

I really was.

"Me too."

SOCCER/NON-AMERICAN FOOTBALL

By the time I woke up the next morning, Mamou had already taken Mom, Dad, and Laleh into town.

The kitchen table was still laden with breakfast: a basket of toasted bread, bowls of nuts, jars of jam, a platter of cheese, and a few slices of some sort of melon. Babou was in his room with the door closed, and the house was quiet and still.

I wondered if mornings were always like this in my grandparents' house.

I wondered if I would ever get used to the temporal displacement.

I wondered when Sohrab was going to show up.

I put the jam back in the refrigerator and grabbed a glass. Mamou didn't keep her glassware in the cupboard: She kept it upside down in a drawer to the left of the sink, which I thought was an interesting way to store glasses.

I grabbed the pitcher of filtered water and opened up my meds.

"Darioush. What are you doing?"

Babou had emerged from his room, dressed in another pair of creased dress pants and a blue button-up.

I dribbled some water down the front of my shirt as I swallowed. "Taking my medicine."

"Medicine?" He set his cup in the sink and picked up one of my pill bottles. "What is this for? Are you sick?"

"Depression," I said. I refilled my glass and took another gulp so I wouldn't have to look at Babou. I could sense the disappointment radiating off him.

I never expected Ardeshir Bahrami to have so much in common with his son-in-law.

"What are you depressed for?" He shook the pill bottle. "You have to think positive, baba. Medicine is for old people. Like me."

"It's just the way I am," I squeaked.

I would never be good enough for Ardeshir Bahrami.

"You just have to try harder, Darioush-jan. Those will not fix anything." He glanced at the table. "Did you have enough to eat?"

"Um. I . . . yeah."

"Good." Babou poured himself a cup of tea and sat down at the table with a bowl of tokhmeh. "When is Sohrab coming?"

"Soon. I think."

"Do you play football in America?"

"Sometimes."

"Sohrab is very good. He plays most days." Babou spat out a shell onto his plate. "It's good you met him. I knew you would be friends."

"Um."

I didn't know how Babou could know that.

He was right, of course.

But how could he be so certain?

I nearly jumped out of my chair when someone finally knocked on the front door.

"Hey," I said.

Sohrab squinted at me. "Hi, Darioush. Ready to go?"

I knelt and pulled my Vans on. "Ready."

"Do you have a kit?" Sohrab held up his red nylon bag, the kind with draw-strings that doubled as straps to make it into a sort of backpack.

I shook my head. I had failed to anticipate the need for soccer/non-American football gear when I packed.

(Not that I owned any.)

"It's okay. I brought extra."

"You sure you don't mind? Sharing, I mean."

Sohrab squinted at me. "Of course not. Come on. Let's go." He opened the door again and then turned to holler back at the kitchen. "Khodahafes, Agha Bahrami."

"Khodahafes, Babou," I said.

Sohrab led me to a park down the street from Mamou's house. A chain-link fence ran all the way around, and it was bordered on three sides by squat stone houses and on the fourth by another of Yazd's boulevards.

The field was full-sized, or pretty close at least, and the sort of vibrant green that only came from constant watering. Nothing else I had seen in Yazd so far was that green—not even Babou's garden, though I would never tell him that.

Sohrab led me to the small, sad-looking public bathroom at the edge of the field. It was clean inside, even if it did have the feta-cheese-and-baby-powder smell of a boys' locker room.

There were no urinals, only a few stalls with sitting toilets—none of the squatting ones, like my bathroom at Mamou's—and I wondered if that was a Social Cue I had missed. What if I was not supposed to pee standing up in Iran?

It wasn't the sort of thing I could ask Sohrab.

How do you ask a guy if it's okay to pee standing up?

"Lots of people play football here." Sohrab started pulling clothes out of his backpack. He tossed me a green T-shirt and a pair of shorts so white, they were blinding in the alien glow of the bathroom's fluorescent lights.

"Darioush, what size shoe do you wear?"

"Twelve," I said.

Sohrab bit the inside of his cheek. "Here," he said, and stepped next to me. "Take off your shoes."

I toed off my Vans, and Sohrab stepped out of his sandals. He wrapped his arm around my side and lined up his foot with mine.

My feet were a bit longer but a lot wider.

I had Hobbit feet.

At least they weren't furry on top.

My stomach tickled where Sohrab had grabbed me. I blushed.

No one ever stood right next to me like Sohrab did.

I wasn't used to guys doing that.

"I wear forty-four," Sohrab said. "I think they will fit you. They will be tight, though."

"Oh." I didn't even realize Iran used a different shoe sizing system. "That's okay. Thanks."

Sohrab dug in his bag and handed me a pair of faded black Adidas.

He avoided my eyes as he passed me the cleats, rummaged through his bag, and pulled out another pair of cleats for himself. They were white (well, they had been, once), and were in imminent danger of experiencing a non-passive failure.

"Uh. Wouldn't you rather use these?" I tried to give back the black Adidas. "I can play in my Vans."

"No. You use them. They are newer."

They were so worn, I wasn't sure they had ever been new, but they were in better shape than Sohrab's white cleats.

"They're yours," I said. "You should use them."

"But you are my guest."

This was another taarof: Sohrab giving me his nicer cleats. And invoking my being a guest was one of the strongest strategies you could employ in taarof.

I felt terrible for using his nice cleats, but I couldn't see any way out of it.

"Thank you."

I took my new kit into a stall to change, which was awkward because I kept banging my elbows into the walls and my knees into the toilet. My boxers were not suited for providing structural integrity while I was running around, and I wished I had thought to bring some compression shorts or something.

I would not have borrowed any of Sohrab's, even if he had offered.

There are some garments you should never share.

I hopped my way into the borrowed Adidas. They fit okay—a little tight, but okay. And they felt light and agile compared to my gray Vans.

Even though the shirt was stretched across my chest, and the shorts kept riding up my butt, I felt very Iranian when I emerged from the stall in my borrowed kit and cleats.

But then I saw Sohrab in his red shirt and shorts, and his white cleats. He looked fit and ready for a real game.

It made me feel very inadequate.

I was only a Fractional Persian, after all.

"Ready?"

"Um."

I wasn't so sure I wanted to play anymore.

But Sohrab squinted at me, and the knot of nerves in my chest melted a little bit.

Some friends just have that effect on you.

"Ready."

Two boys waited on the field for us. Sohrab hollered at them in Farsi and then waved his hand for me to jog after him.

"This is Darioush. Agha Bahrami's grandson. From America."

I said, "Salaam."

"Salaam," Iranian Boy Number One said. He talked out of the side of his mouth, which made it seem like he was half smiling. He was almost my height, but he was rail thin, and he had his hair spiked up in front, almost like a Soulless Minion of Orthodoxy.

I held out my hand, and he shook it, though it was loose and fleeting and felt kind of weird.

"Nice to meet you. Um."

"Ali-Reza," he said.

Ali and Reza are both popular Iranian names—maybe even more popular than Sohrab—though both are technically Arabic in origin.

I held out my hand to the other boy, who had lost the genetic lottery and ended up with the dreaded Persian Unibrow. I thought he would be hairy everywhere else too, but his hair was cut shorter than Sohrab's, and he had pale, hairless arms.

"Hossein," he said. His voice was thick and dark like coffee. He was shorter than me too—shorter even than Sohrab—but with his unibrow and the ghost mustache haunting his upper lip, he looked older: ready to get a job interrogating temporally-displaced Fractional Persians as they arrived at Customs in Imam Khomeini International Airport.

Hossein didn't smile at all as he glanced from me to Sohrab.

"Thanks for letting me play with you," I said.

Sohrab squinted at me.

Ali-Reza elbowed Hossein and said something in Farsi. Sohrab's neck turned red, and his jaw twitched, like he was grinding his teeth a little bit.

"Um."

Sohrab didn't let me ask. "Come on, Darioush."

Like I said, I hadn't been on a soccer team—a real one, not just one in physical education class at Chapel Hill High School (Go Chargers)—since I was twelve. Dad had signed me up for the neighborhood soccer club when I was seven. I was okay at it, but according to our coach I wasn't aggressive enough.

And then I got diagnosed with depression, and I started on my first round of medication, and I couldn't focus on the game at all. I was too slow to track the other players, or the ball, or even the score.

One week, I left every single practice in tears because Coach Henderson (father of our midfielder, Vance Henderson, who I was destined to smack across the face less than a year later) kept humiliating me in front of the whole team. He didn't understand why I had gone from being an okay-but-not-very-aggressive center-back to a complete and utter failure. All he could see was that I wasn't trying hard enough.

I didn't know how to talk to people about being medicated back then. And Dad kept saying I just needed more discipline.

Mom finally put her foot down and insisted it was okay for me to quit, scuttling Stephen Kellner's dreams of me playing professional soccer before they even made it out of dry dock.

It was another of Stephen Kellner's many disappointments in me.

At least he eventually got used to them.

We only used half the field. For a simple two-on-two, using the entire thing would have been illogical.

Sohrab was our nominal forward, which left me de facto defender, but really, both of us played all over the field.

Ali-Reza was supposed to be the forward for his and Hossein's team, but Sohrab played so aggressively, Ali-Reza spent most of his time helping Hossein ward off Sohrab's relentless assaults on their goal.

Coach Henderson would have loved Sohrab's aggressiveness.

Not that Ali-Reza wasn't aggressive too. I had to fend off my share of goals, which I mostly did, through some combination of luck, coincidence, and latent memories of my pre-medication training.

It seemed I had misread the situation between Sohrab and Ali-Reza, who had acted like friends, but were clearly engaged in some sort of personal vendetta that could only be settled through soccer/non-American football.

They fought much more fiercely than Trent Bolger and Cyprian Cusumano, and I was shifting the balance of their vendetta by preventing Ali-Reza from scoring.

The best was when I executed a perfect sliding tackle, stealing the ball from Ali-Reza and passing it down to Sohrab.

I felt very Iranian in that moment, even covered in grass stains.

Ali-Reza hissed and ran back after Sohrab, who dodged Hossein and scored again.

"Pedar sag," Ali-Reza spat as he followed Sohrab back toward center field.

Sohrab stopped and said something to Ali-Reza, which ended up with them shouting in Farsi so fast I couldn't make out a single word. Ali-Reza shoved Sohrab, who shoved him back, and I thought things were going to escalate from there until Hossein started shouting too.

I didn't catch much of that, either, except I could make out *nakon*, which means "don't," so I figured he was telling them to stop it.

Sohrab shook his head, ran over to me and slapped my shoulder. "Good job, Darioush."

"Um. Thanks," I said. "Uh."

But Sohrab ran off again before I could ask what happened.

We played forever.

We played until I couldn't run any more.

We played until my shirt was soaked and translucent with sweat, and my boxers were causing some Level Eight Chafing.

I once again wished for more supportive undergarments.

I hadn't been keeping count, but Sohrab announced we won, by three goals.

He collided with me and gave me a sweaty hug and a slap on the back, then threw his arm over my shoulder as we headed back to the locker room.

"You were great, Darioush."

"Not that good," I said. "Not as good as you."

"Yes," Sohrab said. "You were."

I almost believed him.

Almost.

"Thanks."

I decided to put my arm over Sohrab's shoulder too, even if I felt kind of weird doing it, and not just because of the sweat running down the back of Sohrab's neck.

Sohrab was so comfortable touching me.

I liked how confident he was about that.

Hossein and Ali-Reza walked ahead of us, fingers intertwined behind their heads in what Coach Fortes liked to call Surrender Cobra. Huge ovals of sweat seeped through the backs of their shirts. They hadn't said a thing since we called it quits.

"Uh."

Sohrab squinted at me.

"You play with them a lot?"

"Yes."

"They seem . . . um . . ."

"They do not like to lose."

"Are you guys friends?"

Sohrab shrugged. "Ali-Reza is very prejudiced. Against Bahá'ís."

I thought about that: How back home, all Persians—even Fractional Persians like me and Laleh—were united in our Persian-ness. We celebrated Nowruz and Chaharshanbeh Suri together in big parties, Bahá'ís and Muslims and Jews and Christians and Zoroastrians and even secular humanists like Stephen Kellner, and it didn't matter. Not really.

Not when we were so few in number.

But here, surrounded by Persians, Sohrab was singled out for being Bahá'í.

He was a target.

"What does *pedar sag* mean?"

Sohrab's jaw twitched. "It means 'your father is a dog.' It's very rude."

"Oh."

I thought about that too: How in America, it was much worse to call someone's mother a dog, rather than their father.

"Ali-Reza said that to you?"

"It's fine," Sohrab said. "Ali-Reza is like that. It doesn't bother me so much."

Usually, when I said something like that, I meant the opposite.

I let everything bother me too much. It was one of the reasons Stephen Kellner was always so disappointed in me.

"You know what, Sohrab?" I said. "I think Ali-Reza is just mad because you're so much better than him."

Sohrab squinted at me again. He shook me by the shoulder and rubbed my head, sending sweat flying off the ends of my hair. He didn't seem to care.

"You know what, Darioush? You are better than him too."

Back home, at Chapel Hill High School, we didn't shower after physical education. I don't know why, given how terrible I smelled after running laps or doing mountain climbers, or even playing Net Sports with overly aggressive players like Fatty Bolger and Chip Cusumano. But class ran until five minutes before the bell, which was just enough time to get changed, slather myself with extra deodorant, and run to geometry on the other side of the school.

(Go Chargers.)

So I was a little alarmed when Sohrab pulled soap and shampoo out of his nylon drawstring backpack.

"Uh," I said. "It's okay. I'll shower when I get back to Mamou's."

"You're dirty." He pointed to the grass stains down my legs and across my arms.

"I don't have a towel."

Sohrab pulled a pair of towels out of his bag.

I couldn't figure out how they had fit in there, especially with two kits and two pairs of cleats. Sohrab's backpack had exceeded the normal laws of space-time.

Sohrab tossed the towels onto the wooden bench between us and pulled off his shirt, peeling the wet fabric away from his flat chest and stomach. He was still breathing hard, his abdomen expanding and contracting.

I turned away, to give him privacy and also because I was so embarrassed.

Sohrab was in really good shape.

Also, it was weird to get all the way naked. I had never taken my underwear off next to another guy.

I wasn't even standing that close to Sohrab. But I felt the heat radiating off his skin, like a warp core about to breach.

My skin was still flush from our game, which was good. Sohrab couldn't tell I was blushing all over as I pulled off my own sticky shirt, wrapped the towel around my waist, and pulled my borrowed shorts and not-borrowed boxers out from underneath.

Sohrab was right: I did need a shower.

New life-forms were evolving in the primordial swamp festering between my legs.

"Over here," Sohrab said, which was unnecessary, since the spray of the showers echoed from around the corner.

I turned to follow him. He had his towel over his shoulder, like he didn't have a care in the world.

My skin prickled, the sensation spreading up to my ears, down my neck and shoulders, all the way to my toes. I nearly tripped over my own feet.

I couldn't breathe.

"Uh."

There were no stalls. There were just open shower heads.

Red Alert.

Hossein and Ali-Reza were already under the sprays, talking in Farsi and laughing about something. They were both tanned and lean, their stomach muscles highlighted by the reflection on their wet skin.

I felt like a space-borne leviathan, just standing in the same room with them.

Sohrab hung his towel on the wall. I bit my lip, sucked in my stomach, and did the same. I got under the closest spray, turned away from the other guys, and tried to breathe.

I thought I was having an anxiety attack.

I had never been diagnosed with an anxiety disorder, but Dr. Howell said that anxiety and depression often went hand in hand. Comorbidity, he called it.

It was an ominous-sounding word.

It made me anxious.

Sometimes my heart would pound so fast I thought I was going to die. And then I would start sobbing for no reason.

I couldn't let the guys see me do that.

That wasn't something True Persians did.

The guys had gone quiet. I could barely make out their voices over the spray.

I scrubbed my armpits, and scratched at the grass stains on my elbows until my skin was pink and angry. Hossein and Ali-Reza were arguing with Sohrab in whispered Farsi.

Sohrab cleared his throat behind me.

"Darioush?"

"Um. Yes?"

"What is wrong with your . . . penis?"

My throat clamped up. "Nothing," I squeaked.

Sohrab said something to the other boys, in Farsi again, and they answered, more insistent.

Sohrab cleared his throat again. "It looks different?"

"Uh. I'm not circumcised?"

It was not a question. I just wasn't sure if *circumcised* was a word Sohrab knew how to translate to Farsi.

"Oh!" He started talking to Ali-Reza and Hossein again, no doubt explaining my penis to them.

I didn't think my skin could get any redder than it was, but I was pretty sure I had started glowing like a protostar about to undergo its first burst of fusion.

Ali-Reza laughed, and then he said, in English so I could understand, "It looks like the Ayatollah's turban."

Ayatollah Khamenei was Iran's Supreme Cleric: the absolute religious and governmental authority. His photograph was all over, on signs and walls and newspapers, with his fluffy white beard and a dark turban wrapped around his head.

It was the most humiliating comparison of my life.

Hossein said something in Farsi, and Ali-Reza laughed again.

And then Sohrab said, "Ayatollah Darioush," and all three of them laughed.

At me.

I thought I understood Sohrab.

I thought we were going to be friends.

How had I misjudged him so badly?

Maybe Dad was right.

Maybe I would always be a target.

Even for things I couldn't help. Like being from America. Like having a foreskin.

Those things were normal back home, but not in Iran.

I would never fit in. Not anywhere.

I wiped my face to hide my sniffling while Sohrab and Hossein and Ali-Reza laughed about my penis in Farsi. It didn't matter that I couldn't understand them.

I didn't bother with my hair. I scrubbed the grass off my shins, rinsed off at warp 9, then grabbed my borrowed towel and slunk out of the shower. I would have run if I hadn't been worried about slipping on the wet floor.

The guys' laughter followed me, bouncing off the tiles, between my ears, rattling around in my head.

I wanted to die.

I wasn't allowed to say that, not out loud. The one time I did—and it was only hyperbole—Dad freaked out and threatened to send me to a hospital.

"Don't ever joke about that, Darius."

I didn't really want to die, anyway. I just wanted to slip into a black hole and never come out.

I pulled my pants back on. I didn't have any extra underwear. I hadn't thought about that.

Was it wrong to go commando in Iran?

I was certain there had to be a Social Cue against that, but my options were limited.

And what was the point and purpose of following Social Cues, anyway? I was never going to fit in.

I pulled my shirt back on, fighting to get it over my wet hair and down my back.

"Oh." Sohrab had come around the corner. I wiped at my face to make sure he couldn't see anything. "Are you leaving, Darioush?"

"Yeah." I hated that my voice still squeaked.

Bare feet slapped on the tiles as Ali-Reza and Hossein followed. "Khodahafes," Hossein said.

And then Ali-Reza said, "Nice to meet you, Ayatollah."

It was a new record for me: Less than forty-eight hours in Iran, and I already had a new nickname, one more humiliating than anything Trent Bolger and his Soulless Minions of Orthodoxy had ever come up with.

I dropped my borrowed towel on the floor, wiped my nose with the back of my hand, and made my escape.

Dr. Howell says that crying is normal.

He says that it's a healthy reaction.

He says it helps the body excrete stress hormones.

Having Hossein and Ali-Reza and Sohrab—Sohrab—make fun of my penis had me excreting a lot of stress hormones.

I was not ashamed of my penis. It's just that Stephen Kellner isn't circumcised, and even though it was ubiquitous in Iran, Mom thought it was important for the son to look like the father.

Like I said, we didn't shower after physical education at Chapel Hill High School. And I wasn't on any of Chapel Hill High School's Sportsball Teams (Go Chargers), so I never had to shower after any practices.

And even if I had been on a team, the showers in the Chapel Hill High School locker room were individual stalls with curtains and everything.

I had never showered with other guys looking at me before.

Maybe my penis really was weird-looking.

Okay. I will admit I was pretty sure I was not weird-looking, because there was the Internet.

I knew I didn't look any different.

Though I still hoped I was going to grow some more.

That's normal.

Right?

The front door was locked, so I went around back. Babou was
still at the kitchen table, sipping tea and eating tokhmeh, when
I stepped inside. I wondered if he had been there the whole
time, caught in a temporal causality loop while I was out playing soccer/non-American football and being humiliated for
having an intact foreskin.

He spat out an empty shell and glanced at me as I struggled
to toe my shoes off.

I had been in such a rush to leave, I had put Sohrab's worn
black Adidas back on, and they were much tighter on my Hobbit
feet than my Vans.

I hated them.

"Darioush," he grumbled. "Did you have fun? Did you win?"

"Um. Yeah. We won."

"You played with Sohrab's friends?"

"Yeah."

"Where is Sohrab? He didn't come back?"

I shook my head.

"Darioush-jan. You don't want to invite him to dinner? Next
time ask him over after you play."

"I don't think I'm going to play again."

Not ever.

I couldn't take any more penile humiliation.

Babou scooted his chair back and stared at me. "Eh? Why
not?"

"Um."

I could not tell my grandfather the boys had compared my
penis to Iran's Supreme Cleric.

"They don't like me very much."

"What?" Babou got up and took me by the shoulders. "Why do you think that, Darioush-jan? It's probably a misunderstanding."

It was the sort of thing Stephen Kellner would have said.

I blinked and blinked because I didn't want Babou to witness my stress hormones build up to a containment breach.

"Why are you crying, baba?"

"I'm not."

"You know, in Iran, boys don't worry about these things so much."

"Okay."

"You can't let these things bother you."

I sniffed. "I'm gonna take a shower."

I hadn't really finished back at the soccer field. I was still covered in grass and I hadn't actually washed my hair.

Being humiliated was very distracting.

"Okay. Don't worry, Darioush. Everything will be fine."

It was easy for Ardeshir Bahrami to say that.

He didn't know what it was like to be a target.

In the privacy of my shower, I scrubbed off the last bits of green and washed my hair. I stayed in there as long as I could. I didn't want anyone to hear me sniffling.

When the water started to cool off, I decided I was done. I wrapped myself in one of Mamou's towels. It felt much warmer and softer than Sohrab's scratchy one.

I sniffled, turned on the Dancing Fan, and hid in my bed.

I didn't actually sleep. I couldn't. Sohrab's laughter kept

dancing around in my skull. And the way he had said "Ayatollah Darioush."

I was so sure Sohrab was like me. That he knew what it was like to be different.

I was convinced we were destined to be friends.

But Sohrab Rezaei was just another Soulless Minion of Orthodoxy.

Someone knocked on my door.

I was on my side, studying the tiny imperfections in the lemon rind texture of the wall. "Uh. Yeah?"

After a second, the door creaked open. "Darioush?" Mamou asked. "Do you want a snack? Something to drink?"

I glanced over my shoulder. "No thanks. I'm not hungry."

"You sure? We have tea. And cookies."

"I'm sure."

"Are you okay?"

"Yeah. I'm just tired," I said. "We played a long time."

Mamou slipped into my room and maneuvered around the Dancing Fan. I gripped my covers a little tighter, because I hadn't actually gotten dressed after my shower. Mamou leaned over me and kissed me on the forehead. She played with my hair, which had air dried into a curly mess. "Okay, maman. Get some rest."

I didn't, though. A few minutes later Dad came to check on me too.

"Darius?"

"Yeah?"

"Are you going to get up?"

"No."

"We're waiting on you for tea."

"I'm not thirsty."

"You have to come have tea with us," Laleh complained from the door.

I was not in the mood for tea.

It was the first time in my life I had ever not wanted tea.

"I don't feel like it."

Dad dodged the Dancing Fan and sat beside me on the edge of the bed, generating a gravity well to try and pull me out.

Standard Parental Maneuver Alpha.

"You need to get back on a proper sleep schedule. Come on. Get up."

"I will. In a little while."

"Now, Darius."

"Dad . . ."

"I'm serious. Let's go."

Dad grabbed my blankets, but I clenched them harder to stop him.

"Dad," I whispered, "I'm, uh, naked."

I did not think I could survive any more penile humiliation today.

Dad cleared his throat. "Laleh, why don't you go on?"

"Secrets don't make friends!" she said.

Sometimes my sister was very nosy.

"It's not a secret, Laleh. It's just none of your business."

"Hey! That's not nice."

"So?"

Dad interrupted us before we could devolve into an argument.

"Go on, Laleh," Dad said. He glared at me to be quiet. "We'll be right there."

I waited for the *flap-flap-flap* of Laleh's bare feet on the hallway floor to recede.

And then Dad said, "Better not pick a fight if you're not dressed for one."

"I wasn't trying to pick a fight."

"I wouldn't make a habit of sleeping naked in your grandmother's house, though."

"I didn't mean to. I showered and then I just got in bed without thinking."

I mean, I usually slept naked at home, where there was a door I could lock, but I had no intention of doing that in my grandmother's house.

I had no intention of going number three in Mamou's house, either. Not under any circumstances.

It would have been too weird.

Dad shook his head. "I understand. I used to sleep naked all the time. Up until you were born." He got this sly grin.

"Uh."

"How do you think you got made?"

"Dad. Gross."

Dad laughed at me—laughed!—and I kind of laughed too. It was an uncomfortable laughter, but still better than Sohrab's and Ali-Reza's and Hossein's laughter.

It was deeply awkward.

"Okay. Come on. I know you're tired, but you've got to stay awake until bedtime."

Dad rubbed the dense black shrub of my hair and tugged on the ends.

I was certain he was going to start on me about how long it was again. But then—

"Stephen!" Mamou called from the kitchen. "The tea is ready!"

Dad exhaled through his lips.

I blinked.

We were supposed to get along now.

"Babou said you went and played soccer. He said you made a friend."

"Um."

"I'm so proud of you, Darius."

Dad pushed the hair off my forehead and kissed it.

"Go ahead and put some clothes on. Let's have some tea. It'll be dinnertime soon."

"Okay."

THE DESSERT CAPITAL
OF THE ANCIENT WORLD

Dad closed the door behind him, and the Dancing Fan chose that moment to fall over.

I dug some clean clothes out of my suitcase and set the Dancing Fan back on its rubber feet.

I also grabbed the tin of FTGFOP1 First Flush Darjeeling out of my Kellner & Newton Messenger Bag. It had gotten dented on its journey through time and space, but the lid was still snug and sealed.

Dad and Laleh were in the living room, sipping cups of Persian tea. "Where's Mom?"

"Shower," Dad said. "Tea's in the kitchen."

Mamou was rinsing rice at the sink. It was a huge, double-basined one, and the windows above it faced out into Babou's garden. It made me all prickly and nervous.

I wondered if Sohrab was supposed to come help Babou again.

I wondered how I was going to avoid him.

"You're up, Darioush-jan."

"Yeah. Um." I realized I had not wrapped the tin of FTGFOP1 First Flush Darjeeling or anything. "I brought you something. I meant to give it to you yesterday, but . . ."

"You were too tired yesterday, Darioush-jan. It's okay."

Mamou dried off her hands and took the tin.

"It's tea?"

"From Portland. Well, I mean, it's from a place called Namring, in India. But it's from a store in Portland. My favorite."

Mamou popped the lid and unsealed the tea. "It looks good, maman. Thank you. You are so sweet. Just like your dad." She pulled me close and kissed me on both cheeks.

If I had been drinking tea at that moment, I would have imitated Javaneh Esfahani and shot it out of my nose.

No one had ever called Stephen Kellner sweet.

Not ever.

I said, "I hope you like it."

"You have to make it for me sometime." She set the tin on the counter and led me to the table, where she had arranged the tea tray with sweets. "Darioush-jan, do you like qottab?"

Qottab are these little pastries filled with crushed almonds and sugar and cardamom, then deep-fried and coated with powdered sugar.

They are my favorite sweet.

According to Mom, Yazd is pretty much the dessert capital of Iran, and had been for thousands of years. All the best desserts originated there: qottab, and noon-e panjereh (these crispy rosette things dusted in powdered sugar), and lavoshak (the Iranian version of Fruit Roll-Ups, but made with fruits popular in Iran, like pomegranate or kiwi). Yazdis had even invented cotton candy, which was called pashmak.

I was fairly certain that, if you traced the lineage of all the desserts in the world, each and every one originated in Yazd.

With one side of my family coming from the dessert capital of the ancient world, I was doomed to have a sweet tooth.

It wasn't like I ate sweets all the time or anything. I couldn't, not with Stephen Kellner constantly monitoring me for dietary indiscretions. But even when I only ate dessert once a month, I never lost any weight.

Dr. Howell said it was a side effect of my medications, and that a little weight gain was a small price to pay for emotional stability.

I knew Dad thought it was a lack of discipline. That if I ate better (and hadn't given up soccer), I could have counteracted the effects of my medication.

Stephen Kellner never struggled with his weight.

Übermensches never do.

Someone knocked on the door. A familiar knock.

My stomach squirmed. I thought about how I had accidentally kept Sohrab's cleats.

"Darioush, can you get the door please?"

"Um." I swallowed. "Okay." I licked a bit of powdered sugar from my fingers, but Dad was watching me, so I grabbed a napkin and wiped the rest off. I had only eaten one qottab, which I thought showed excellent discipline on my part.

Sohrab was standing there, holding my Vans in his right hand, looking at something on his iPhone with his left.

I didn't expect Sohrab to have an iPhone.

I don't know why.

"Oh," he said, and tucked the phone in his pocket. He shuffled back and forth on his feet. "Darioush. You left these."

"Thank you. Um. Yours are in the kitchen."

I stood back to let Sohrab in. He slipped off his shoes and padded toward the kitchen in his black socks.

I always wore white socks, the kind that didn't show when I wore my Vans. I did not like high-rise socks. And I did not like black socks, regardless of length, because they made my feet smell like Cool Ranch Doritos, which is not a normal smell for feet to have.

Sohrab had pants on, so I couldn't tell if he pulled his socks all the way up—which was the fashion back home, if you were a Soulless Minion of Orthodoxy—or if he folded them over, like Dad used to do when he mowed the yard, before he delegated that duty to me.

I suspected Sohrab pulled them all the way up.

"Sohrab!" Mamou pulled him close and kissed him on both cheeks. My stomach churned. Mamou had no way of knowing that Sohrab had made fun of my foreskin only a few hours earlier. She didn't know he'd called me Ayatollah Darioush. But I still felt the burn of jealousy behind my sternum.

I really hated myself for that.

I hated how petty I was.

Mamou started talking to Sohrab in rapid-fire Farsi. All I caught was "chai mekhai," a phrase I had memorized because it meant "Do you want tea?"

"Nah, merci," Sohrab said, and then something else I couldn't follow. Whatever he said, it was magical, because Mamou didn't even offer again.

He had defeated taarof in a single sentence.

"I'm sorry," Mamou said, "I forgot."

Sohrab squinted at her. I hated that he was squinting at my grandmother. "It's fine. Thank you."

"You're fasting?" Laleh said from my side. She had snuck up to inspect our visitor.

"Yes. I can't eat or drink until sunset."

"Not even tea?"

"Not even tea."

"Not even water?"

"Only if I get sick."

I hadn't realized Sohrab's fast included water. I wondered if it was wise to work up a sweat playing soccer/non-American football if you couldn't hydrate after.

Then I remembered the locker room, and I decided I didn't care if Sohrab passed out from dehydration or not.

Dad cleared his throat from behind me.

"Oh. Uh. Dad, Laleh, this is Sohrab. We played soccer together. Football."

Dad gave Sohrab a firm Teutonic handshake. Laleh looked up at Sohrab and then back to me. She could sense the tension hidden between us like a cloaked Romulan Warbird.

"I'm going to put these away," I said, holding up my Vans. "Thanks."

Sohrab followed me down the hall.

"Darioush. Wait."

I kept going. The back of my neck was heating up. I didn't want to start crying again. And if I did, I didn't want Sohrab to see me.

He brushed my shoulder but I shrugged him off.

"I'm sorry," he said. "About before."

He followed me into my bedroom at the end of the hall and closed the door behind him.

"It's fine." I kept my back to him and took as long as I could to put my shoes away. I tucked the laces inside and lined them up perfectly parallel at the foot of my bed.

"No. It was not nice. I should not have said it. I should have stopped them."

I sighed.

I wanted Sohrab to leave.

"It's okay. I get it."

Sometimes you're just wrong about people.

"Thank you for bringing these back. They're the only shoes I brought."

"Darioush. Please." Sohrab rested his palm on my shoulder. It was warm and tentative, like he thought I would pull away.

I thought I would too.

"I was . . ." He paused, and I looked over to see him swallow, his sharp Adam's apple bobbing up and down. "It was nice. You know? Not being the one that Ali-Reza was making fun of."

I mean, I could understand where Sohrab was coming from.

It sucked being a target all the time.

"But he is not my friend, Darioush. Or Hossein. I'm not like them."

"Okay."

"I'm sorry. Really."

Sohrab smiled—not a squinty one, but almost like a question—and I knew he really meant it.

"It's okay. I just took it wrong is all."

"No." Sohrab squeezed my shoulder. "I was very rude. And I am sorry. Will you give me another chance?"

I thought I had been wrong about Sohrab.

But maybe I had been right.

Maybe Sohrab and I really were destined to be friends.

Maybe we were.

"Okay."

Sohrab's smile brightened into a squint. "Friends?"

I smiled too.

It was impossible not to.

"Friends."

You can know things without them being said out loud.

I knew Sohrab and I were going to be friends for life.

Sometimes you can just tell that kind of thing.

I knew my dad wished I was more like him. Our problems went deeper than my hair and my weight. It was everything about me: the outfits I picked for school photos, the messiness of my bedroom, even how inaccurately I used to follow the directions on my LEGO sets.

Stephen Kellner was a firm believer in adhering to the included directions, which had been diligently prepared by a professional LEGO engineer. Designing my own models was tantamount to architectural blasphemy.

Another thing I knew:

I knew my sister, Laleh, wasn't an accident.

A lot of people thought so, because she was eight years younger than me, and my parents weren't "trying for another child," which is kind of gross if you think about it. But she was not an accident.

She was a replacement. An upgrade. I knew that without anyone saying it out loud.

And I knew Stephen Kellner was relieved to have another chance, a new child who wouldn't be such a disappointment. It was written across his face every time he smiled at her. Every time he sighed at me.

I didn't blame Laleh for that.

I really didn't.

But sometimes I wondered if I was the one who was an accident.

That's normal.

Right?

You can learn things without them being said out loud too.

That night at dinner, I learned Ardeshir Bahrami did not like Stephen Kellner very much. At all.

Maybe it was because Mom stayed in America for Dad. She left her family, her country, her father, for Stephen Kellner.

Maybe it was because Ardeshir Bahrami—a True Persian in every sense of the word—was culturally predisposed to reject any and all Teutonic influences intruding on his Iranian family.

Maybe it was because Dad was a secular humanist, and Babou was religiously predisposed to dislike him. Zoroastrianism is patrilineal, which meant that even though Mom had inherited Babou's religion, she couldn't pass it on to me and Laleh.

Maybe it was all three.

We sat around Mamou's dining room table—Sohrab stayed to eat with us, once the sun had set—and somehow Dad had ended up seated next to Babou, who had decided to keep up a running commentary on the meal.

"You probably don't like this stew, Stephen." he said. "Most Americans don't like fesenjoon."

"I love it," Dad said. "It's my favorite. Shirin taught me how to make it."

It was true: Dad really did love it.

133

And fesenjoon is a hard food to love at first.

It kind of looks like mud.

Worse than mud, even: It looks like the sort of primordial goo that could generate new amino acids, which would inevitably combine to initiate protein synthesis and create brand new life forms.

Babou was right that non-Persians (and even some Fractional Persians) tended to regard fesenjoon with suspicion, which is a shame, because it's just chicken, ground walnuts, and robe. It's salty and sweet and sour and perfect.

"You eat it the American way," Babou said. He nodded at Dad's hands, where he held his knife and fork. Babou—and Mamou and Sohrab and Mom, for that matter—used forks and spoons, which is how a lot of Persians ate.

Dad smiled with his lips closed. "I never got used to eating with my fork and spoon."

"It's fine, Stephen," Babou said. He scooped up a spoonful of rice and said something to Mom in Farsi, who shook her head and answered in Farsi too.

Dad glanced at Mom and then back at his plate.

This was a thing that happened sometimes, when we were around Persians. They would switch from Farsi to English between sentences, or sometimes even within them, and me and Dad would be left out.

Dad's ears looked a little pink. It was like looking into a distorted mirror at one of our family dinners, with Stephen Kellner playing me and Babou playing Stephen Kellner.

There was something deeply wrong about seeing Stephen Kellner embarrassed.

My own ears burned. Harmonic resonance.

"Darioush," Sohrab said. He sat next to me, his plate piled twice as high as my own with rice and stew.

He hadn't eaten since breakfast, after all.

"Tell me about your school. In America."

"Um," I said.

"What are your classes like?"

"They're okay. I take economics, which is kind of cool. Physical education. English. Um. Geometry, but I'm not very good at that."

"You're not good at maths?"

I thought it was very interesting, how Sohrab used the British version of *math*.

"Not really."

I glanced at Dad, but he was too busy shoveling rice into his mouth to comment on my math grades. Not that he was ever that bad about it. School was maybe the one thing he was mostly okay about. He knew how hard I studied.

But I knew without him saying it out loud that he was disappointed I didn't have the knack for it. I would never be an architect like him. He'd never be able to update his messenger bag to say "Kellner & Son" or "Kellner & Kellner."

It wasn't the biggest disappointment I had ever dealt him, but I could tell it still stung.

"What about friends? You have lots of them?"

The fire in my ears spread to my neck and cheeks.

"Um. Not really. I guess I don't fit in much."

As soon as I said it, I glanced at Dad, because Stephen Kellner was categorically opposed to self-pity. But thankfully, he was still occupied with his fesenjoon.

Sohrab's smile faded as he studied me.

"It's because you are Iranian?"

"Yeah. I guess."

He used his spoon to pick the meat off a chicken leg and scoop it up with some rice. "You're the only Iranian at your school?"

"No. There's a girl too. She's full Iranian, though."

"Your girlfriend?"

I choked on a bit of rice.

"No!" I coughed. "We're just friends. Her name is Javaneh. Javaneh Esfahani. Her grandparents are from Isfahan."

"That's what the name means," Sohrab said. "Esfahani. From Isfahan."

"Oh."

Babou cleared his throat and pointed his spoon at me. "Darioush," he said. "How come you don't know this?"

"Um."

He turned to Mom. "It's because you don't teach him," he said. "You wanted him to be American, like Stephen. You don't want him to be Persian."

"Babou!" Mom said. She started arguing in Farsi, and Babou argued right back. He kept pointing his spoon at me.

"Darioush. You don't want to learn Farsi, baba?"

"Um."

I mean, of course I did. But I couldn't just say that. Not without making Mom feel guilty.

I sunk down in my chair a bit.

But then Sohrab came to my rescue. He cleared his throat.

"Who wants tah dig?"

Tah dig is the layer of crispy rice from the bottom of the pot.

It's universally acknowledged as the ultimate form of rice.

More than one family has forgotten their arguments when it came time to divide the tah dig.

"Thanks," I mumbled.

Sohrab squinted at me and handed me a wedge of tah dig.

"You're welcome, Darioush."

I led Sohrab to the door to say good-bye.

"Mamou said you are going to Persepolis tomorrow."

"Yeah. I think so."

"She asked if I wanted to come too."

"Oh. Cool."

"I won't go if you don't want me to, Darioush. It's time with your family."

"No. It's okay. I want you to. Really."

I was facing hours trapped in a car with Stephen Kellner, and Sohrab being there might actually make it bearable.

"Okay. See you in the morning?"

"Yeah. See you."

I didn't hold out much hope for Dad and me continuing our nightly *Star Trek* tradition, but I went in search of Babou's computer anyway.

Across from Laleh's room was a sunroom—though it was dark now—with a huge window covered in Venetian blinds and a well-loved beige couch in front. Against the opposite wall, a large television stood on an antique wooden table. DVDs and cases orbited in a ring around it, mostly Farsi-language dubs of Bollywood movies.

On either side of the television, and above it, the Bahrami Family Portrait Gallery extended into a new wing.

Fariba Bahrami loved photographs.

One picture was of Mom in the hospital, cradling a newly born baby Laleh. Dad had his arms wrapped around them both, looking ridiculous but somehow still radiating Teutonic stoicism in his light blue scrubs. Beneath Dad's elbow, there stood a young, still-squeaky me, bouncing on my toes to catch a glimpse of my new baby sister.

There were so many pictures. Some were of Dayi Jamsheed and his kids, and Dayi Soheil's family. I recognized them from pictures Mom had showed me. Others I recognized from home, because Mom had sent them to Mamou, like one of Laleh from last Halloween. She was dressed up as Dorothy from *The Wizard of Oz*.

Laleh was totally obsessed with *The Wizard of Oz* last summer. The Judy Garland version. She would watch it and then run around the living room a few times and then watch it again, all day long.

Mom braided Laleh's hair last Halloween—her curly Persian hair made perfect pigtails—and she'd found a blue-and-white gingham dress. Dad had brought home bright red sneakers with lights in the soles for Laleh to wear as her Ruby Slippers.

Mom and Dad took Laleh trick-or-treating, while I was assigned to monitor the house and disburse candy as necessary.

I was not cool enough to be invited to the parties where the

Soulless Minions of Orthodoxy celebrated Halloween. In fact, I wasn't even cool enough to get invited to a mid-level party. I was a D-Bag, in social status if not in name quite yet. So I sat at home, watching *Star Trek: First Contact* (the scariest of all *Star Trek* films) and giving out Reese's Peanut Butter Cups to the neighborhood kids as they wandered by.

Despite his opposition to my own dietary indiscretions, Stephen Kellner insisted there was no finer candy for trick-or-treaters than Reese's Peanut Butter Cups.

At least we were not the house with raisins.

"What are you looking for, Darius?" Mom watched me from the doorway, cradling two cups of tea. They were the glass kind, the ones with gilded rims and no handles. Many True Persians used cups like that, but I had never mastered the trick. I always burned my fingers.

"The computer. I thought maybe Dad and I could watch *Star Trek* on it."

"Probably not, with the Internet censors."

"Oh."

Mom sat on the couch and patted the cushion next to her. I took my tea from her, but then I put it on the coffee table before I scorched my fingerprints off.

"So? What did you think of Yazd?"

"Well. It's different. But not as different as I thought it would be."

"Oh?"

"Yeah. I mean, it's not like *Aladdin* or anything."

Mom laughed.

"And it's more modern. Sohrab has an iPhone, even."

Mom sipped her tea and let out a long, contented sigh. She ran the fingers of her left hand through my hair and stared at the Bahrami Family Portrait Gallery until she found a photo of my tenth birthday party.

"Your hair," she said.

When I was ten, I had decided I wanted to wear my hair like Lt. Commander Data, the *Enterprise*'s android operations officer. Every morning, Mom helped me blow dry my hair and brush it back into perfectly straight lines, and then gel it until it was as stiff as a bicycle helmet.

"The Android Look was not a good one for me."

Mom laughed.

"What are we going to do for your birthday this year?"

"Um. I dunno."

My birthday was April 2, which was the day before we left Iran.

According to Mom, even though I was born on April 2, she went into labor with me on April Fools' Day.

When her water broke, and she told Dad, he thought she was joking.

It wasn't until she got in the car without him that Dad realized it was really happening.

Sometimes Mom said I was her April Fools' Joke.

I knew—without her saying—that she didn't realize how bad it made me feel.

When I took my teacup/glass to the kitchen, Babou had his nose in the cupboard.

"Darioush. What is this?" He pulled out the FTGFOP1 First Flush Darjeeling and shook the tin around.

"It's a gift. For having us here."

"This is tea?" He popped open the tin and peered in. "This is not Persian tea. I will teach you how we make Persian tea."

I already knew how to damn Persian tea with hell.

"Um."

"Come. Darioush." Babou grabbed the teapot off the stove—it was nearly empty—and dumped the dregs into the sink. "We will make it fresh."

Babou rinsed out the pot once and banged it on the counter in front of me. The back of my neck prickled.

Having my foreskin compared to a turban was still the most humiliating moment of my life, but being taught how to make Persian tea—when I had been making it for years—came in a close second.

"We put the tea in like this," he said, scooping loose tea from the huge frosted glass jar on the counter. The leaves were black, short, and sharp, but they were bursting with fragrance. Bergamot, mostly—kind of lemony—but there was something else in there too, something I couldn't place. It was earthy, kind of like feet (not Cool Ranch Doritos), but kind of like the wet mulch in the flower beds outside of Chapel Hill High School's student entrance.

I leaned over the pot to get a better whiff, but Babou pushed me back.

"What are you doing? This is for drinking, not for smelling."

"Uh."

Tea—good tea, at least—was for smelling too.

When I took cupping classes at Rose City Teas, we always had to smell the tea leaves both before and after they had been steeped. Not that I could ever admit to taking cupping classes. Charles Apatan, Manager of the Tea Haven at the Shoppes at Fairview Court, would have called that elitist too.

"Four scoops," Babou said. "And we crush the hel. You know hel?"

"Cardamom."

"Yes." He shook out five green pods from a smaller frosted glass jar. "We crush it like this." He rolled the bottom of the teapot around on the cardamom pods to pop them open, then scooped them up and dropped them in with the tea leaves. "Cover it with water."

Babou grabbed the kettle. The lid was still off, from where the teapot had been sitting. Steam billowed around his hand like the scalding breath of Smaug the Ever-Boiling, but Ardeshir Bahrami's skin was part dragon hide. He filled the teapot, flipped the lid closed, then put it and the kettle back on the burner.

"Now we let it sit."

"Dam it."

"Yes. Ten minutes."

"Okay."

"Not before. It will be too light."

"Okay."

"Now you know. Next time you can make it."

"Okay."

Babou made me stand with him in a Level Five Awkward Silence while the tea dammed.

It was upgraded to a Level Six Awkward Silence when Dad came in to take his medicine. He glanced back and forth between me and Babou for a second.

"You okay, Darius?" he asked, which broke the silence, but not the awkwardness.

I nodded.

Dad shook out his pills and filled a glass of water.

Babou's mustache twitched. "Stephen," he said, "you take these pills too?"

Dad dry-swallowed and then drank his water—the entire glass—in one long gulp. He almost blushed.

Almost.

"Yes," he said.

And then he said, "Hey. Is that tea ready?"

I glanced at the timer on my phone.

"Another two minutes."

"Mind pouring me one? I'll get *Star Trek* set up in the living room."

"What about the censors?"

"I've got the whole season on my iPad."

It shouldn't have surprised me. Übermensches were known for their foresight.

But I honestly had not expected Stephen Kellner to bring it up on his own.

"Oh. Okay. Cool."

"Thanks." Dad nodded at Babou and went back into the living room.

I played with the hem of my shirt and waited for the tea to finish.

When I got to the living room, Captain Picard had already started the opening narration.

And Dad was sitting on the couch with his arm around Laleh.

"Uh."

"Sorry, Darius," Dad said. "But you've seen it before. And your sister was so excited to watch."

I blinked. It didn't make any sense.

Star Trek was supposed to be me and Dad's special thing.

What was he doing, watching it with Laleh?

I mean, it was inevitable that Laleh would acquire a taste for *Star Trek*—eventually. She was my sister, after all. And Stephen Kellner's daughter. It was in her genetic makeup.

But I thought I would get to keep that bit of Dad to myself for a little while longer.

It was the only time I ever got to be his son.

The credits faded out, and the episode title came up. "Sins of the Father," which was about Worf going back home to face accusations that his father had committed treason.

It seemed weirdly appropriate.

"Come sit," Dad said.

He patted the couch beside him.

"Um."

We were supposed to get along in Iran.

But did that mean we had to cancel the only time we actually spent together?

Maybe it did.

I sat against the edge of the couch and balanced my tea on

my kneecap, but Dad reached out and pulled me closer. He left his arm across my back for a second.

"Your shoulders are getting broad," he said.

Then he let go of me and leaned over to kiss Laleh on the forehead.

And I sat with Stephen and Laleh Kellner as they watched *Star Trek*.

It wasn't even dawn when a voice began chanting.

It was far away, tinny, like the speakers in a drive-thru.

But it was beautiful, even if I couldn't tell what it was saying.

When it faded away, I didn't go back to sleep, because Mom knocked on my door.

I pulled the covers closer around my neck. I had on my boxers, but still.

"Yeah?"

"Oh. You're up."

"Yeah. The chanting woke me. The call to prayer. Right?"

Mom smiled. "The azan."

"It's beautiful." I'd heard it the last couple of days, but I never got a chance to ask about it. And it felt different, waking up to it instead of hearing it while I was making tea or eating lunch.

"I forgot how much I missed hearing it."

"Yeah?"

Mom turned on the light. The Dancing Fan chose that moment to fall over.

We both stared at it for a second.

Mom shook her head. "I can't believe Babou still has that old thing."

"You always say Yazdis don't throw anything away."

Mom snorted. "Come on. You'd better get dressed. Your grandfather wants to hit the road in half an hour."

"Okay."

The sun was still kissing the horizon when I stepped out of the house. I pulled the hood of my jacket up to warm my ears.

Everything was quiet.

Everything, that is, except the house behind me, where Mom was shouting at Laleh to get her shoes on, and Mamou was shouting at Mom to remember the water bottles and snacks.

Dad bumped his elbow against me, his hands deep in the pockets of his gray Keller & Newton jacket.

"Um."

The shouting inside was drowned out by the sound of a thousand furious wasps as Babou drove the Bahrami family vehicle up to the curb.

Ardeshir Bahrami drove a dull blue minivan that looked like it had come from a different age of this world. It was boxy and angular, and it poured so much smoke out of its exhaust pipe, I was certain the Forges of some Dark Lord were firing deep within its catalytic converter.

I wondered if they had emissions tests in Iran. It seemed impossible the Bahrami family vehicle could pass any sort of inspection.

Babou stopped in front of the house, but the cloud of smoke kept going, enveloping the minivan in a black shroud before dissipating into a thin trail of intermittent puffs.

I decided to call it the Smokemobile.

I would have christened it, but the sale of alcohol was illegal in Iran, so there was no bottle of champagne to smash upon its blue hull. I could have used a bottle of doogh—the carbonated yogurt beverage that True, Non-Fractional Persians enjoyed—

but (a) it usually came in plastic bottles, which would not shatter, and (b) it would have made a terrible mess.

Babou stepped out and leaned over the hood. "Fariba-khanum!"

Mamou dragged a half-asleep Laleh out of the house and deposited her in the Smokemobile. Dad buckled her in, while Mamou ran back inside.

"Fariba-khanum!" Babou shouted again.

Mom came out next, hoisting a bag of snacks.

"I can take that."

"Thank you, sweetie."

I stuck the snacks in the trunk and contorted my way into the backseat next to Laleh, but then Mom turned around and ran back inside too.

"Shirin!"

And then Babou followed Mom inside.

Dad met my eyes, the tiniest of smiles curling his lips. "Now we see where your mom gets it from." He pulled himself into the van and took the middle seat.

I wondered if it was all that safe for Babou to drive in his condition, especially such a long distance—supposedly it was almost six hours to Persepolis—but when I asked Dad, he shushed me.

"Not now," he said.

I wondered if maybe someone had already brought it up.

I wondered if maybe that's why everyone was in such a bad mood.

Laleh stretched and yawned and leaned against me, burying her face in my side.

Normally, I enjoyed when Laleh did that. Being a pillow felt like the kind of thing a big brother was supposed to do.

I did not feel like a very good big brother that morning.

I shifted and twisted until Laleh got annoyed and leaned against the window instead.

Finally, Mamou and Mom came out. Mom took her seat next to Dad, while Mamou took the passenger seat.

"Where's Babou?" Dad asked.

"He forgot his tokhmeh for the trip," Mamou answered.

Mom said something to Mamou in Farsi.

"Yes. Every time!"

Babou hurried back out with a huge bag of tokhmeh and buckled himself in.

"Okay," he said. "Bereem."

Sohrab was waiting for us in front of his house. It was hard to see much in the dawn light—the sun was rising behind the house— but with the curtained windows glowing, it looked warm and cozy.

I scooted into the middle spot so Sohrab could sit by me. Laleh huffed and wiggled a bit closer to the window.

"Hey," I said, once Sohrab was finished saying hi to Mamou and Babou in a long stream of Farsi that seemed to consist mostly of taarofing.

"Good morning, Darioush."

"Ready to go?"

He clicked his seat belt.

"Ready to go."

※ ※ ※

Ardeshir Bahrami was a madman behind the wheel.

There were no handles to hold on to—Dad called them "Oh-Shit-Handles," even though he was categorically opposed to colorful metaphors—so I gripped the seat cushion and tried not to flatten Sohrab or Laleh whenever Babou executed an unexpected lane change.

Mom and Mamou, who were no doubt acclimated to Babou's driving, swayed with the Smokemobile's inertia. And Stephen Kellner, who loved to drive his German Road Machine at unsafe velocities, was right at home, leaning into each turn like a race car driver.

The streets were still mostly empty as we merged onto the highway, but Babou drove as if he was dodging enemy fire, pulling off one evasive maneuver after another.

It must have been a Social Cue.

Like I said, it was supposed to be a six-hour drive to Persepolis.

Ardeshir Bahrami made it in four and a half.

When we finally pulled into the parking lot, my body had to adjust to sub-light speeds before I could pour myself out of the Smokemobile's backseat and follow Sohrab to the ticket office.

I think ticket offices are some sort of universal constant, whether it's the ruins of Persepolis—"Takhte Jamsheed," Sohrab kept calling it, the Throne of Jamsheed—or the International Rose Test Garden back home. One day, when humans colonize Mars, there will be a ticket office to see Olympus Mons.

The real one. Not the smoldering caldera of my former pimple.

Babou glowered at the cashier and started arguing about the price of admission. Haggling over prices was another Persian

Social Cue, one I had observed when I went with Mom to the Persian Grocery back in Portland.

Laleh had spent most of the drive asleep against the humming window.

I guess I did feel kind of bad about that.

But she had woken up refreshed and anxious to run through the gates and explore. She kept twisting the ends of her soft yellow headscarf around her fingers. It had sunflowers on it.

"Your headscarf looks nice, Laleh," I said, taking her hand to stop her fidgeting.

She squeezed my hand. I loved the way my sister's hand fit in mine. "Thank you."

Babou was still haggling, but Mom stepped up and whispered something in his ear. Babou shook his head, but then Mom thrust a wad of bills under the glass partition before Babou could stop her. The man at the counter seemed alarmed at Mom's directness, but he handed Babou our tickets and wiped the sweat from his forehead.

Ardeshir Bahrami was an intense negotiator.

"Come," he said. He took Laleh's other hand, and she let go of me to match his stride.

My sister wanted to look at every single stall in the bazaar that sprawled between the ticket office and the entrance to the ruins, but Babou managed to maneuver her away from them all. Apparently his evasive driving skills extended to navigating Laleh past potential distractions.

"Your sister has so much energy," Sohrab said.

"Yeah. Too much."

"You are a good brother, Darioush."

I didn't know if that was the truth. But I liked that Sohrab thought that about me.

A row of trees hid the ruins from view. We followed the path—made of sun-bleached wooden beams—up a short hill. Ahead of us, Laleh wiggled out of Babou's grasp and rabbited through a crumpled stone archway that had stood for thousands of years. Sohrab and I jogged to catch up.

Even though the trees and manicured lawns were green, Persepolis itself was brown and dry. Pillars of stone reached for the sun, their surfaces smoothed by wind and age. I had to crane my neck to see their tops, but the sky was so bright and the sun was so high I started sneezing.

"Wow," I said when I regained the power of speech.

Dad paused beside us. "Wow is right. Look at it."

Many of the stone pillars were broken. Some were cracked but still standing, barricaded with Plexiglas to keep people from touching them. Others had already experienced non-passive failures. Huge chunks of brown rubble lay forlorn across the loose rocky ground. Tufts of grass poked out from a few shady spots, but mostly, it was dry and stark.

I felt like I had stepped onto the surface of the planet Vulcan, and was finally going to master the Kolinahr discipline, embracing logic and purging myself of all emotions.

Dad pulled his sketchbook out of his Kellner & Newton Messenger Bag—Dad was never far from his sketchbook—and stepped off the wooden planks onto the gravel to sketch the nearest row of broken pillars.

Laleh and Babou had already wandered off, so Sohrab led me to a giant statue of a lamassu.

A lamassu is pretty much the Persian version of a sphinx: a mishmash animal, with the head of a man, the body of an ox, and the wings of an eagle. As far as I knew, no riddles were involved in mythological encounters with lamassu, but there was probably some extremely high level taarofing.

This lamassu was one of a pair. Its mate had been decapitated at some point, but still, the statues towered over us, mute sentinels of a fallen empire.

"The Gate of All Nations," Sohrab said. He gestured around to the lamassus and pillars surrounding us. "That's the name in English."

It wasn't much of a gate anymore, since anyone of any nation could have easily stepped around it instead of walking through. But it was still amazing.

Behind the lamassu, more columns sprouted from the ground like ancient trees in a petrified forest, forty feet tall, spindly but still miraculously upright. Giant stone slabs formed the remains of what must once have been a breathtaking structure.

Sohrab held my shoulders and guided me through the Gate of All Nations, then turned me toward another long wood-planked path where Mom and Mamou were waiting for us.

"This is the palace of Darioush the First," Sohrab said. "Darioush the Great."

"Wow," I said.

My vocabulary had failed me.

"Pretty cool, right?" Mom said. She looked back toward the entrance. "Where's your dad?

"Sketching the pillars."

"Go get him, would you?" She tucked a strand of hair back under her turquoise headscarf, and then did the same for her mother. "We should stay together."

"What about Laleh and Babou?"

Mamou said, "They'll be fine."

I ran back to grab Dad.

"Mom says we should stick together."

"All right."

But Dad had to get sketches of the Gate of All Nations too, until Mom finally lost her patience and came to get him herself.

She waved her arm at the crowds around us. "Everyone is going to think you're planning a drone strike," she whispered, her voice sharp as vinegar.

Shirin Kellner could be formidable when she needed to be.

"Sorry," Dad said. He slipped the sketchbook back into his Kellner & Newton Messenger Bag.

Dad knew better than to argue with Mom when she used her vinegar voice.

He bumped elbows with me as we followed Mom.

I didn't understand why he did that.

"Huge, huh?"

"Yeah."

"I'm grateful you're getting to see this."

"Me too."

Dad almost smiled.

Almost.

Maybe he was doing his best.

"Darioush!" Sohrab called. He waved me forward.

"Coming!"

⚜ ⚜ ⚜

It wasn't like the Ruins of Persepolis were an entire city.

At its height, Persepolis had covered a huge area. Not as big as Greater Portland, maybe, but still. The part we were in, the part with the actual ruins—Takhte Jamsheed—was small enough to fit in our neighborhood back home.

Sohrab led me through the Apadana, the complex's main palace. There was not much of it left: several enormous pillars, even taller than the Gate of All Nations; and some ornate staircases, though their wide, shallow steps had a bizarre rise-to-run ratio; and a bunch of stone arches whose structural integrity fields had held up impressively well over thousands of years.

The whole thing smelled like sun-baked dust—it made me think of Mom running the vacuum, which was weird—but it wasn't old or musty. The wind from the mountains around Shiraz kept a light breeze spinning through the Apadana, quieter and more subtle than the Dancing Fan could ever hope to be.

In pictures, old buildings are always white and smooth. But in real life, Persepolis was brown and rough and imperfect. There was something magical about it: the low walls, all that remained of some ancient hall, and the pillars looming over me like giants in an ancient playground.

According to Sohrab, many of the buildings were never finished before Alexander the Great sacked Persepolis.

Alexander the Great was the Trent Bolger of Ancient Persia.

Dad followed us into the Apadana and pulled his sketchbook back out.

"These arches are incredible." Dad pointed to a huge set that looked at least four stories high.

"Yeah."

"Stephen," Sohrab said. "You like architecture?"

"That's what I do back home," Dad said. "I'm an architect."

Sohrab's eyebrows shot up. "Really?"

Dad nodded and kept sketching.

I wanted to ask him if the ruins reminded him of Vulcan, the way they reminded me.

I wanted to ask him if he wanted to come exploring with me and Sohrab.

But I didn't know how.

Stephen Kellner stared at the arches above us and bit his lip. He rubbed his thumb against the page to make a shadow and kept sketching.

"Come on," I said to Sohrab as we left Dad behind.

"Your dad is an architect?"

"Yeah. He's a partner in a firm."

"That's what I want to do. Someday."

"Really?"

"Yes. That or civil engineering."

"Wow."

To be honest, I wasn't really sure what the difference was between the two.

I couldn't say that out loud.

"It's a lot of school, though."

"Yes. Not easy for Bahá'ís."

"Oh?"

Sohrab nodded, but he didn't elaborate.

Instead, he said, "Come on, Darioush. There's much more to see."

※ ※ ※

We found Laleh and Babou standing in front of a wall.

It was not a plain wall: Like everything else in Persepolis, it was oversized, carved, and the color of cargo pants.

"Eh! Sohrab. Good. Darioush hasn't seen this," Babou said. "Come see, baba."

Laleh was sagging against Babou's leg. I put my hand on top of her headscarf and rubbed it a little. Laleh sighed and shifted her weight from Babou's leg to mine.

Babou nodded at the wall. "Look."

I craned my neck to try and make out all the details.

It was a relief, carved directly into the stone. A bearded man sat on a throne, holding a staff in one hand and a hyacinth in the other.

Maybe he was preparing for Nowruz. Lots of people like to add sonbols to their haft-seen.

Carved in relief, the figure's beard looked like it was made of enormous stone beads, each with a little swirl in the center, countless tiny galaxies of rock.

"It's you." Babou poked me in the chest.

"Me?"

I was certain I would never be able to grow a beard so luxurious as the one hewn into the wall above me. Stephen Kellner's fair-haired Teutonic genes would prevent it.

"It's Darioush the Great," Sohrab said.

"Oh."

Babou said, "He built many of these things."

Until they got burned to the ground by angry Greeks.

Well, Macedonians, technically.

Babou looked right at me. "Darioush was a great man. Strong. Smart. Brave."

I didn't feel strong or smart or brave.

Like I said, my parents were setting themselves up for disappointment, naming me after a titanic figure like that.

Darius the Great was a diplomat and a conqueror. And I was just me.

"Your mom and dad picked a good name for you."

Babou put his arm on my shoulder. I swallowed and followed his gaze to stare at the carving.

"Mamou thought it was too much driving to come here. To see this. But it's important for you to know where you come from."

I didn't understand Ardeshir Bahrami.

Yesterday I wasn't Persian enough because I didn't speak Farsi, because I took medicine for depression, because I brought him and Mamou fancy tea.

He made me feel small and stupid.

Now he was determined to show me my heritage.

Maybe Ardeshir Bahrami experienced Mood Slingshot Maneuvers too.

Babou squeezed my shoulder and then led Laleh away, leaving me and Sohrab alone.

"Babou is right," Sohrab said. "It's good to see where you come from."

"Yeah," I said. "I guess."

"You don't like it?"

"No. It's just . . ."

Sohrab had grown up with this history all around him.

He knew where he was from.

There was no ancient emperor for him to measure up to.

"I don't know."

"It's okay, Darioush," he said.

He put his arm over my shoulder and led me down the path after Babou and Laleh.

"I understand."

L aleh and I taught Sohrab how to play I Spy on the drive back to Yazd. When it got too dark to play any more, Laleh fell asleep with her face mashed into my side. I unwound her headscarf so it wouldn't get tangled as she shifted against me.

As we reached the outskirts of Yazd, Babou slowed the Smokemobile down so much, it felt like we were coasting down the evening streets on maneuvering thrusters only.

"Ardeshir?" Mamou said.

Babou looked back and forth at the road signs and said something in Farsi. Mamou put her hand on his arm, but he shook it off and snapped at her.

In front of me, Mom's shoulders bunched up.

"What is it?" I asked, but Mom shook her head. Laleh stirred against me, yawned, and rubbed her face into my stomach. My shirt was wet where she had drooled a little bit.

I looked to Sohrab, but he was staring at his hands folded in his lap.

Mamou and Babou argued back and forth until Babou slammed on the brakes—not that it did much, since we were barely crawling forward—and pulled over. The Smokemobile's exhaust plumed around us.

Mamou unbuckled her seat belt, but Mom reached forward to put an arm on her shoulder. She and Mamou started whispering in Farsi, while Babou sat in the driver's seat with his arms folded and his chin on his chest.

Mom popped her own seat belt and tried to get up, but Dad caught her. "What's going on?"

"I'm driving us the rest of the way."

Dad glanced at Mamou and Babou and then back to Mom.

"Let me."

"You sure?" Mom's voice caught, like she had swallowed tea the wrong way.

"Positive."

Dad opened the sliding door, letting in a cloud of the Black Breath that nearly suffocated us all. Once Dad got out, Babou climbed in next to Mom and slid the door shut with the finality of a guillotine.

Dad settled into the driver's seat of the Smokemobile—the most un-Audi car imaginable—and buckled himself in. "You'll have to guide me."

Stephen Kellner, Teutonic Übermensch, had never asked for directions in his life.

"Take the next right."

While Mamou guided Dad, Mom whispered to Babou in Farsi and wound her arm through his.

I cleared my throat and glanced at Sohrab again.

"What happened?" I whispered.

Sohrab bit his lip. He leaned in close so no one else would hear.

"Babou got lost."

※ ※ ※

Like I said. You can know things without them being said out loud.

I knew that Babou would never get to drive the Smokemobile again.

I didn't say anything when we dropped off Sohrab. Just waved good-bye.

Some things were too big to talk about.

Sohrab understood that.

When we got back to Mamou's, Laleh crawled over me and sprinted inside to pee. She'd been complaining since she woke up that her bladder was about to experience a non-passive failure.

Mamou led Babou inside, talking low in Farsi, while Dad waited for Mom at the door after letting Laleh in.

I stooped under Dad's arm where it rested against the door frame and walked into the house. When I looked back, Dad was holding Mom, kissing her hair as she shook and cried against him.

I didn't know what to do.

Darius the Great might have known. But I didn't.

I went to the kitchen to make some tea.

Babou's unnecessary and humiliating lesson in how to dam tea had one benefit: I now knew where Mamou kept her tea and hel.

When it was ready, I poured a cup and knocked on the sunroom door. "Babou? Do you want some tea?"

"Come," he said, which made me think of The Picard.

Babou had changed into a plain white shirt and loose white pants with a drawstring waist, and he had hitched them halfway up his torso. He sat on the floor with a blue-patterned Persian tablecloth spread before him, picking through sabzi with Laleh's help. The warm glow of a table lamp softened the planes of Babou's face and brightened his eyes. Even his mustache seemed friendlier.

"Darioush-jan. Come. Sit." He nodded at the couch behind him, then went back to paring the stalks of fresh cilantro from the colander next to him. Every so often, he'd hand some to Laleh for her to sort out the bad leaves.

"Um." I handed Babou his tea and a sugar cube. Up close, he looked less warm—almost gray.

I hated seeing Babou like that.

I think I liked it better when I only saw him on a computer screen.

That's normal.

Right?

"Did you see your mom?" He pointed his knife at a weird wrought-iron-looking frame on the wall with six oval photos in it, all of Mom when she was young: Mom as a baby, Mom as a little girl playing with Dayi Jamsheed and Dayi Soheil, Mom lined up with the family behind the haft-seen for Nowruz. There was this one stunning portrait of teenaged Mom looking over her shoulder toward the camera, tugging her headscarf toward her face.

Shirin Kellner (née Bahrami) could have been a supermodel.

"I never thought she would move to America," Babou said. "But she did well."

I could tell there was more that Babou wanted to say but didn't.

"She did well," Babou repeated. "She married your dad."

It was the first nice thing—well, almost-nice thing—Babou had said about Dad.

"And she had you and Laleh."

Laleh looked up at the sound of her name, and Babou gave her a handful of basil leaves from the colander, wrapped in a damp paper towel. He said something to her in Farsi, and Laleh hopped up and ran off.

Babou shifted the sugar cube around in his mouth, clacking it against his teeth. "Your dad is a good man," he said. "But he is not Zoroastrian. You and Laleh are not either."

"Oh."

I was used to being a disappointment to Dad, and being a disappointment to Babou didn't seem that different. But I hated that he was disappointed in Laleh too, for something she couldn't change.

I swallowed.

Babou looked up at me. There was something sad and lonely in his eyes, in the way his mustache drooped over his frown.

I wanted to tell him I was still his grandson.

I wanted to tell him I was glad I was getting to know him.

I wanted to tell him I was sorry about his brain tumor.

I didn't tell him any of that, though. I sipped my tea, and Ardeshir Bahrami sipped his. The silence between us hung heavy with all the things we couldn't say. All the things we knew without them being said out loud.

Mamou was at the kitchen table, drinking her own cup of tea, when I brought the basket of cleaned sabzi into the kitchen.

"Darioush-jan. Did you make this tea?"

"Um. Yeah?"

"It's cinnamon?"

"I added a pinch."

"It's good, maman!"

"Thanks." I poured myself a fresh cup. "I was worried Babou wouldn't like it."

"Babou doesn't notice, you know? His taste buds are not that good."

"Oh."

"Did you have a nice time, maman?"

"Yeah. Um. Babou showed me Darius the First."

"Where your name came from."

I nodded.

"I wish you had seen it sooner. I wish you lived here."

"Really?"

"Yes, of course. I miss you. And I wish you could know your history better. You know, for Yazdis, family history is very important."

"Um."

"But I am happy for you, living in America."

I sipped my tea. "Is Babou okay?"

Mamou smiled at me, but her eyes had turned sad. Fariba Bahrami had the kindest eyes in the entire galaxy. They were huge and brown, with little soft pillows under them. Mom called them Bette Davis eyes.

I had to google who Bette Davis was. It turns out someone wrote a whole song about her eyes.

Mamou said, "Babou is okay."

I knew he wasn't okay. Not really. She didn't have to say it out loud.

"I love you, Mamou." I set down my tea and hugged her.

"I love you too, maman." She kissed me on the cheek, and then she smiled again. "Do you like broccoli?"

"Uh. Sure."

I had no strong feelings on broccoli. And I wasn't prepared for the conversation's sudden and inexplicable course correction. Fariba Bahrami was a Level Ten Topic Changer when she needed to be.

"I'll make you some tomorrow. You want anything before bed?"

"No. I'm okay."

I washed our dishes while Mamou put away the sabzi Babou and Laleh had picked through. "You are like your dad," she said. "He always helps in the kitchen too."

"He does?"

"I remember, when we came for the wedding. Your dad always did the dishes. He wouldn't let me help at all. Your dad is so sweet."

There it was again.

Stephen Kellner: sweet.

"You are sweet too, Darioush-jan."

"Um."

Mamou pulled me down to kiss me again. "I'm so glad you came."

"Me too."

PERSIAN CASUAL

Dad woke me up the next morning, shaking my shoulder.

"You naked?"

"What? No."

"Good. Happy Nowruz, Darius." Dad rubbed my hair.

He didn't even comment on its length.

"Happy Nowruz, Dad."

Like I said, there were special rules for *Star Trek*—or at least there used to be, before Dad changed them on me—rules where we got to be a real father and son.

At Nowruz, the same rules applied. But this time, our father-son relationship had an audience.

The Dancing Fan had been creeping up on Dad, a relentless Borg drone determined to assimilate us both, but as soon as he glanced at it, it stopped moving.

Resistance was futile.

"Better get dressed. Your uncle Soheil is coming soon."

"What time is it?"

"Almost ten. Come on. Before the kitchen gets taken over."

Dad poured me a cup of tea and sat next to me as I ate my sangak and feta cheese.

Noon-e sangak is a flatbread baked on a stone. It's kind of chewy, unless you toast it—which I did, using the gleaming, deluxe toaster oven Mamou kept on the counter. It was all brushed steel with digital readouts and touch-sensitive controls.

It was the U.S.S. *Enterprise* of toaster ovens.

Back home, we had bacon and eggs for breakfast on holidays (or on days when Mom was craving bacon, which usually happened if she was stressed at work), but you couldn't get bacon in Yazd. It wasn't halal, which meant it was forbidden in the Islamic Republic of Iran. So I ate flatbread and cheese for breakfast, just like every other teenage boy in Iran. Just like Darius the First probably did when he was growing up.

I felt very Persian indeed.

"Happy Nowruz, Darioush," Mom said, kissing me on the head while I washed my dishes from breakfast. She was back to using my Iranian name.

"Happy Nowruz, Mom."

She had her hair in curlers, and she was wearing a long, puffy white robe. My stomach experienced a gravitic inversion.

"Uh. Are you dressing up for the party?" But I already knew the answer.

"Just a little bit."

"Should I dress up too?"

"Whatever is fine. It's just family. Wear something casual."

I knew she was lying.

"Okay."

"Where's your sister?"

"Watching Iranian soap operas with her grandfather," Dad said without looking up from his sketchpad. He had been refining his sketches of Persepolis ever since we got back. "He said it would improve her Farsi."

I kind of wanted to go watch Iranian soap operas with my grandfather and improve my Farsi too.

"If we're not careful, my father may try to kidnap her," Mom said.

"Where was he when Laleh was two?"

Mom leaned down to kiss Dad on the temple, which I had noticed was her favorite place to kiss him when other people were around.

"The shower is all yours, honey," she said.

Dad pulled Mom down for another kiss, this one at the corner of her mouth, which was how Dad liked to kiss Mom when they had an audience. "Thanks."

As soon as Mom went into the living room, I turned to Dad.

"Persian Casual?"

Dad flipped his sketchpad closed.

"Persian Casual," he agreed.

Persian Casual covers a wide gamut, from slightly more-formal-than-business-casual to just-shy-of-black-tie-or-full-military-dress. Button-up shirt and dress pants are the bare minimum; maybe a suit jacket, depending on the crowd. Back home, it meant a tie too, but no one wore ties in Iran. It was considered a "Western" fashion.

Dad ran out of room in his luggage for any of his suit jackets, and I didn't fit in mine anymore, so that left us at a disadvantage as far as looking more impressive than everyone else.

That was the whole point and purpose of Persian Casual, as far as I could tell: to make sure you and your family looked more impressive than everyone else, usually by tricking people into thinking the occasion was more casual than it really was.

Dad had lots of practice with Persian Casual. He knew how to anticipate it. He made sure we were dressed up, though some-times it backfired. The only thing worse than being perpetually underdressed was being garishly overdressed. Then everyone would whisper behind our backs (in Farsi, of course) about how ostentatious we were.

Mom insists the entire concept of Persian Casual is all in our heads.

She always says we look fine, even if we're in shorts and T-shirts while everyone else is in button-ups and jackets.

She says we're just being self-conscious.

Maybe it's a Social Cue.

I waited for Dad to finish before I went to my own bathroom (with the squatting toilet, which honestly wasn't that bad once I got used to it) to shower and get dressed. With a house full of people all trying to achieve Persian Casual, there wasn't much hot water left. I wore my dark gray dress pants and a turquoise button-up with these subtle leaf patterns on it, the kind you could only see in a certain light.

It was kind of slimming. I liked the way it looked on me.

I almost felt handsome.

Almost.

Dayi Soheil arrived a little after noon, with his wife and two sons. Dayi Jamsheed wasn't supposed to arrive until later.

Dayi Soheil looked exactly like Babou, a younger version from some parallel quantum reality where Babou was capable of smiling. Dayi Soheil and his wife, Zandayi Simin, took turns kissing me on both cheeks, hugging me, kissing me again, until Dayi Soheil stepped back and patted my stomach.

"Where did this come from, dayi? All those medicines?"

"Um."

Even Stephen Kellner had never pointed my stomach out to me.

I didn't know what to say.

"Darioush-jan," Zandayi Simin said, "welcome to Iran!"

Zandayi means "mother's brother's wife."

My zandayi's voice was deep and smooth, like an Elven queen's. Her accent was thicker than Dayi Soheil's too: All her consonants were sharpened, and she said "welcome" as "velcome."

"Thank you, Zandayi. Um. Eid-e shomaa mobarak."

That is the traditional Nowruz greeting for someone older than you.

My aunt and uncle smiled at me. It was the kind of smile you give a toddler who has finally managed, after months of intensive training, to use the potty on his own for the first time.

Dayi Soheil took my face in his hands. "Eid-e toh mobarak, Darioush-jan!"

That is how you wish a happy Nowruz to someone younger than you.

Dayi Soheil kissed me on each cheek again, patted my belly once last time, and went inside.

I was so ashamed.

"Happy Nowruz, Darioush!" Sohrab announced when I answered the door.

He was dressed Persian Casual too, though his shirt was white with a sort of striped texture to it that caught the light down his sides. He'd done something to his hair, so it stood up in soft spikes that shone in the hallway light.

I had put gel in my hair too, but all that did was make the black curls shinier and stiffer.

Sohrab smelled nice, like rosemary and leather, but he hadn't overdone it. He had avoided the genetic predisposition many True Persians had toward using too much cologne.

"Eid-e toh mobarak," I said.

You could also use *toh* for someone you were very close to.

Sohrab squinted at me, then held the door open for the woman behind him to enter. She was short—almost squat—but her hair was so huge, once it was freed from her headscarf, that it took up the whole room.

Sohrab said, "Maman, this is Darioush. Agha Bahrami's grandson."

Sohrab's mom leaned her head back to look me up and down.

"*Eid-e shomaa mobarak*, Khanum Rezaei," I said.

"Happy Nowruz!" she said. Her voice was throaty and sandy. And loud.

"It's nice to meet you."

She smiled, and her eyes crinkled up just like Sohrab's. "Thank you." She pulled me down by my shoulders and kissed me on both cheeks, then let go of me to find Mamou.

"Is your dad coming? Or your amou?"

Sohrab chewed on the inside of his cheek for a moment.

"No. Just me and my mom. We always come for Nowruz. Amou Ashkan goes to Feast."

"Feast?"

"The Bahá'í celebration. Most of the Bahá'í families go."

"Oh."

I was going to ask more, but then I heard Sohrab's mom let out a cry and charge across the sea of Bahramis separating her from her target.

"My mom loves Mamou," he said, and his squint was back. "She is special. You know?"

I did know. Sohrab didn't have to say it out loud.

We all had to take pictures behind the haft-seen.

Laleh and I sat on chairs from the dining room, while Mom and Dad stood behind us.

Persians have mastered the ancient and noble art of the awkward family photo—in fact, we probably invented it. True, Non-Fractional Persians refuse to smile in photos, unless they are tricked into it, or have been talked into it with a combination of pleading, guilt-tripping, and high-level taarofing.

Dad smiled behind me. He had very straight, very white teeth—exactly what you'd expect from his Teutonic heritage and years of aggressive dentistry—and Laleh smiled, because she was Laleh, and Laleh was always smiling.

But Mom just pursed her lips, which is as close as she came to smiling unless you surprised her.

I tried to smile too, but my face felt weird and rubbery, and it came out as a half smile, half-constipated look.

Dayi Jamsheed snapped a few pictures of us, and I thought we were done.

I was wrong.

Everyone needed pictures: with their own family units, with Mamou and Babou, with me, Laleh, Mom, and Dad. I kept getting pulled into different photos, with different arms over my shoulders or around my waist every few minutes. My family was everywhere.

And even though I hated getting shuffled around and grabbed by my love handles, my rubbery constipated face did relax into a smile.

I had never been surrounded by my family before. Not really.

When Dayi Jamsheed started herding us together into a big group photo, my eyes started burning. I couldn't help it.

I loved them.

I loved how their eyelashes were long and dark and distinct, just like mine. And how their noses curved around a little bump in the middle, just like mine. And how their hair cow-licked in three separate places, just like mine.

"Darius? You okay?" Dad said. He'd gotten squeezed into the very back, with me, since we were taller than everyone else.

"Um. Yeah," I clucked.

Dad put his hand on my back and gave me a little wiggle.

"You're so lucky to have this big family."

I was lucky.

That well inside me was ready to burst.

Mamou turned around—she and Babou were seated in the very front, the binary suns of the Bahrami family solar system—and she smiled at me.

For the first time in Bahrami family history, she had all her grandchildren in one place.

I loved my grandmother's smile more than anything.

Dayi Jamsheed handed his camera—a big SLR—off to Sohrab, while Sohrab's mom pointed someone's iPhone at us.

She had another two tucked under her arms, and one held between her chin and her chest.

It was deeply redundant.

"Yek. Doh. Seh," Sohrab said. He studied the picture for a second. "Good!"

Babou stood and said something to Mamou. Whatever it was must have been bad: The room went silent, like the house had experienced an explosive decompression.

Maybe we had.

And then Babou started shouting.

It was incoherent and garbled and venomous.

Sohrab's mom's eyebrows formed perfect arches above her eyes, threatening to disappear into her hair, as my grandfather screamed at my grandmother for no reason I could understand.

Sohrab studied the floor and fiddled with the camera in his hands.

Mom's face had turned chalky.

But Mamou was the worst.

She was still smiling, but it didn't reach her eyes anymore.

At last, Babou stormed off toward his room.

No one said anything. We were all waiting for the atmospheric pressure to return to normal. As Mamou stood, I leaned in and tried to hug her, but it ended up as an awkward half hug. Mamou shifted and wrapped her arms around me. Her face was wet against my shoulder.

I hated that she was crying.

I hated that Babou had treated her like that.

"Thank you, maman. I will be fine."

"What happened?"

"Nothing. It's okay."

Mamou kissed me on the cheek and then pulled away, disappearing into the bathroom with Mom right behind her.

Without our binary stars holding us together, our orbits decayed until the Bahrami family solar system succumbed to entropy and broke apart.

"He does this sometimes," Sohrab said. "Gets angry. For no reason. Because of the tumor."

"Oh."

"That's not how he really is."

Ardeshir Bahrami had always seemed severe to me, for as long as I had known him. Even when I was a child and he was a scary figure on Mom's computer monitor with a gruff voice and a bushy mustache.

So I wasn't sure I believed Sohrab. Not entirely.

But it was nice to imagine a version of my grandfather that didn't make my grandmother cry.

"Maybe we should make some tea," I said.

That's all I ever knew how to do. Make tea.

"Sure."

The kitchen was empty. Everyone had abandoned ship after the photo fiasco. But the steam-filled air was bursting with the scents of turmeric and dill and rice and salmon and dried Persian limes. Mamou had a huge piece of fish in the oven, and sabzi polow cooking on the stove, and plates of every kind of torshi known to mankind—even the lemon one, which was my favorite.

Sohrab's stomach grumbled.

"Your fast is over today. Right?"

"At sunset."

The kettle was already steaming, but the teapot was empty except for the dregs of the last batch. I shook it out over the sink and started a new pot.

While we waited, Zandayi Simin came in with an empty teacup. "Oh. Thank you, Darioush-jan."

She said something in Farsi to Sohrab, who nodded back at her. He looked at me and then back to her.

His cheeks were turning red.

I didn't know anything could make Sohrab blush.

It made me like him even more.

"Um," I said.

"Darioush-jan," Zandayi Simin said, "I am so happy to meet you."

"Me too," I said.

I started blushing a little bit myself.

"I love you very much."

"Um."

She said something to Sohrab again, and then said, "My English is not very good."

"No," I said. "It's terrific."

"Thank you," she said. "Sohrab will help to . . ." She looked at him.

"Translate," he said.

She nodded. "Any questions you have."

"Oh." I swallowed. I had only spoken to Zandayi Simin a few times over the Internet. Usually she just talked to Mom in Farsi.

I had so many questions inside me.

All I knew about our family was the little bits I heard from Mom.

I wanted to know what our family's stories were.

I wanted to know the things Mom wouldn't think to tell me. Things she knew but never said out loud, because they were a part of her.

I wanted to know what made the Bahrami family special.

"Uh."

My neck started to prickle.

I wanted to know about growing up in Iran.

I wanted to know what my cousins were like when they were kids.

I wanted to know what Zandayi Simin had done with her life.

My aunt was offering me a treasure—a hoard of jewels, worthy of Smaug the Terrible (the dragon, not the water boiler). And I was too paralyzed to reach out and select a gem.

"Um."

Zandayi Simin smiled patiently at me.

"Simin-khanum," he said. "Tell him about Babou and the aftabeh."

Zandayi Simin laughed. "Sohrab!" She said something in Farsi, something that made him blush harder, but he laughed too.

"Darioush-jan. You know what aftabeh is?"

MY COUSIN, THE RINGWRAITH

In some ways, Nowruz is the Persian version of Christmas: You spend it with your whole family, and you eat mountains and mountains of food, and nearly everyone takes the day off.

Mom always pulled me and Laleh out of school. I never told anyone why. I'm pretty sure Laleh did, but like I said, Laleh was a lot more popular than me.

Another way Nowruz is like Christmas: presents.

Mamou and Babou—who had finally reemerged, acting as if nothing unusual had transpired—gave me a crisp white button-up shirt. It was a little like the one Sohrab wore, except it had blue pinstripes.

Dayi Jamsheed and Dayi Soheil gave me five million rials each.

I did not know the exact exchange rate for Iranian rial (IRR) and United States dollar (USD), only that there was a considerable difference.

My uncles gave the same to Laleh, who screamed and ran around shouting, "I'm a millionaire! I'm a millionaire!"

Laleh had been sneaking the Nowruz desserts—baqlava and bahmieh—all afternoon. She'd also had three cups of tea, and thus nine cubes of sugar, which meant she had enough fuel to power an electro-plasma system.

There was a mountain of qottab waiting for after dinner too.

I didn't tell Laleh that.

Sohrab followed me back to my room as I put away my shirt and money. "I got you something, Darioush," he said.

"You did?"

I felt terrible. I hadn't gotten Sohrab anything.

How could I have predicted I would make a friend in Iran?

Sohrab produced a small package, wrapped in advertisements from an Iranian newspaper. He tried to hand it to me, but I remembered the appropriate Social Cue.

"I can't," I said.

I wasn't just taarofing.

I couldn't stand how selfish I felt.

"Please."

"Really."

"Go on, Darioush. Taarof nakon."

He shoved the present toward my chest.

Resistance was futile.

"Okay, Sohrab. Thank you."

I peeled the paper off and a silky white shirt slithered onto my hands. It was a soccer/non-American football jersey, with a green stripe across the shoulder, a red one across the chest, and the lightly drawn outline of a cheetah's head on the stomach.

"Wow," I said. The smooth jersey slid through my fingers as I inspected the logo on the chest.

"It's Team Melli. Iran's national team. From the World Cup."

I pulled the jersey over my head—the collar of my Persian Casual shirt stuck up underneath—but still, I felt like a real Iranian. Even though the cheetah's head stretched over my stomach.

"I love it," I said. "Thank you."

I blinked a couple times, because I didn't want Sohrab to notice my mood was performing a severe Slingshot Maneuver. I knew soccer/non-American football jerseys weren't cheap. Sohrab could have used that money on some new cleats for himself, but he had gotten me the jersey instead.

"Are you okay, Darioush?"

"Yeah. Yeah." I blinked some more. "It's just really, really nice."

It made me feel like I belonged.

"I didn't get you anything. I'm sorry, Sohrab."

Sohrab squinted at me. "Don't be. I wanted to surprise you."

Sohrab's mom appeared in the doorway behind her son, camera in hand.

I used the distraction to wipe at my eyes and sniff a bit.

"Sohrab! You gave him the shirt."

"Baleh, Maman."

"I love it. Thank you, Khanum Rezaei."

"It was all Sohrab."

"It's perfect." I glanced over at him.

Sohrab's mom held up the camera. Sohrab threw his arm over my shoulder and smiled into his mom's telescoping lens.

"Yek. Doh. Seh."

I tried to smile, but I probably just looked surprised. Or constipated.

No one ever threw their arm over my shoulder the way Sohrab did. Like it was perfectly fine to do that sort of thing to another guy. Like that was a thing friends did to each other.

Sohrab had no walls inside.

I loved that about him.

Khanum Rezaei snapped a photo and checked it. She leaned her head way back and looked over the top of her glasses. "It's good!"

"Thank you," I said again. "So much."

"Sohrab knew you would like it." She squinted at me and slipped out into the hallway.

Sohrab was still leaning against me, patting my shoulder.

"This is the nicest gift anyone has ever given me."

Sohrab squeezed my shoulder again and rubbed the back of my head.

"I'm glad you like it, Darioush."

We ate at sunset.

Our family did not have to fast, but Mamou wanted to make sure Sohrab and his mom were not left out. Mahvash Rezaei—that's what Mom called her, Mahvash-khanum—was so complimentary about everything, I thought Mamou was going to throw the rice server at her to get her to stop talking.

There weren't enough tables and chairs for all the Bahramis (plus two Rezaeis) gathered, so we stood around, holding our plates and eating one-handed as best we could. Laleh ignored all the stews and rice and went straight for the bowl of cucumbers, which she ate whole, like candy bars.

"Darioush-jan," Dayi Jamsheed said. "You don't like khiar?"

"Um. Not really." I didn't understand the point and purpose of cucumbers. The taste wasn't bad, but they had this weird slimy texture that I couldn't get over.

"You are not very Persian," he said. "Not like Laleh."

I looked down at my Team Melli jersey, which I still had on over my button-up.

This was the most Persian I had ever been in my entire life, and it still wasn't enough.

"You are more like your dad. He doesn't like them either," he said. And then he grabbed a cucumber for himself and wandered off.

Dad was in the kitchen, funneling dishes into the dishwasher as fast as they came.

I rinsed off my plate and then started helping with the rest, piled up in the sink.

"Good dinner?"

"Yeah."

"You don't have to help. I got it."

"I don't mind," I said. "Mamou said how much you help with the dishes. She said you're sweet."

Dad almost blushed at that.

Almost.

"She told your mom I was going to spoil her. She said men in Iran don't do dishes."

"Oh."

"I'm glad to do it, though. Your grandmother has enough on her plate." He angled another dish into the dishwasher and chuckled. "Proverbially speaking."

"Yeah."

"What do you think of your uncles?"

"They're . . . I don't know. Dayi Jamsheed told me I wasn't

Persian. Because I don't like cucumbers." I handed Dad the last plate and started gathering the forks and spoons. "And Dayi Soheil called me fat."

Dad nearly dropped the plate.

"He what?"

"Well. Not really. He just, like, patted me on my stomach. But that was the implication."

"I think he was just being affectionate, Darius."

Stephen Kellner always gave everyone the benefit of the doubt.

Everyone except me.

"There you are," Mom said. She closed the door behind her and took the silverware from me. "You two get out there. I'll take care of it."

But Dad said, "I don't mind, love." He glanced at the door. "Spend time with your brothers."

For a moment, I wondered if Dad was trying to avoid the living room. If he was avoiding the critical mass of Bahramis by taking shelter in the kitchen.

But that was impossible.

Stephen Kellner never avoided anything.

"Let me," Mom said. She hip-checked Dad out of the way with a smirk, but then she stood on her toes to kiss him on the temple. "Go on."

"Okay. Come on, Darius."

He hooked his arm around my shoulder and led me back into the living room.

After dinner, Dayi Jamsheed's kids pushed all the furniture

in the living room against the walls, leaving the large red and green carpet in the center of the room for us to dance on.

Dayi Jamsheed had four kids: his sons Zal and Bahram, and his daughters Vida and Nazgol.

First off: My cousin Nazgol got her name from the Farsi word for *flower*.

She was not a Ringwraith—a Nazgûl—and I was pretty sure she had never read *The Lord of the Rings,* so it wasn't like I could joke about it with her.

Second: Dayi Jamsheed must have been part-Übermensch himself. The decision to name his son Bahram Bahrami must have sprung from the same well of Teutonic Nihilism that led Stephen Kellner to choose Grover as my middle name.

What kind of name is Darius Grover Kellner?

It was like I was destined to be a target.

Here's the thing:

All Iranian songs have the exact same drumbeat.

Maybe only True, Non-Fractional, Cucumber-Loving Persians can tell them apart.

At first, only the ladies danced. They formed a circle, swaying their hips and flipping their wrists and taking tiny steps in intricate patterns on the floor. Mamou had this stained glass partition separating the living room from the dining room, and the light filtering through it cast constellations of color across my family's faces.

Khanum Rezaei found her way to the center of the circle, where she danced with her headscarf in hand, flicking and flailing it around to the beat. Laleh laughed and tried to copy her, though my sister's flailing was somewhat more violent.

Sohrab and I hung back in the corner. He had this cool way of snapping by clasping his hands and rubbing his index fingers against each other, but no matter how I tried I couldn't get it, so I tapped my foot along instead. We swayed together, laughing and bumping shoulders.

It was the most fun I had ever had.

The song changed again, to one I recognized because it got played at Persian parties back home. It sounded like the infernal spawn of a Persian drum beat and a dozen Celtic fiddles.

Mamou screamed, "I love this one!" at the top of her lungs. She leaped into the middle of the circle to join Mahvash Rezaei and Laleh. The three of them kicked their feet, jumped and stomped, so vigorously they rattled the photos on the walls.

Sohrab joined in next, dragging me by the arm, and I jumped and laughed and tried to follow, but I was about as graceful as an android when it came to dancing.

Mamou took my hand, and I took Sohrab's, and we made a chain until we were all dancing and spinning and stomping and jumping and smiling.

But even as I laughed, I thought about how Mamou and Mrs. Rezaei and Sohrab had danced this dance together before. How they had celebrated Nowruz together before.

How Mamou had kissed Sohrab on both cheeks and invited him inside for tea before. More times than anyone could count.

My chest imploded. Just a little bit.

I hated how Sohrab had a larger share of my grandmother's life than I did.

I hated how jealous of him I was.

I hated that I couldn't make it through a Nowruz party without experiencing Mood Slingshot Maneuvers.

But then Sohrab caught my eyes and smiled so wide at me, his eyes all crinkled up, and I smiled back at him and laughed.

Sohrab understood me.

And I understood him too.

And it was pretty much the most amazing thing ever.

In the kitchen, I found Dad sitting with Dayi Jamsheed, Dayi Soheil, and Babou, all with little plates of tokhmeh in front of them, playing an intense game of Rook.

Rook is a card game that, as far as I can tell, is encoded into all True Persians at the cellular level. At any gathering of four or more Persians, it was certain at least one would have a deck of cards tucked into their breast pocket.

In Rook, you played in pairs, partnered with whoever sat across from you. Through some quantum-mechanical entanglement, Dad and Babou had ended up as teammates.

I couldn't believe Stephen Kellner was playing Rook.

I couldn't believe he was playing with Ardeshir Bahrami.

I couldn't believe he looked like he was actually having fun.

Stephen Kellner having fun with Ardeshir Bahrami.

I didn't understand. I didn't know how to play Rook, not really, and last I'd heard, neither did Dad. At Persian parties we'd stand together in the corner, watching all the older Persian men play, laughing at the arguments that inevitably ensued even if we couldn't understand a word that was said.

Babou grunted and nodded, and Dad threw the eight of

hearts onto the table. While Dayi Jamsheed played, Dad looked up at me and smiled.

Smiled.

Like he was right at home.

I didn't know how he did it. How he adapted himself to get along with all the Bahrami men, like a chameleon.

He really was the Übermensch.

The kitchen was too hot. The breeze had died when the sun went down, and now the stuffy air hung still in the kitchen windows. The kettle belched steam, relentless as Smaug the Golden.

I grabbed a qottab when Dad wasn't looking and skirted past the table, out the door to the backyard.

MAIN SEQUENCE

Something smelled sweet.

Jasmine blossoms.

I'd never smelled fresh jasmine before. It was intense, but soft as a fleece blanket. I liked jasmine in Rose City's Dragon Pearl Jasmine, but that paled next to the scent of the fresh flowers. Mamou and Babou had planted the tiny white blooms along the perimeter of their yard, in little wooden boxes painted a soft blue.

I slid down against one of the planters and breathed in. My chest felt heavy, like someone had dropped a planet on me.

Inside, my family sat around, playing Rook and talking so I couldn't understand them. Dancing dances they had danced with each other for years. Sharing jokes and stories I would never be a part of. Eating khiar and drinking doogh like True Persians.

Even Dad had found a way to fit in.

I didn't belong.

"Darioush?"

It was Sohrab.

"What is the matter?"

I wiped my eyes and studied my feet. Sohrab slid down the wall next to me and pulled his knees against his chest.

"Nothing."

There was no squint in Sohrab's eyes.

I hadn't noticed how big they were before.

"Why are you crying?"

"I'm not," I said, except my throat had clamped and I sounded like a frog.

Sohrab leaned closer and bumped shoulders with me.

"Did someone say something to you?"

I shook my head and kept silent.

Sohrab reached above us and plucked a jasmine flower out of the nearest shrub. He twirled the tiny blossom back and forth and waited for me to talk.

"It's just hard," I said. "Everyone knows everyone. And everyone speaks Farsi. And everyone knows the dances. And I . . ."

"Don't you remember Simin-khanum?" Sohrab said. "She loves to have you here."

"It's not the same, though. Dayi Soheil thinks I'm fat. And Dayi Jamsheed says I'm not Persian. But they like my dad. He's in there playing Rook." I hiccuped. "Everyone is disappointed in me."

"Darioush." Sohrab bumped my shoulder again.

"No one wants me here."

"Everyone wants you here. We have a saying in Farsi. It translates 'your place was empty.' We say it when we miss somebody."

I sniffed.

"Your place was empty before. But this is your family. You belong here."

I rubbed my eyes with the heels of my hands.

It was nice to imagine. Even if I didn't believe him.

"Thanks, Sohrab."

⚹ ⚹ ⚹

When I had finally finished excreting stress hormones, I said, "Don't tell Babou. Or my dad."

"What?"

"That I was . . . you know."

"Oh." He chewed the inside of his cheek. "You don't talk to your dad?"

"Not really."

"Why?"

"Um." How was I supposed to explain the vast gulf between Stephen Kellner, Teutonic Übermensch, and me, a D-Bag?

I sighed, bumping against Sohrab's side. We had sagged closer together while I calmed down.

"It's just . . . everything I do, he's unhappy with me. How I cut my hair. What I eat. The backpack I take to school. My job. Everything. He's always disappointed in me. He's always trying to change me. To make me do things the way he would do them. To make me act how he would act."

"Darioush . . ."

"You know what he told me? He told me people wouldn't pick on me so much if I was more normal. What does that even mean?"

"I don't know." Sohrab bumped me again. "You get picked on? At school?"

"Yeah. Some of the guys tease me. A lot."

"Sorry."

"It wouldn't be so bad if Dad would just say that they're wrong. That they're wrong about me. That they're wrong to do that. But he acts like it's my fault. Like if I could make myself into a Soulless Minion of Orthodoxy they'd leave me alone. And it's not just school. It's everything. It's every mood I have. It's like Dad's convinced I'm going to . . ."

"To what?"

I swallowed.

"Darioush?"

"So. I'm depressed. I mean, I have depression. Clinically."

"Did something bad happen? To make you so sad?"

Some people meant it judgmentally when they asked, but not Sohrab.

He said it like I was a puzzle, one he was enjoying putting together.

Even if the pieces didn't quite make sense.

"No. I'm just messed up. My brain makes the wrong chemicals."

My ears burned.

"Nothing bad has ever happened to me."

I felt terrible saying it out loud.

Dr. Howell—and Dad too—always told me not to be ashamed. But it was hard not to be.

"How long have you had it?"

"I dunno. A while," I said. "It's genetic. Dad has it too."

"But you don't talk to him about it? When you are sad, like now?"

"No."

Sohrab chewed on his bottom lip.

"Sometimes," I said, "it feels like he doesn't really love me. Not really."

"Why?"

I told Sohrab about telling stories. I told him about soccer and about Boy Scouts. I told him about all the steps Dad and I had taken away from each other. And how we never really went back.

Sohrab was a good listener. He never played devil's advocate or told me what I was feeling was wrong, the way Stephen Kellner did. He nodded to let me know he understood, and laughed if I said something funny.

But eventually, even the topic of Stephen Kellner ran its course.

I played with the hem of my Team Melli jersey, twisting it around and around my index fingers.

"What about you?"

"Me?"

"You never talk about your dad. And he's not here. Is he . . ."

Sohrab looked away and bit his cheek again.

"I'm sorry. I just wondered."

"No." He looked up at me. "It's okay. Most people already know. And you are my friend." Sohrab pulled down another jasmine blossom to play with. "My father is in jail."

"Oh."

I had never known anyone who knew someone in jail.

"What happened?"

"You saw in the news about the protests? Years ago. When there were elections?"

"I think so?"

I would have to ask Mom to be sure.

"There were protests here, in Yazd too. My dad was there. Not protesting. He was on the way to work. He owns the store with Amou Ashkan."

I nodded.

"The police came. They were dressed like protesters too."

"Plainclothes?"

"Yes. He was arrested with the protesters. He has been there since then."

"What? Why?"

"He is Bahá'í. It's not so good if you're arrested and you're Bahá'í. You know?"

I shook my head. "But Mamou and Babou aren't Muslim. They don't get much trouble."

"But it's different for Zoroastrians. The government doesn't like Bahá'ís."

"Oh."

I never knew that.

I felt even more ashamed.

Sohrab had been pretty much fatherless for years, but here I was, complaining about Stephen Kellner who, while imperfect, was certainly less terrifying than the Iranian government.

"I'm really sorry, Sohrab."

I bumped my shoulder against his, and he let out a sigh and relaxed a little.

"It's okay, Darioush."

I knew without him saying that it wasn't.

Not really.

Sohrab and I sat out in the garden talking as the evening chill descended on us. The fine, dark hairs on Sohrab's arms stood at attention. "We should go inside. It's getting late. I think my mom already left."

I shivered. "Okay."

My foot had fallen asleep. It felt like I was walking on glass shards as I followed Sohrab inside.

I did feel better, though. Sohrab had that effect on people.

Everyone had left. Dad and Babou sat alone at the kitchen table, sipping tea and talking quietly.

"I don't know," Dad said. "It's like he's always making things hard on himself."

"It's too late to change him," Babou said. "You can't control him, Stephen."

"I don't want to control him. He's just so stubborn."

My ears burned. I waited for them to notice me and Sohrab standing in the doorway.

"Don't worry so much, Stephen. At least he made friends with Sohrab. He is going to be fine."

"You think so?"

Babou nodded.

Dad stared into his tea. His Adam's apple bobbed up and down.

And then he said, "I think Sohrab might be the first real friend he's ever had."

Deep inside my chest, a main sequence star collapsed under its own gravity.

I hated that Dad thought that about me.

I hated that he was right.

I hated that Sohrab could hear him.

"Uh," I said, louder than I needed to.

Dad looked back and saw me. His ears turned bright red too.

I wanted him to say something. To take it back.

But Stephen Kellner never said things he didn't mean.

It was Sohrab who rescued me.

"Khodahafes, Agha Bahrami. Eid-e shomaa mobarak."

"Khodahafes, Sohrab-jan."

"Uh. Good night," I said.

I led Sohrab to the living room, which looked like it had been host to a Level Twelve Party by twenty or thirty Soulless Minions of Orthodoxy.

Like I said, alcohol was illegal in Iran (not that it stopped everyone, but it stopped the Bahrami family), so there were no empty bottles or red Solo cups to pick up, but there were dirty plates and teacups and piles of split tokhmeh shells and several white powdered-sugar handprints on the walls.

There could only be one culprit for those. They were at perfect Laleh height.

At the door, Sohrab kicked off the pair of Babou's garden slippers he had worn outside. He still had on his black socks. I never wore socks with sandals, but Sohrab had managed to pull it off.

He was a True Persian.

"Thanks," I said.

"Darioush. You remember what I told you? Your place was empty?"

"Yeah."

"Your place was empty for me too," he said. "I never had a friend either."

I almost smiled.

Almost.

"See you tomorrow?"

"Yeah. If you like. I mean, I think so."

Sohrab cocked his head to the side, like I had said something funny, but then he shook his head and squinted at me. "Okay. Khodahafes, Darioush."

"Khodahafes."

THE BORG OF HERBS

lank. Clank.

The Dancing Fan was still dancing, its rubber feet beating out the same syncopated Persian rhythm I'd been listening to all night, but that wasn't what woke me.

I slipped out of my bedroom, sticking to the rugs where I could. The floor tiles were cold as my feet slapped against them.

Clank. Swish.

It was coming from the kitchen.

"Mom?"

She stood at the sink in her robe, Mamou's bright pink rubber gloves pulled up to her elbows. Her hair was still done up Persian Casual, all curls and falls, though several locks had managed to escape their careful arrangement.

The counters to the right of the sink were stacked high as the Gate of All Nations with pots and pans, plates and glasses, and teacups.

So many teacups.

"Hi, sweetie."

"What're you doing?"

"I couldn't sleep."

"Can I help?"

"It's okay. Go back to bed."

I could tell she was just taarofing.

"I can't sleep either."

"All right. You mind drying these?" She nodded to the serving platters in the dish rack. "You can stack them on the table."

I pulled a tea towel from the drawer next to the stove, then grabbed the ceramic rice platter and dried it off. The enormous dish was white with concentric rings of tiny green leaves on it.

"Hey. Didn't we send this with the Ardekanis last year?"

Mom pushed her glasses back up the bridge of her nose with her forearm. "Yeah. For their anniversary."

"Oh, yeah."

Mamou and Babou had been married for fifty-one years.

I thought about all the fights they must have had, and all the times they had forgiven each other.

I thought about the little secrets they knew about each other that no one else knew.

I thought about how they might not reach their fifty-second anniversary.

"Mom?"

"Yeah?" Her voice had gone all pinched, like the neck of a deflating balloon.

"I'm sorry. About Babou."

She shook her head and scrubbed the soup pot hard enough to bore a hole through it. "No. I'm sorry. I wish I had brought you and Laleh sooner. It's not fair you only get to see him like this. So tired. And just . . . well, you saw."

She stopped scrubbing and blew a hair out of her face.

"Yeah."

"His doctors say it's going to get worse."

I swallowed and looked for a dry spot on my towel.

"You know what I remember?"

"What?"

"There was this day . . . I was seven or eight, and me and Mahvash had gone to the park to play. We were friends growing up. Did I tell you that?"

She had not told me that.

It was weird, imagining Mom having childhood friends.

But I liked that Mom was friends with Mahvash, and now I was friends with her son.

"Anyway, we had gone barefoot, because it was a cool morning. But when lunchtime came around, we tried to leave the grass, and the pavement was too hot."

Mom got this funny smile on her face.

"When we didn't make it home, Babou came and found us. But he didn't know why we were there, and he hadn't brought us any shoes."

"Oh, no," I said.

"So he carried Mahvash back home, piggyback, and left me in the park. He told me it would teach me to be more responsible."

That sounded like something Babou would do.

"But when he came back, he had forgotten to swing by our house and get shoes for me. So he had to carry me home too."

That made me smile.

"He was so strong," Mom said. And then she sniffled.

I put down my towel and tried to give Mom a sideways hug, but she shook me off.

"I'm okay." She pushed her glasses up again. "I'm sorry I didn't teach you Farsi."

"What?"

I didn't understand. Our conversation had made a particularly confusing Slingshot Maneuver.

"It was my job to teach you. To make sure you knew where you came from. And I really screwed up."

"Mom . . ."

She put down her sponge and turned off the sink.

"It was hard for me, you know? Moving to America. When I left here, I was sure I was going to come back. But I didn't. I fell in love with your dad and stayed, even though I never really felt at home. When you were born I wanted you to grow up American. So you would feel like you belonged."

I understood that. I really did.

School was hard enough, being a Fractional Persian. I'm not sure I would have survived being Even More Persian.

Mom shook her head. "You're so much like your dad. In so many ways. But you're my son too. I tried to do better as you got older, but I think it helped your sister more than it helped you."

I mean.

It would have been nice to learn Farsi like Laleh.

"I'm sorry, Darius."

Now that it was just us—all the True Persians had gone to bed—I was back to my American name.

Mom leaned over to kiss the side of my head and then turned the faucet back on. "You'd have an easier time talking to your grandfather if you could speak to him in Farsi. He was never very comfortable in English, even before."

That was something I already understood. Back home,

when we Skyped, it was Mamou who did most of the talking in English.

"He really does love you, you know. Even if he doesn't always say the right things. He loves you."

"I know," I said.

"I think he loves you more, since he never gets to see you. It makes it more special."

"Yeah. I love him too."

That may have been an exaggeration.

I mean, I loved the idea of Babou.

But the idea was very different from the reality.

Laleh was the first one up the next morning. She ran up and down the hallway, singing at the top of her lungs, her feet pattering on the tiles as she danced. She cracked my door and peeked into my room.

"Morning, Laleh."

"Sobh bekheir!"

"You want some breakfast?"

"Baleh."

"Okay. I'll be right there." I pulled on a pair of socks and followed her to the kitchen.

Thanks to me and Mom, you could hardly tell there had been a Nowruz party the night before. I even wiped down the countertops and stove.

Laleh stuck her nose in the refrigerator. It was stacked so full of leftovers, the light up top didn't hit anything below the first shelf.

"Noon-o paneer mekham."

Laleh had entered Farsi-only mode, though at least she was sticking to phrases that I could understand.

I pulled the feta cheese out from the highest corner of the refrigerator door. "You want me to toast the bread for you?"

"Baleh!"

Laleh couldn't reach the plates, but she got out clean butter knives for us. When the toaster oven dinged—I kind of wanted it to make a Red Alert sound or something, it was so futuristic-looking—I lined a basket with one of Mamou's tea towels and filled it with bread.

"You want some tea?"

Laleh nodded and pulled out a piece of sangak bigger than her head. She tossed it on her plate and blew on her fingers where the bread had burned her.

After breakfast, Laleh and I settled in the living room—me to read *The Lord of the Rings*, and her to watch another Iranian soap opera. I had never seen a soap opera in America, so I had no frame of reference, but the Iranian soap operas were absurd.

Every single character seemed to be doing a William Shatner impression.

My sister loved it.

"Look at her coat!" Laleh had finally switched back to English to provide a running commentary for me.

On the television, an older woman sat at a table in a fancy restaurant, wearing a ridiculous white fur coat that made her the exact color (and size) of a polar bear.

"Wow."

Mamou found us like that, Laleh laughing at the television, me reading my book and concurring with my sister when necessary.

"Sobh bekheir!" Laleh said, switching back to Farsi now that she had a receptive audience.

"Sobh bekheir, Laleh-jan." Mamou kissed Laleh, and then me. "You had your breakfast?"

"Baleh."

"There's still warm sangak in the basket," I said. "I can make some more tea."

"Why don't you make me the special tea you brought, maman?"

"Okay."

While I pulled down the FTGFOP1 First Flush Darjeeling, Mamou pulled out a big bowl of qottab covered in plastic wrap from somewhere deep inside the refrigerator, gave me a wink, and carried it into the living room.

I heard Laleh cry out "Yum!" in a voice three octaves below her normal register.

Laleh liked qottab even more than I did.

I put the pot of tea on a tray, along with a few cups, so I could serve Mamou in the living room.

"Thank you, maman," she said. She inhaled long and slow over her cup. "The smell is very nice."

Despite what Ardeshir Bahrami said, it seemed like tea could be for smelling after all.

Mamou closed her eyes and took a long, slow sip.

"It's good, maman! Thank you."

I offered a taste to Laleh, who refused—it was too hot, and it had not been sweetened at all—and then took my own sip.

Mamou smiled and scooted closer to kiss me on the cheek.

"Thank you, Darioush-jan," she said. "Your gift was perfect."

I really loved my grandmother.

Mom emerged around ten o'clock, already dressed. She pulled a headscarf off one of the hooks by the door. "Mamou," she said. "Bereem!"

Mamou emerged from her room, dressed up too.

"Where are you going?"

"We are going to visit my friends," Mamou said.

"It's tradition," Mom said. "On the day after Nowruz."

"It is?"

Mom nodded.

"We never do that back home."

I remembered how Sohrab had looked at me, when he asked if he would see me. How he was surprised I didn't say yes right away.

How could there be a Nowruz tradition I didn't know about?

"Well," Mom said. And then she blinked at me, like she wasn't sure how to answer. "Why don't you go visit Sohrab?"

It was only logical.

"Okay."

I showered and got dressed, and Mom drew me a quick map before she left. Sohrab only lived a few blocks away, but everything looked different if you were walking instead of driving.

When we picked up Sohrab to go to Persepolis, it was still dark out. In the daylight, the Rezaeis' house was older and smaller than Mamou's, the khaki muted enough that I could look at it without sustaining damage to my visual cortex. It had wooden double doors, and each had a differently shaped bronze knocker on it: a horseshoe on the right, and a solid rectangular slab on the left.

The bronze was slightly pitted—like the doors, like the house itself. It felt lived-in and loved.

It made perfect sense for Sohrab to come from a place like this.

I gave the horseshoe knocker three quick raps. Mahvash Rezaei answered. There was a smear of white powder across her forehead, and some had gotten into her eyebrows, too, but she smiled when she saw me—that same squinting smile she had passed down to her son.

"Alláh-u-Abhá, Darioush!"

"Um."

I always felt weird, if someone said "Alláh-u-Abhá" to me, because I wasn't sure if I should say it back—if I was even allowed to—since I wasn't Bahá'í and I didn't believe in God.

The Picard didn't count.

"Come in!"

I pulled my Vans off and set them in the corner next to Sohrab's slender shoes.

There was a wooden partition separating the entryway from the rest of the house, with shelves covered in pictures and candles and phone chargers. The rugs were white and green with gold accents, and they didn't have little tassels on them like Mamou's. The house felt cozy, like a Hobbit-hole.

The air was heavy with the scent of baking bread. Real, home-made bread, not the mass-produced Subway kind.

"Have you eaten? You want anything?"

"I'm okay. I had breakfast."

"Are you sure?" She steered me toward the kitchen. "It's no trouble."

"I'm sure. I thought I should come visit, since it's the day after Nowruz."

I felt very Persian.

"You are so sweet."

Darius Kellner. Sweet.

I liked that Sohrab's mom thought that about me.

I really did.

"You are sure you don't want anything?"

"I'm okay. I had qottab before I came."

"Your grandma makes the best qottab."

Technically, I had not tasted all the possibilities, but I agreed with Mahvash Rezaei in principle.

"She sent some with me," I said, holding out the plastic container I'd brought.

Mahvash Rezaei's eyes bugged out, and I was reminded of a Klingon warrior. Her personality was too big and mercurial to be contained in a frail human body.

"Thank you! Thank your grandma for me!"

Khanum Rezaei set the qottab aside and went back to the counter by her oven. It was dusted with flour, which explained the mysterious white powder on her face.

Her sink was overflowing with whole romaine lettuce leaves,

bathing under the running water. I wondered if it was for the bread. I didn't know of any Iranian recipes that involved baking romaine lettuce into bread, but that didn't mean there weren't any.

"Um."

"It's Sohrab's favorite," Khanum Rezaei said, nodding toward the sink. "He and his dad love it."

Sohrab's dad.

I felt so bad for him.

Also, I felt confused, because I didn't know anyone whose favorite food was romaine lettuce.

Sohrab Rezaei contained multitudes.

"Can you take it outside for me?" Mrs. Rezaei scooped the leaves into a colander, banged it on the sink a few times, and handed it to me. "Put it on the table. I'll go get Sohrab."

The Rezaeis' garden was very different from Babou's. There were no fruit trees, no planters of jasmine, only long rows of hyacinths and a collection of huge pots filled with different herbs. The largest was right next to the kitchen—it was nearly two feet across and three feet high—and it was being assimilated by fresh mint.

Mint is the Borg of herbs. If you let it, it will take over each and every patch of ground it encounters, adding the soil's biological and technological distinctiveness to its own.

There was a charcoal grill in the middle of the garden, the big round kind that looked like a miniature red Starbase. The only table was a Ping-Pong table, close to the door where I stood holding the dripping romaine leaves.

"Khanum Rezaei?"

There was no answer.

Was the Ping-Pong table the one I was supposed to put the romaine on?

Did Iranians say Ping-Pong, or did they say table tennis?

We didn't cover the history of Ping-Pong/table tennis in Iran during our Net Sports Unit in physical education, which now seemed like a ridiculous oversight.

Khanum Rezaei popped up behind me. I almost dropped the lettuce in fright.

"I forgot this," she said, squeezing behind me and flapping a giant white-and-blue tablecloth over the Ping-Pong table. It tented up over the little posts for the net. "You can spread the leaves out to dry some."

"Okay." I did what she asked, spreading the leaves out so they overlapped as little as possible. The water seeped into the tablecloth, turning it translucent.

"Darioush!"

Sohrab grabbed me around the shoulders from behind and swayed me back and forth.

My neck tingled.

"Oh. Hi."

He was wearing plaid pajama pants so huge, he could have fit his entire body down one leg. They were cinched around his waist with a drawstring. I could tell because he had tucked his green polo shirt into his pants.

As soon as Sohrab saw the lettuce, he let me go and ran back inside, talking to his mom in Farsi at warp 9.

I had become invisible.

As I watched Sohrab through the doorway, he seemed

younger somehow, swimming in his pajama pants with his shirt tucked in.

I knew without him saying it that he was missing his dad.

I felt terrible for him.

And I felt terrible feeling sorry for myself. Another Nowruz had come and gone for Sohrab without his father, and I was worried about feeling invisible.

But then Sohrab looked back at me as I watched him from the doorway, and his eyes squinted up again. His smile was a supernova.

"Darioush, you like sekanjabin?"

"What?"

"Sekanjabin. You've had it?"

"No," I said. "What is it?

He pulled a short, wide-mouthed jar out of the fridge, said something quick to his mom, and came back outside. "It's mint syrup. Here." He unscrewed the jar, shook the water off a piece of lettuce, and dipped it in the sauce.

If his face was a supernova before, it became an accretion disc—one of the brightest objects in the universe—as soon as he tasted his lettuce.

I loved that Sohrab could be transported like that.

I took a tiny leaf and tried the sauce. It was sweet and minty, but there was something sour too.

"Vinegar?"

"Yes. Babou always adds a little."

"Babou made this?"

"Yes. You never had it?"

"No. I never heard of it before."

How did I not know my grandfather made sekanjabin?

How did I not know how delicious sekanjabin was?

"He is famous for it. My dad . . . He always grew extra mint, for Babou to use when he made it." He gestured out to the garden. "You saw our mint?"

"Yeah."

"Now it grows too much. Babou hasn't made it for a while."

"Oh."

Sohrab dipped another leaf and then passed me the jar.

It was perfect.

"Thank you for coming over, Darioush."

"It's tradition to visit your friends the day after Nowruz." I took another leaf to dip. "Right?"

Sohrab squeezed my shoulder as he inhaled another piece of lettuce. He nodded and chewed and swallowed and then squinted right at me.

"Right."

After I helped Sohrab polish off every piece of lettuce on the table—two whole heads—he ran to get dressed, while I watched Khanum Rezaei make her bread. She pounded out the dough with her floured palms, then sprinkled a mixture of dried herbs and spices on top.

"Do you like this bread, Darioush-jan? Noon-e barbari?"

"Um. Yeah. Mom gets it from the Persian bakery sometimes."

"You don't make it at home?"

"Not really."

"I'll make some for you. You can put it in the freezer and take it home with you."

"Maman!" Sohrab had reappeared in the doorway, dressed in real pants and a white polo shirt. He said something to his mom in Farsi, something about dinner, but it was too quick. "Come on, Darioush. Let's go."

"Um. Thank you," I said to his mom. I followed Sohrab to the door and laced up my Vans.

There was something he wanted to show me.

THE KHAKI KINGDOM

We headed down Sohrab's street, away from Mamou's. A breeze had picked up, and the air smelled crisp and a little bit dusty.

As we passed an intersection, Sohrab pointed to our right.

"My school is about five kilometers that way."

He put the accent on the *ki* in *kilometers,* instead of the *lo,* which was cool.

"Do you like it?"

"It's okay." He shrugged. "I have class with Ali-Reza and Hossein there."

"Oh."

No matter where you went to school, Soulless Minions of Orthodoxy were unavoidable.

We passed a long white wall, the backside of a row of shops. The sun shone off it.

I sneezed.

"But you have friends there too. Right?"

"Some. Not as good as you, Darioush."

I smiled, but it turned into another sneeze.

"Sorry. Are they all Bahá'ís?"

"No. Only a few." He chuckled. "Most people are not like Ali-Reza, Darioush. They aren't so prejudiced."

"Sorry." My ears burned. "Your school is all boys. Right?"

"Yes."

We reached a crosswalk. Sohrab chewed his cheek and looked at me while we waited for the cars to pass.

"So you don't have a girlfriend, Darioush?"

I swallowed. "No."

I tried to keep my voice neutral, but no matter how you answer that question, people will always read too much into it. The fire in my ears spread to my cheeks.

"How come?"

I didn't know how to answer that.

It wasn't like I could lie to Sohrab.

I think Sohrab realized how uncomfortable I was, though, because before I could say anything else, he said, "It's okay. I don't have one either."

I almost smiled.

Almost.

He said, "It's different here. Boys and girls don't . . ."

He chewed on his sentence for a moment.

"There is not much interaction. Until we are older. Yazd is very conservative. You know?"

"Oh. I guess."

I didn't know. Not really.

But before I could ask, Sohrab looked away and pointed.

The khaki wall on our right had given way to a wide green park. Scrubby trees dotted the lawn, casting dappled shadows over the benches scattered around. A squat public bathroom stood in the corner, surrounded by a chain-link fence.

Who puts a fence around a bathroom?

The breeze came up again, stirring the grass. Sohrab closed his eyes and breathed in.

"This is our favorite park," he said. "We come here for Sizdeh Bedar."

Sizdeh Bedar is the thirteenth day after Nowruz, when Persians go for a picnic.

Persians are crazy about picnics, especially Sizdeh Bedar. Back home, every family makes too much of whatever dish they are most famous for—dolmeh and salad olivieh and kotlet—and we commandeer an entire park so there's room for pretty much every Persian, Fractional or otherwise, in a fifty-mile radius.

Because Nowruz moves around every year, depending on the equinox, so does Sizdeh Bedar, which means it sometimes falls on my birthday. But somehow I could never manage to correctly calculate it.

"It's April first this year. Right?"

Sohrab looked up as he did the calculations from the Iranian calendar to the Gregorian one.

"April two."

"Oh. That's my birthday."

"You'll still be here?"

I nodded.

"Good. We can celebrate both."

Sohrab grabbed me by the shoulder and led me toward the bathroom.

"We play football here, sometimes. When the field is too full."

"Oh." I hoped we weren't about to play soccer/non-American football. I wasn't ready for that. "Cool."

"Come on," Sohrab said, leading me around the back of the squat building. "I want to show you something."

Sohrab spared me a brief squinty smile, then stuck his fingers in the chain-link fence surrounding the bathroom and started to climb. The metal flexed and bowed under his slender weight as he wedged the toes of his sneakers into the diamond-shaped gaps.

"Come on!" he said again as he scrambled onto the bathroom's roof.

I was heavier than Sohrab, and the fence's structural integrity was highly dubious. I was certain it would experience a non-passive failure if I tried to climb it.

"Darioush!" Sohrab called. The roof clattered as he shifted his feet. "Come see!"

I bit my lip and grabbed the fence. The sun had been shining on it all day, and the links were hot beneath my fingers. I clambered up after Sohrab, convinced the fence was going to peel off the building like the lid of a soup can just before I reached the top. But it held, and Sohrab offered a black-smudged hand to pull me up onto the roof. My own hands were crisscrossed with perfect black mesh marks too, and they smelled like old coins.

I rubbed my palms together but only managed to smear the dirt around even worse.

Sohrab laughed and threw his arm over my shoulder, which no doubt left a black handprint on my shirt.

"Look." He nodded straight ahead.

"Wow."

I did not know how I had missed the two turquoise points sticking up above the pale flat rooftops spread before us. They looked like the jeweled spires of some Elven palace from a prior age of this world, made of mithril and sapphire and magic and will.

I blinked. It seemed like a mirage—too beautiful to be real—but it was still there when I looked again.

"What is it?"

"The Masjid-e-Jameh. It's a very famous mosque. Hundreds of years old."

"Wow. It's huge."

"Those are just the . . ." He thought for a second. "Minarets. Yes?"

I nodded. Sohrab's English vocabulary was immense.

"And below there are two domes. Huge domes. And the garden and the mosque."

"Wow."

My own vocabulary had become somewhat less immense in the face of the majestic mosque.

The Masjid-e-Jameh towered above the other buildings in Yazd. Everything around it was short and tan, and even the domes were only a few stories high.

From up here, it felt like looking out over a fantasy world, a world wrought by Dwarvish cunning and Elven magic.

"What are those things?" I pointed to the spires sticking up from some of the roofs between us and the Masjid-e-Jameh.

"We call them baad gir. Wind catcher."

"Oh."

"It's ancient Persian air-conditioning."

"Cool."

Sohrab left his arm resting on my shoulder as he pointed out the other buildings nearby: newer, smaller mosques, and bazaars, and farther away, looming over Yazd, the mountains we were going to visit soon. I could smell his deodorant—something medicinal, like cough syrup mixed with pine needles—and then I couldn't remember if I had put on my own deodorant after showering.

I leaned down to surreptitiously sniff my armpit. It did not smell like "mountain breeze"—whatever that is supposed to smell like—but it didn't smell like cooked onions, either, which is what I usually smelled like when I forgot my deodorant and began producing biotoxins.

We sat on the ledge of the roof for a long time, swinging our legs and surveying the khaki kingdom laid out before us. Clouds blew by, and the breeze tossed my hair and kept it from turning into a Level Eight Fire Hazard.

Across the street from us, a pair of women walked down the sidewalk. One was older, with a blue headscarf so faded it was practically gray. It reminded me of the old rag Dad used to polish his dress shoes.

The younger woman wore a shiny red headscarf, and a stylish jacket that came down to her hips. Mom said those were called manteaux, which was yet another word Farsi may or may not have borrowed from the French.

I did not understand the Iranian obsession with French loan words.

The minarets of the Jameh Mosque sparkled in the sunlight as I used my tongue to dig a piece of lettuce out from between my teeth.

I could still taste the sweet and minty sekanjabin.

My grandfather made it.

"Hey Sohrab?"

"Yes?"

"What did you mean yesterday? After Babou . . . when you said that wasn't how he really is?"

"He was not himself. Because of the tumor."

"But you've known him a long time. Right?"

Sohrab nodded. "He and Mamou helped. So much. When my dad went to prison."

"What was he like? Before?"

Sohrab let his arm fall from my shoulder and folded his hands in his lap. He chewed on his lip for a moment.

"I remember one time. Three, four years ago. Mamou and Babou came to our house for ghormeh sabzi. My mom loves to make it."

Ghormeh sabzi is a stew made with tons of herbs and greens. I always found it suspicious, because it had red kidney beans in it that looked like tiny eyes, corpse lights lit in the swamp of the green stew to draw weary Hobbitses to their graves.

"Babou had just got his new phone. He needed me to help him with it. Babou is not very good with technology."

"Really?"

"Yes. I help with their computer too. So they can Skype with your mom."

"Oh. Thanks."

"Of course. I love your grandparents."

Sohrab bopped me on my shoulder. "Anyway. He was trying to put his background photo to a picture of you. From school."

"Me?"

"Yes. He was so proud. He always talks about his grandchildren in America. Always."

It didn't make sense.

Ardeshir Bahrami, proud of me?

He didn't even know me.

Sohrab was more of a grandson to him than I would ever be.

"He talked so much about you. When you came here, I thought I already knew you. I knew we would be friends."

My throat squeezed shut.

I loved how Sohrab could say things like that without feeling weird. How there were no walls inside him.

"I wish I could have known him back then," I said. "I wish . . ."

I was cut off by the azan sounding. Up on the rooftop, it was loud and clear, richer than I had ever heard it before.

We listened to the voice in the speakers chant, and I imagined everyone in the Jameh Mosque kneeling to pray, and all the people in Yazd heeding the call, and even farther out, a neural network spread throughout the entire country and to the Iranian diaspora across the whole planet.

I felt very Persian just then, even though I didn't understand the chanting. Even though I wasn't Muslim.

I was one tiny pulsar in a swirling, luminous galaxy of Iranians, held together by the gravity of thousands of years of culture and heritage.

There was nothing like it back home.

Maybe the Super Bowl.

When it finished, I wiped off my eyes with my sleeve.

I would have felt nervous excreting stress hormones in front of someone else, but not Sohrab. Not when he told me he felt like he already knew me.

Maybe I already knew him too.

Maybe I did.

"It's beautiful," Sohrab said.

"Yeah."

"We only pray in the morning and night. Not to the azan."

"Oh."

"Sometimes I wish we had it. It feels . . ."

"Like you're connected?"

"Yes." He picked up a loose sliver of tile and tossed it off the roof.

I scratched at the collar of my shirt, wishing it had tassels on it, because the silence between us had grown suddenly heavy. It was not unpleasant, but it was full, like the hush before a sudden downpour.

Sohrab swallowed. "Darioush. Do you believe in God?"

I looked away.

Like I said, I didn't really believe in any sort of higher power, The Picard notwithstanding.

I found my own chunk of roof to throw off.

"I guess not," I said.

I felt ashamed and inadequate.

Sohrab kicked his heels against the fence beneath us and studied the shadows we cast on the ground below.

"Does it bother you?"

"No," Sohrab said.

I could tell without him saying that it did.

"Sorry," I whispered.

Sohrab shook his head and tossed another tile to clatter on the ground below.

"Who do you turn to?" He closed his eyes and swallowed. "When you need succor?"

I knew he was thinking about his dad.

I put my hand on his shoulder. It was awkward—I didn't know how Sohrab could just do stuff like that without thinking about it—but after a second it felt okay.

"I guess . . . that's what friends are for."

Sohrab looked up and almost squinted.

Almost.

He put his arm over my shoulder, and I reached across him so we were linked.

"I'm glad we are friends, Darioush," he said. He reached up and mussed my hair. I liked how he did that. "I'm glad you are here."

"Me too."

"I wish you could stay. But we will always be friends. Even when you go back home."

"Really?"

"Yes."

I squeezed Sohrab's shoulder. He squeezed mine back.

"Okay."

A TACTICAL WITHDRAWAL

We hadn't watched any *Star Trek* on Nowruz, of course—that would have been impossible—but the day Sohrab showed me the rooftop, Dad brought out his iPad after dinner.

"I'm making tea . . . mind waiting for me?"

"You've seen it before," Dad said. "You know your sister gets impatient."

By the time I finished, Laleh sat pressed up against Dad with his arm around her, well into the first act of "Allegiance."

They looked happy and content without me.

Like I said, I knew Laleh was a replacement for me. I had known that since she was born. But I had never minded it before. Not that much.

Star Trek was all Dad and I had. And now Laleh had replaced me at that too.

The quantum singularity in my chest churned, drawing more interstellar dust into its event horizon, sucking up all the light that drew too close.

I took a sip of my tea and then went back through the kitchen and out into the garden.

The jasmine was in blossom again. Everything was silent, except for the occasional rattle of a car cruising down the street.

I loved the quiet. Even if it sometimes made me think of sad things. Like whether anyone would miss me if I was dead.

I sipped my tea and breathed in the jasmine and wondered

if anyone would be sad if I was killed in a car accident or something.

That's normal.

Right?

"Darius?"

"Yeah?"

"Why didn't you come watch?"

"Like you said. I've seen it before."

Dad sighed at me.

I hated when he sighed at me.

"Don't be like that."

"Like what?"

"You're being selfish."

"Selfish?"

"Your sister wanted to spend time with you. You spend all day off with Sohrab, wandering around doing who knows what, and Laleh's here all alone."

I was pretty sure Babou had been home all day too, so Laleh had hardly been "all alone."

"You really hurt Laleh's feelings, storming off like that."

I didn't storm off.

I made a tactical withdrawal.

"You guys started without me. Again."

"I didn't want your sister to wander off."

"Well, would that be so bad? For us to watch it without her?"

"She's your sister, Darius."

"This was supposed to be our thing. You and me. This was our time together. And she's ruining it."

224

"Did it ever occur to you that I might actually enjoy watching it with her?"

Stephen Kellner had never hit me. Not ever.

But this felt like it.

What was it about me that made it so easy for him to cast me aside?

Was it because I was such a target?

I swallowed and took a deep breath. I didn't want my voice to squeak.

"Fine. Then watch it with her."

"Don't be upset, Darius."

"I'm not upset, okay?"

Stephen Kellner didn't like it when I got upset.

He didn't like it when I had feelings.

"Darius . . ."

I shoved myself off the ground.

"I'm going to bed."

Even when Dad stopped telling me stories, he made a point of saying "I love you" every night before I went to bed.

It was a thing.

And I always said "I love you" back to him.

It was our tradition.

That night, Dad didn't tell me he loved me.

I didn't tell him either.

Mom knocked on my door the next morning, long before the azan. We were going to see the Towers of Silence.

I had to wait in bed a few minutes for my own Tower of Silence to go away.

So far I had stuck to my plan not to go number three in my grandmother's house, but it was making my mornings increasingly awkward.

"Darioush!"

"I'm awake."

Mom was back to calling me by my Iranian name.

I wished she would make up her mind.

I stood in the cool morning, my hands stuffed in my pockets.

Déjà vu.

But this time, it was Stephen Kellner who pulled the Smokemobile around.

Laleh and I crammed ourselves into the back. Babou climbed into the middle next to Mamou. His mouth was set in a perfect line. Dad kept trying to meet my eyes in the rearview mirror, but I avoided him.

Laleh was wide-awake. Wide-awake and angry. Her eyes were puffy, her voice scratchy. "I don't want to go."

"You're going," Mom said from the passenger seat. "We all are."

It was clearly a running argument.

Laleh groaned and buried her face in my side.

It reminded me of when she was little—really little—and I would get to hold her whenever Mom and Dad needed a break. Even if she was wound up, she'd eventually fall asleep on my lap, her face mashed into my shoulder, arms limp, mouth drooling.

That was my favorite version of Laleh. When all I had to do was hold her, and she loved me more than anything. And *Star Trek* was something only Dad and I did.

I didn't want to share. Not *Star Trek*.

I hated how selfish I was.

But then Laleh wrapped her arms around me and squeezed. She let out this soft sigh.

She was mad at Mom and Dad, but she was content with me.

It was so hard to stay mad at my sister, even if I wanted to.

And it was Dad who had decided to replace me, anyway.

Not Laleh.

The drive to the Towers of Silence wound around the base of the mountains outside Yazd. I sat in the back and tried not to throw up as Stephen Kellner navigated the undulating roads at unsafe velocities.

"Here!" Mom shouted.

My neck nearly snapped when Dad slammed the brakes. He pulled into an unmarked gravel parking lot.

The Smokemobile sputtered and fell silent when Dad pulled out the key. The Black Breath enveloped us again, heavy with the scent of burnt hair and scorched popcorn and a hint of The End of All Things.

※ ※ ※

The rising sun painted the khaki hills red and pink as we hiked the dusty trail. Mom and Dad led the way, Dad offering an arm to Mamou here and there. Babou took the slope on his own, more slowly. For a moment I wondered if he needed help, but then I remembered how he had clambered over the roof to water his fig trees. And how Sohrab said we were supposed to watch him until he was done. So I hung back to keep an eye out and hoped he wouldn't fall.

Laleh walked with me. When her energy ebbed, and she started to whine, Babou turned around and took her hand.

"Laleh-khanum," he said. "Don't you want to see the top? It is very beautiful."

"I don't care!" Laleh pouted, stretching her complaint out until it snapped.

I had learned to recognize the early warning signs of an impending Laleh-tastrophe.

I jogged forward and took Laleh's other hand. "Come on, Laleh. We're almost to the top."

But my sister slowed her pace even more, pulling Babou and me to a stop.

I turned and knelt down in front of her. "This is important, Laleh. It's part of our family history."

But I knew such appeals did not usually work with Laleh, not when she was this far gone. She was immune to logic.

There was only one way to get her to calm down.

"And when we get back to Mamou's, I can take you into town. Sohrab's uncle owns a store. We can go and get faludeh."

Laleh drew in her lower lip as she mulled it over.

My sister could never resist a good bribe.

"Promise?"

"I promise."

"Okay." Laleh let go of Babou's hand and sprang forward to catch up with Mamou.

When I stood up, Babou looked at me for a second.

"You are a very good brother, Darioush-jan."

I blinked.

It was the nicest thing Ardeshir Bahrami had ever said to me.

Yazd stretched below us, stray pockets of fog tucked into the shadows where the morning sun had yet to burn them away. Line after line of baad girs marched into the distance, and the azure minarets of the Jameh Mosque sparkled when they caught the light.

The Towers of Silence, where Zoroastrians buried their dead—it was called sky burial—had stood sentinel over Yazd for thousands of years.

"My grandfather was buried here," Babou said. "He was named Darioush also. And my grandmother too."

I sucked on the tassels of my hoodie as he led me around the tower, following the crumbling wall that enclosed us. We stood within a stone ring, a hundred feet across, with a gentle slope from the outer walls down toward the center, where bodies were once laid to rest in concentric circles: men on the outside, women in the middle, children in the center.

It was empty now. There hadn't been a sky burial in decades, not since it was outlawed. And there was no one else around, because tourists don't like getting up so early in the morning.

I wondered if I was a tourist.

It felt like a tourist thing, coming to see the Towers of Silence.

And it had felt like a tourist thing, going to visit the ruins of Persepolis. Even if they were part of our family history. Even if they were our heritage.

How could I be a tourist in my own past?

The wind was strong and cool. It stirred the dust we kicked up with our shoes, and blew my hood up around my hair.

I pulled it back down and let my tassels fall out of my mouth.

Babou sighed. "Now we have to put them in cement. It's not the same."

"Oh."

He stopped and pointed across a valley to another mountain. "There is another one. See?"

"Yes."

"Many of Mamou's ancestors there."

"Wow."

"Our family has been in Yazd for many years. Many generations, born and raised here. And then put here when they died."

Our family was woven into the fabric of Yazd. Into the stones and the sky.

"Now your dayi Soheil lives in Shiraz. And your mom lives in America. Even Dayi Jamsheed talks about moving to Tehran. Soon maybe there will be no more Bahramis in Yazd."

My grandfather seemed so small and defeated then, bowed under the weight of history and the burdens of the future.

I didn't know what to say.

The singularity in my stomach was back, pulsing and writhing in sympathetic harmony with the one I knew lived deep inside Babou.

In that moment I understood my grandfather perfectly.

Ardeshir Bahrami was as sad as I was.

He rested his hand on my neck and gave me a soft squeeze.

That was as close to a hug as he had ever given me.

I relaxed against him as we studied the landscape below us.

That was as close to a hug as I had ever given him.

Like I promised, when we got back from the Towers of Silence, I took Laleh to Ashkan Rezaei's store. We swung by Sohrab's house along the way. He squinted when he opened the door.

"Hi, Darioush! Hello, Laleh-khanum."

"Hi," Laleh whispered. She twisted her hand in mine and looked down, hiding the roses blossoming on her cheeks.

It looked like my sister had a crush.

It made sense. If my sister had to have a crush on someone, Sohrab was a good choice, even if he was way too old for her.

"Hey. We're going to your amou's store. For faludeh. You want to come?"

"Of course!"

Laleh grabbed Sohrab's hand, so she was swinging between us. Despite her complaining, she had enjoyed herself at the Towers of Silence: She peppered Sohrab with every conceivable detail about the morning as we walked.

I gave Sohrab a sympathetic shrug.

I loved that Laleh could talk to him so easily.

When we got to the store, I let go of Laleh's hand to get the door, and she ran straight for the counter. Sohrab squinted at me and followed her.

"Sohrab-jan! Agha Darioush! Who is this?"

"This is my little sister. Laleh."

"Alláh-u-Abhá, Laleh-khanum. What a beautiful name. Nice to meet you."

Laleh blushed again. "Hi," she said to the gray-tiled floor.

I took Laleh's hand and gave it a wiggle. "Do you want faludeh, Laleh?"

She shook her head and stared downward, studying the toes of her white sneakers.

Even the lure of dessert wasn't enough to overcome Laleh's sudden and inexplicable shyness.

Mr. Rezaei said, "We have ice cream too, Laleh-khanum, if you like."

Persian ice cream is mixed with saffron and pistachios.

I didn't like it as much as faludeh, but it was still terrific.

"Bastani mekhai, Laleh-jan?" Sohrab asked.

"Baleh," she said.

"Darioush?"

"Faludeh. Please."

I sent Laleh to wash her hands, while Sohrab and his amou talked in Farsi. Sohrab kept smiling. Not his usual squinty smile, but a softer one.

I liked watching Sohrab talk to his uncle. He was different than he was with his mom. More relaxed.

Maybe he felt like a kid again when he was with his amou, in a way he couldn't with his mom, because he had to be the man of the house.

I wished Sohrab could be a kid again all the time.

I don't know if Ashkan Rezaei always gave out such large servings of faludeh, but I was grateful Stephen Kellner wasn't around to witness my dietary indiscretion.

Sohrab was fairly restrained—he only put a little splash of

lime juice on his faludeh—but I doused mine in enough sour cherry syrup to turn it into Klingon Blood Wine.

I grabbed napkins for us, and Ashkan Rezaei handed Laleh a perfect sphere of sunny yellow bastani.

"Noosh-e joon," he said.

Laleh finally looked up. "Merci," she whispered.

She bypassed her spoon and started licking her bastani straight out of its little paper bowl.

I reached out to shake Mr. Rezaei's hand. "Khaylee mamnoon, Agha Rezaei."

"You're welcome," he said, swallowing my hand with both of his. I noticed the backs of his hands were very hairy, like his chest. "Come back soon, Agha Darioush."

Laleh's tongue was turning yellow, and it had clearly gone numb from the cold, but that didn't stop her from carrying on a full conversation with Sohrab in Farsi as we walked home.

I didn't know why she had decided to make the switch, but it made me angry.

I didn't have to bring her along for ice cream.

I didn't have to include her. I didn't have to spend time with her.

The singularity swirled inside me, a black hole threatening to pull me in.

First Laleh had taken *Star Trek*, and now she was threatening to take Sohrab too.

"How's your ice cream?" I asked, to try and gain a foothold in the conversation.

"Good," Laleh said. And then she turned back to Sohrab and started up in Farsi again.

Sohrab glanced at me and turned back to Laleh. "Laleh," he said. "It's not polite to do that. Darioush can't understand you."

I blinked.

No one had ever made people speak in English around me before.

Not even Mom.

"It's okay," I said.

"No," Sohrab said. "It's not polite."

"Sorry, Darius," Laleh said.

"It's fine."

I looked at Sohrab. He squinted at me with his spoon in his mouth.

"Thanks."

"Darioush," Sohrab said. "Can you stay out?"

"Oh. I think so."

I deposited Laleh in the kitchen with Mamou, who tried to feed Sohrab more Nowruz leftovers—it seemed they were self-replicating, and we might never run out—before we left again.

I could tell, from the turns we took, that Sohrab was leading us back to the park near the Jameh Mosque.

It was becoming our spot.

"Darioush," he said, once we had settled onto the roof of the bathroom. He crumpled up a newspaper that had somehow found its way onto the rooftop. "What's wrong?"

"What do you mean?"

Sohrab chewed on his bottom lip for a second and squished the newspaper until it was a tiny sphere.

"You seem very sad."

"Oh."

"Are you mad about Laleh?"

"No," I said.

And then I said, "Not really."

Sohrab nodded and waited for me.

I liked that about Sohrab. That he would wait for me to figure out what I wanted to say.

"Me and my dad used to watch *Star Trek* every night. You know *Star Trek*?"

Sohrab nodded.

"It used to be our thing. But now he wants to watch it with Laleh instead."

"He doesn't want to watch with you too?"

"No," I said. "I don't know." I sucked on one of my tassels for a second and then spit it out when I realized I was doing it in front of Sohrab.

I didn't want Sohrab to think I sucked on my tassels.

"It's just . . . it's not just the *Star Trek* thing. Like, with Farsi. She can speak it and I can't. And everyone here likes her better. So where does that leave me?"

"Darioush," he said. "You remember what I told you? Your place was empty before?"

"Yeah."

"Laleh can't take your place. Why would you think that?"

"I don't know," I said.

"Sometimes I just get stuck thinking things."

"Sad things?"

I nodded and played with the hem of my shirt.

I didn't know how to explain it any better than that.

"It's hard for you? Your depression?"

"Yeah. Sometimes."

Sohrab nodded.

And then he put his arm across my shoulder and said, "But you know what? Laleh is not my best friend, Darioush. You are."

My ears burned.

I had never been someone's best friend before.

Sohrab swayed me back and forth.

"Don't be sad, Darioush."

"I'll try," I said.

I was Sohrab's best friend.

I almost smiled.

Almost.

I didn't have to say it out loud.

Sohrab had to know he was my best friend too.

Star Trek Time was becoming a regular thing again, now that our nights weren't so busy. Now that our days had slowed down.

Now that being in Yazd didn't feel so different from being at home.

It had become a regular thing, except that Laleh was there.

And I wasn't.

Despite what Sohrab said, it was hard not to think about her taking my place when she and Dad snuggled up on the living room couch to watch "Captain's Holiday," which is one of the best episodes of *The Next Generation*'s third season. It's about The Picard racing against time-traveling aliens to solve an ancient mystery.

Even though I hate time travel, I love that episode.

It's terrific.

It's also notorious for Captain Picard's vacation attire: extremely short silver swim trunks that only a Frenchman could pull off.

Laleh found them ridiculous.

"What is he wearing?" she asked, so loud that I could hear her from the kitchen, where I sat drinking tea and reading *The Lord of the Rings*.

Dad shushed Laleh. "Captain's Holiday" was one of his favorite episodes too.

I almost went and joined them.

Almost.

But then Laleh started talking again, making fun of the special effects.

So I drank my tea and I read my book, and I did my best to ignore the sound of Dad and Laleh laughing.

"Darius?"

I looked up from my book. The ending credits music was playing in the living room.

"Yeah?"

"You okay?"

"Yeah."

"Want me to grab your medicine?"

"Sure. Thanks."

I poured a glass of water while Dad pulled down our bottles. He handed me mine and then shook out his own pills.

"Better get to bed soon. Early start tomorrow."

"Okay."

Dad pulled my head down to kiss me on my forehead. He hadn't shaved since we arrived in Iran, no doubt in an attempt to cultivate a rugged Iranian five-thirty shadow, and his chin scratched against the bridge of my nose.

"Love you, Darius."

Dad held my face for a moment and looked in my eyes.

I didn't know what he wanted. What he expected from me.

But at least he said it.

"Love you, Dad."

The next morning, Mamou invited Sohrab and his mom over for breakfast. Laleh took the opportunity to educate Sohrab about *Star Trek: The Next Generation*, now that she was a self-proclaimed expert.

While Laleh distracted Sohrab, I poured a glass of water and took my medicine.

I don't know why I didn't want him to see it. He had seen my foreskin, after all. And he knew all about my depression anyway.

But I still hated that he was seeing me have to take pills.

Somehow it felt more intimate than just being naked in front of each other.

That's normal.

Right?

"Finish your breakfast, Laleh-jan," Mamou said. "Let Sohrab eat. We have to go."

We were going to see Dowlatabad.

Dowlatabad is one of the most common place-names in Iran. It's like Springfield back in the United States: There is one in every province.

The one in Yazd was a garden, not a separate city (at least, not as far as I could tell), and it was famous for its landscaping and its mansion and its giant baad gir.

The adults walked ahead, with Laleh riding on Dad's shoulders, while Sohrab and I walked behind in companionable silence.

That was one of the things I liked best about Sohrab: We didn't have to talk to enjoy each other's company. We just walked and enjoyed the Yazd morning. Sometimes we would catch each other's eye and smile or squint or even chuckle.

The sun was shining, but the air was still shaking off the night's chill. I really should have worn a hoodie, but instead I had on a long-sleeved shirt with my Team Melli jersey over it.

I really loved that jersey.

I felt very Persian in it.

Birds whistled above us.

I sneezed.

"Afiat basheh," Sohrab said.

"Thanks." I sneezed again. "Sorry. How far is it?"

"Not far. Closer than Masjid-e-Jameh."

"Okay."

"Darioush. When are we going to play football again?"

I bit my lip and stared down at my Vans. They were getting dusty.

I wasn't sure I could endure another episode of penile humiliation in the showers.

But Sohrab said, "We don't have to play with Ali-Reza and Hossein, if you don't want to. We can go to a different field."

That's another thing I liked about Sohrab: He knew what I was thinking without me having to say it out loud.

And a third thing I liked about him: He gave me time to think things over.

Penile humiliation notwithstanding, I actually did have fun

playing soccer/non-American football with Sohrab. And we couldn't really play with only the two of us. Not if we were going to be on the same team.

I always wanted to be on the same team as Sohrab.

"I don't mind," I said at last. "We can play with the others."

"You sure? I won't let them tease you again. I promise."

"I'm sure," I said. "We can play whenever."

Sohrab squinted at me. "Let's go this afternoon. When we get back. Okay?"

"Okay."

"You are so good at it, Darioush. You should play for your school. When you go home."

I imagined running onto a field in the Chapel Hill High School team kit. Go Chargers!

"Maybe I will."

Fir and cypress trees lined the walkways of Dowlatabad Garden. We walked in the dappled shade, enjoying the mist blown off the burbling fountains. The path was paved with broken stones on one side and gleaming white diamond-shaped tiles on the other.

It was so peaceful.

"My dad loved to come here," Sohrab said.

I liked that he felt safe talking about his dad to me.

"Do you get to visit him?"

Sohrab chewed his cheek and didn't answer.

"Sorry."

"No. Don't be. It's okay, Darioush."

He sat on the edge of a fountain, and I sat beside him, bumping shoulders.

I don't know why people say "joined at the hip." Sohrab and I were joined at the shoulder.

I let him take his time.

"We got to see him at first. For the first few years. Once a month."

The fountain gurgled.

The wind rustled the trees.

"Was it bad?"

"Not too bad. He was here, in Yazd. The prison was not good, but at least he was close."

Sohrab's jaw twitched.

I bumped his shoulder again, more to cheer him up than anything.

But then he said, "Four years ago they transferred him."

"Oh?"

"To Evin prison. You know Evin?"

I shook my head.

"It is very bad. It's in Tehran. And they put him . . ."

Sohrab stared up at the branches shading us.

"No one can see him. Not even the other prisoners."

"Solitary confinement?"

"Yes."

"Oh," I said.

Sohrab sighed.

I wanted to make it better, but I didn't know how.

Sohrab had Father Issues.

I suppose I had Father Issues too, though they paled in comparison.

Maybe all Persian boys have Father Issues.

Maybe that is what it means to be a Persian boy.

"I'm sorry, Sohrab."

I rested my hand on his shoulder, and he let out a long, low breath.

"What if I never see him again?" he whispered.

I squeezed Sohrab's shoulder and then stretched my arm all the way across it, so I was kind of holding him.

Sohrab bit his lip and blinked and squeezed out a few stress hormones of his own.

Just a few.

"You will," I said.

Sohrab wiped his face with the back of his hand.

I felt so helpless.

Sohrab was hurting and there was nothing I could do. Nothing except sit there and be his friend.

But maybe that was enough. Because Sohrab knew it was okay to cry in front of me. He knew I wouldn't tell him not to have feelings.

He felt safe with me.

Maybe that's the thing I liked about Sohrab best of all.

After a minute, he cleared his throat, shook his head, and stood up.

"Come on, Darioush," he said. "There is more I want you to see."

"**D**arioush. Look up. We're here."

"Wow."

The roof of leaves ended abruptly. We stood at the end of a long fountain, and that fountain led to a huge eight-sided mansion, and out of that mansion rose a baad gir. A wind tower.

It was a true tower—not like the Towers of Silence, which were more mounds than anything.

The baad gir of Dowlatabad Garden was even taller than the spindly columns of Takhte Jamsheed. It soared a hundred feet above us, smooth along its bottom half, slotted along the upper half to catch the wind, with little spade-shaped ornaments at the top. Spines dotted the surface of the spire.

It reminded me of the Barad-Dûr, although it lacked the flaming Eye of Sauron atop it to complete the picture. And it was khaki colored, not black.

I sneezed.

"It's huge!"

"Yes, huge." Sohrab squinted at my astonishment. "Come on. It's better inside."

"We can go in?"

"Of course."

It was the most colorful place I had seen in Yazd. Maybe the most colorful place in the entire world.

One entire wall was taken up with a huge stained glass window. Intricately wrought flowers in every color cast dancing rainbows into the mansion.

We were swimming in light.

We were accelerating to warp speed.

"Wow," I breathed.

It felt like the kind of place where you were supposed to whisper.

"You say that a lot."

"Sorry."

"Don't be. I like it. You don't have these things back home?"

"Nothing like this," I said. I stared up at the ceiling: gleaming white lines intersecting and weaving together into a twenty-four-sided star, which cascaded outward into interlocking diamonds as they followed the curvature of the inner dome.

I had stepped into a world of Elven magic. Into Rivendell, or Lothlórien.

The cool air from the baad gir above us rippled the hair on my arms.

"Nothing like this."

This time, when we went to play soccer/non-American football, I knew to pack a towel. And more supportive underwear.

I still didn't have cleats—Sohrab said I could borrow his again—but I had my Team Melli jersey to wear, which was even better.

I still felt kind of sick when I thought about being naked again, but the worst had already happened, and I knew Sohrab would stick up for me if it came to it.

When we got to the locker room, Sohrab tried to pass me his nicer cleats again.

"You should wear these," I said. "I can use the white ones."

"You take them. These are better."

"But . . ." I had been outmaneuvered once more. My taarof skills were still very poor. "I feel bad. You can't give me your nice cleats."

"Okay, Darioush. Thank you."

Success!

When I finished dressing, Sohrab looked me over and squinted.

"You look like a football star, Darioush."

My ears turned so red, they matched the stripe across my chest.

"Thanks."

"Ready?"

"Ready."

Ali-Reza and Hossein were out on the field again, engaged in a two-on-eight game against a group of clearly outmatched younger kids. Sohrab and I watched for a minute as Ali-Reza bowled over one of his opponents and scored a goal.

I shook my head. It was the sort of overly aggressive maneuver only a Soulless Minion of Orthodoxy would engage in.

Sohrab grabbed my shoulder. "Come on!"

He ran into the pack and insinuated himself onto the younger team. In a flash, he hooked the ball from Ali-Reza and tore up the field toward the goal. It was completely undefended.

The kids whooped and laughed as Sohrab scored. They didn't mind at all that we had infiltrated their team.

I hung back to defend our goal with a boy in overlarge cleats—he must have had Hobbit feet like me—and Persian hair even longer and curlier than mine.

"Salaam," he said. He had a thick accent, but it was cool. I liked the way he formed his vowels.

"Um. Salaam."

He pointed at my Team Melli jersey.

"Nice," he said in English.

I guess he could tell I didn't speak much Farsi.

"Thanks."

The young Iranian Hobbit—I decided to call him Frodo—ran up toward midfield. Now that Sohrab was playing, Ali-Reza and Hossein had lost their tactical advantage, and our team kept pressing forward.

Sohrab scored three more times, with assists from some of our new teammates, before Hossein held on to the ball and waved us all out to huddle midfield.

Frodo and I jogged out to join the circle. Everyone was talking in Farsi, arguing back and forth too fast for me to make anything out.

Like Frodo when he wore the One Ring, I had slipped back into the Twilight world, hidden from the Iranians around me by my inability to speak Farsi.

Since I was Frodo, I decided that made the Hobbit next to me Samwise.

But then Sohrab said, "English. Darioush can't understand."

And Hossein said, "Okay. Sohrab and Ayatollah pick first."

Samwise looked at me. "Ayatollah?"

My ears burned hotter than Mount Doom.

Sohrab saved me again. "We are changing teams," he explained. "Six and six. You are with me, Darioush. Captains."

Me. Darius Kellner. A captain.

Just like The Picard.

"Asghar," Sohrab said to Samwise. "You are with us."

Sohrab and Ali-Reza took turns picking the other boys. We got Mehrabon, a non-Reza Ali, and Behruz, who was the shortest kid there but had the darkest mustache.

It was deeply impressive.

"Okay," Sohrab said. He nodded at me.

I cleared my throat.

"Make it so."

Playing soccer/non-American football with Sohrab, Asghar-Samwise-Frodo, and the rest of my team was genuinely fun. Even if Asghar and the other guys had all decided to call me Ayatollah.

I hated it at first, but as far as I could tell, none of them knew the real reason.

"It's because you are in charge," Sohrab said. "That's what I told them."

Our team cheered my new nickname whenever I nailed a tricky pass or managed a good save. I almost started to like it.

Almost.

But no matter what, Sohrab always called me Darioush.

We played until my calves burned and my lungs were in danger of experiencing a non-passive failure. We played until Asghar had to hunch on the side of the field, hands on his knees, and fight the urge to vomit. We played until Hossein and Ali-Reza got tired of us scoring goals on them. And we scored a lot of goals.

Asghar and the other guys made us promise to play again the next day. Sohrab said yes right away. Apparently he was something of a fixture on the field, though he had missed several games since he started hanging out with me.

He had given that up for me.

He didn't have to do that.

Ali-Reza pretended like he might not return—he had suffered a crushing defeat, after all—but I knew he would be back when Hossein said, "Different teams next time."

Sohrab hung back, kicking the ball around with me while the others cooled off and headed for the locker room.

I knew why he was doing it. But he didn't say anything or make a big deal out of it.

That's the kind of friend he was.

But that didn't make things any less awkward when it was just him and me in the locker room.

In fact, it might have been more awkward.

Once again, Sohrab stripped himself completely, like it was totally normal for guys to be naked around each other. His skin was a volcano, with sweat running down every valley.

My face was experiencing some extreme thermal flux of its own. "Thanks for letting me borrow these," I said as I tucked the laces back inside my borrowed cleats.

"You're welcome." Sohrab slung his towel over his shoulder. "It's nice to share with you, Darioush."

I peeled off the sweaty Team Melli jersey, acutely aware

that all my soccer/non-American football stuff had come from Sohrab, whether bought or borrowed.

I felt very inadequate as a friend.

But then it came to me: the way to make it up to him. Sohrab desperately needed a new pair of cleats. And I was an Iranian millionaire.

"Come on. The water should be warm again."

Sohrab faced me and talked while we showered, which was weird, but at least there was a spray going and soap partially covering me. I didn't feel quite so exposed, especially when I could turn away to rinse off and listen to him.

Sohrab told me all about the guys we had played with: how the games had started out with just Sohrab and Ali-Reza, and then Ali-Reza invited Hossein, and Sohrab invited Asghar, and one by one the group had coalesced like a solar system forming around a brand-new star.

I was amazed Sohrab could carry on a casual conversation about the dynamics of Yazd's soccer/non-American football-playing youth while soaping up his penis.

I was even more amazed I managed to talk back to him while I scrubbed my belly button and my stomach jiggled like some sort of gelatinous non-humanoid life-form.

Maybe I was learning to have less walls inside me too.

Maybe I was.

On the way home, Sohrab said, "Thank you for playing, Darioush."

"Thank you for asking me."

Sohrab squinted at me. "I told you. Remember? Your place was empty."

I smiled back at him. "Yeah."

"But not anymore."

"Not anymore."

"Mamou," I said. "I want to get Sohrab some nice soccer cleats. Uh. I mean football cleats."

"Okay, maman. Do you know what size?"

"Forty-four."

"Okay. I'll have Dayi Soheil bring them next time he comes. They have better shopping in Shiraz."

"I'll grab my money."

"It's okay, Darioush-jan, you don't have to."

"Yes I do. He is my friend. I want to do something nice for him."

"You are so sweet."

I was amazed I didn't have to taarof about it.

"Can I help?"

Mamou was up to her elbows in suds.

"It's okay, Darioush-jan."

"I can rinse for you."

"If you want. Thank you."

I was amazed I didn't have to taarof about that either.

I stood next to Mamou and rinsed the dishes for her as she hummed along to the radio.

I was so used to unrecognizable Persian beats, at first I didn't recognize what Mamou was humming. What the radio was playing.

"Uh."

It wasn't Farsi. It wasn't Persian music at all.

It was "Dancing Queen."

"Mamou?"

"Yes?"

"Are we listening to ABBA?"

"Yes. They are my favorite."

I thought about that: how Fariba Bahrami, who had lived in Iran her entire life, was in love with a band from Sweden.

I wanted to know where she heard them for the first time.

I wanted to know what other music she liked. And movies. And books.

I wanted to know everything she loved.

"Darioush-jan."

"Yeah?"

"I am almost done. Can you make me some of your special tea?"

"Sure." I dried my hands and started the water. Mamou finished the last few dishes and then pulled half a watermelon out of the fridge. She carved it into cubes while I dammed the FTG-FOP1 First Flush Darjeeling and poured us each a cup.

"You don't keep the leaves in?" Mamou asked.

"It gets bitter if you let it steep too long."

"Oh. Thank you, maman. I love this tea."

I loved my grandmother.

Before, she had been photons on a computer screen.

Now she was real, and full of the most amazing contradictions.

I wanted to know more.

I wanted to know everything about her.

It was like the well inside me had finally cracked open.

And I finally had my chance.

"When did you start listening to ABBA?"

CHELO KABOB

Sohrab and I played soccer/non-American football every day after that, except for Friday.

On Friday, Mamou was making chelo kabob.

That morning, I found her elbow deep in an enormous glass bowl of ground beef, burnished a bright gold from all the turmeric she'd added.

"Sobh bekheir, maman," she said.

"Sobh bekheir."

"There is tea in the kettle. It's in the living room."

That was the safest place for it.

Fariba Bahrami was making chelo kabob, which meant the kitchen was about to become a battlefield, like Helm's Deep.

"Thanks. Is there anything I can help with?"

"I will let you know. Thank you."

"Okay."

Even Fractional Persians like me and Laleh dream sweet, exquisite dreams of chelo kabob.

Back home, we only had it on special occasions: birthdays and holidays and report card days, so long as I made a B average.

Stephen Kellner was surprisingly cool about that. He said he wanted me to try my hardest. He didn't want me to be afraid of getting a bad grade, as long as I was learning.

That was good, because I pretty much always got a C in math, but I got A's in history and English, so that kept my GPA in good enough shape to maintain a regular supply of chelo kabob.

When we made chelo kabob at home, Mom was in charge of the chelo—she knows the secret to perfect tah dig—and Dad was in charge of the kabob.

Mastery of grilled meats is an essential component in the makeup of a Teutonic Übermensch.

Mom must have mentioned Dad's preternatural kabob skills, because Mamou put him to work packing the ground beef for kabob koobideh onto skewers.

Dad patted the meat around the wide metal skewers, pinching them between his index and middle fingers up and down the length of the blade to seal them on, while Mom helped Mamou cut chicken breast into cubes using a cartoonishly oversized cleaver.

I was certain the event would end in bloodshed; in bodies piled sky-high, like the Battle of the Pelennor Fields.

I washed the dishes when they let me, enjoyed the smells of kabob in the making, and waited for the horns to sound.

"Darioush. Come help me, please."

Babou summoned me to the garden.

"We need to put the tables up."

I half expected Babou to wheel a Ping-Pong table out, like the Rezaeis had in their yard, but instead he had me drag three fabric-topped card tables out from the shed in the corner. I unfolded the legs and helped him line them up beneath the canopy of fig leaves.

Babou grunted and nodded at me but didn't really speak. His shoulders were hunched, and as I followed him to the shed to collect some dark wooden folding chairs, I noticed how slowly he shuffled his feet.

I remembered what Mom said, about how strong Babou was, that day he carried her home from the park.

I wondered if it was the same park where Sohrab and I sat on a rooftop and watched the sun set over our Khaki Kingdom.

I wondered if Babou had ever carried any of my cousins piggyback.

I wondered what else I had missed out on. What else I was going to miss.

I didn't understand Babou—I wasn't even sure if I liked him, to be honest—but I did not want him to die.

Soon there would be one less Bahrami.

"Darioush-jan. Go ask Khanum Rezaei to bring more sabzi when she and Sohrab come."

"Okay."

Mrs. Rezaei opened the door before I even knocked. She had her hair pulled back and arranged in huge curlers. With her forehead exposed and her eyebrows stretched upward by the strength of her hair, she reminded me even more of a Klingon warrior preparing for battle.

"Alláh-u-Abhá, Darioush-jan," she said, and pulled me in. "Come in. Sohrab is in the back."

"Um. Alláh-u-Abhá." Mrs. Rezaei's smile widened, and I was glad I had decided it was okay to use the greeting with her even though I wasn't Bahá'í.

"Babou asked me to ask you to bring more sabzi for tonight. If you can."

"Sure, sure. Your grandma makes the best chelo kabob."

I hoped she would not be offended that Stephen Kellner had a hand in making the chelo kabob this time. Klingons could be notoriously contentious when it came to their food.

While Mrs. Rezaei sorted out which sabzi to take, I found Sohrab in the backyard.

He was kicking his soccer ball/non-American football around, barefoot and shirtless. Sweat plastered his short hair to his temples and the nape of his neck. He waved when I came out and put his hands behind his head in Surrender Cobra. His flat chest rose and fell, rose and fell, and his stomach muscles rolled with each breath.

I knew if I got close enough to him, the intense thermal radiation he was emitting would scorch me.

"Hi, Darioush," he said. He squinted at me, but he could barely breathe.

"Hey. What were you doing?"

"Push-ups. Sit-ups. Wind sprints. Drills."

"Wow."

I had underestimated Sohrab's dedication to soccer/non-American football.

Maybe I should have been practicing too.

Sohrab breathed and squinted and breathed and squinted.

I sneezed.

"Babou wanted me to ask your mom to bring some sabzi tonight. For chelo kabob."

"Mamou makes the best chelo kabob! I eat way too much, every time."

"Me too," I said. "I mean, when my mom and dad make it."

Sohrab pressed his right foot into his left, scratching at the top of it with his big toenail. The silence between us hung heavy and close. My ears warmed their way toward a Red Alert.

Sohrab swallowed. The little hollow in his collarbone stood out against his glowing skin.

"You want to play awhile?"

He knew the perfect way to puncture the silence.

"Yeah."

It was true what everyone said:

Fariba Bahrami did make the best chelo kabob in the world.

Maybe in the entire Alpha Quadrant.

We ate in the shade of Babou's fig trees, crowded around the card tables or sitting on the ledges of Babou's herb planters. Unlike the Rezaeis' garden, Babou's hadn't been assimilated by fresh mint, but it was only a matter of time.

Resistance is futile.

Baskets of sabzi—parsley and watercress and tarragon and basil and mint, stalks of green onion, fresh radishes carved into flowers—sat on each table. There were lemon wedges to squeeze onto our meat, and tiny glass dishes overflowing with bright ruby sumac, which was for sprinkling over everything.

It's supposed to help with digestion, which is good, because I do not know a single Persian—Fractional or otherwise—who doesn't overeat when chelo kabob is on the menu.

"I told you." Sohrab bumped my shoulder. "Your grandma makes the best."

"Yeah."

I used the point of my spoon to break off a segment of kabob koobideh. Of all Persian foods, kabob koobideh is probably the most suspicious-looking, even more than fesenjoon. Each kabob looked like a soft brown log, shiny with oil and fat, dimpled where Dad had pinched it to seal it onto the skewer.

It was deeply suggestive.

My cousin Nazgol, who may have actually been a Ringwraith, sat on my other side, watching Laleh cut her kabob and mix grilled tomato into her rice. Nazgol turned to me and popped the petals of a radish flower into her mouth.

"You want some?"

"No thanks."

"It's good for you. Here." She tried to press a piece of radish to my lips as I laughed and turned away.

"Nakon, Nazgol-khanum," Sohrab said. "Leave him alone."

Nazgol shrugged and turned to offer the radish to Laleh, who popped it into her mouth and then scrunched her face up.

Sohrab watched Laleh gag. He caught my eye and chuckled.

"Thanks," I said. "I'm gonna grab some more. You want any?"

"Na merci, Darioush." He squinted at me. And then he said, "Maybe a little."

"Okay."

I took both our plates into the kitchen, where the platters of kabob and rice took up every square inch of available counter space. When dinner was through, the dishes would pile even higher than the mountain Mom and I had washed after Nowruz.

Chelo kabob was a serious endeavor.

Dad was refilling his plate with grilled vegetables as I scooped more saffron rice onto my own. For once he didn't comment on my food choices, even though a second helping of rice was a classic dietary indiscretion. He was too busy fielding advice and criticism about kabob preparation from all the Bahrami men.

"You have to use enough salt. This is very important," Dayi Jamsheed said.

"You have to pinch it better, or it falls off the skewer," Dayi Soheil said.

"You have to make sure the grill is very hot," Babou said. "But not too hot."

I almost felt sorry for Dad.

Almost.

I met his eyes, to see if he needed to be rescued.

But he grinned at me and turned back to Babou.

"What I like to do is use oil on my fingers, instead of water," Dad said. "That way they don't stick as much. It's messy, though."

The Bahrami men nodded in approval.

I wasn't jealous of him.

Not really.

Maybe Dad's place had been empty too.

Maybe he'd figured out how to fill it.

Maybe he had.

With so many Persians gathered in such close proximity, it was inevitable they would reach critical mass and ignite a game of Rook.

This time, Babou played with Dayi Soheil against Dad and Dayi Jamsheed.

I did not understand how anyone could play Rook as much as Ardeshir Bahrami.

Sometimes I found him in bed, playing alone, the cards spread across a blanket on his lap as he formulated moves and countermoves with imaginary opponents and an imaginary teammate.

I found a seat in the corner and watched the Bahrami men—and Stephen Kellner—start bidding.

How did he do it?

How could he just join in like that?

"Darioush," Sohrab said. "Are you stuck?"

"Huh?"

"You said sometimes you get stuck. Thinking something sad."

"Oh." I swallowed and pulled at the tassels of my hoodie. "It's nothing."

"Come on." Sohrab pulled me up to my feet. "I won't let you be stuck anymore." He dragged me to the table where Parviz and Navid, Dayi Soheil's sons, sat. Parviz was twenty-three, and Navid was twenty-one, which made them closer to me in age than anyone, except Nazgol the Nineteen-Year-Old Nazgûl.

"Darioush," Parviz said. His voice was rich and creamy, like smooth peanut butter. He barely had an accent: It only came through in the sharpness of his vowels and the lilt in his sentences, as if there was the shade of a question in everything he said. "How come you never told us you play football?"

"Oh. Um."

"Sohrab said you are very good at it."

I tried really hard not to smile.

"He is. You should see him."

"I'm not that good."

"Yes you are! You should have heard Ali-Reza. He was so mad. He said, 'It's not fair! I'm never playing with you two again!'"

Parviz snorted. "You still play with him?"

"I thought he moved," Navid said.

Navid's voice was deep, like his mother's. He'd inherited her elegant, arched lips, and Mamou's long, dark eyelashes. I too had inherited Mamou's eyelashes, which sometimes got me teased at school.

To be honest, though, I liked them.

I really did.

"He was going to move to Kerman," Sohrab said. "But his father lost his job and they had to stay here."

Ali-Reza had been a complete jerk to me—the epitome of a Soulless Minion of Orthodoxy—but I still felt bad for him.

It turned out Ali-Reza had Father Issues too.

Sohrab gave Parviz and Navid a complete play-by-play of our latest game. He made me sound way better than I really was, glossing over the passes I missed and exaggerating all the saves I pulled off.

It became a lot harder not to smile.

I felt like I was ten feet tall.

"After the game, Ali-Reza wouldn't stop complaining. Asghar told me. Ali-Reza said, 'They don't even play football in America.'"

Sohrab threw his arm over my shoulder. He had showered before coming over, and still smelled soapy and fresh, like rosemary. My back warmed where his arm rested.

"But it doesn't matter. Darioush is Persian too."

I was a warp core on full power.

I was glowing with pride.

Navid and Parviz decided that, since I was so Persian, it was time for me to learn how to play Rook. Navid produced a pack of cards from his shirt pocket, the way a smoker would produce a pack of cigarettes, and began dealing.

Sohrab sat across from me and helped my cousins explain the game. I already knew the basics, but I'd never actually tried to play before.

"It's okay," Sohrab said. "Just have fun."

I glanced over at Dad's table. He caught my eye and smiled, like he actually approved of what I was doing.

I worried I would have to play Rook with him when we got home.

I did not think I could stomach it.

Sohrab started out our bidding. The inherent telepathy that made us such a good team at soccer/non-American football helped us with Rook too.

That was good, because I was pretty much terrible at the game.

Sohrab never got mad or impatient, though. And even Navid and Parviz were nice about it. After each round, they gave me advice on what I could have done better. It was probably the slowest game of Rook they had ever played.

It didn't matter, though. We had fun.

When the night wound down, I escorted Sohrab and his mom out and said good night to the living room, where all the ladies sat sipping tea and talking over each other in Farsi.

Mamou pushed herself off the couch to give me a good night hug.

If Mamou made the best chelo kabob in the Alpha Quadrant, it was nothing compared to her hugs, which were easily the best in the Virgo Supercluster, of which our Milky Way Galaxy was only one small part.

When Mamou wrapped her arms around me, a whole new dimension of light and warmth opened up between them.

I sighed and hugged Mamou back.

I wished there was a way I could bundle her hugs up and take them back to Portland with me.

"Good night, maman."

"Good night, Mamou. I love you."

"I love you, Darioush-jan." She held my face. "Sleep well."

Laleh's door was cracked open as I passed by. She was curled up in her bed, completely incapacitated by the amount of chelo kabob she had eaten.

I kind of wished Dad wasn't playing Rook. Maybe I could have convinced him to watch an episode of *Star Trek*. Just the two of us.

But Dad had found his place, and I had found mine. Even if they were further apart.

Like I said, our intermix ratio had to be carefully calibrated.

I went to my room and started up the Dancing Fan. Dayi Soheil had brought Sohrab's new cleats for me, concealed in a grocery bag, and Mamou had left the box on my bed. I opened it up: bright green Adidas, with the three gleaming white stripes on each shoe so crisp and new, they would blind Ali-Reza and Hossein next time Sohrab played against them.

They were perfect.

I wanted to run after Sohrab and give them to him right away.

I wanted to go to the field and play a game.

But then I thought about what he had said—that it was nice to share with me. And I thought maybe I should wait and give them to him later. Like a going away gift or something.

"What's that?" Mom asked from the door.

"Dayi Soheil picked up some cleats for me to give Sohrab. As a gift. He needs new ones."

"They're perfect."

"Yeah."

Mom sat down next to me and ran her fingers through my hair. "You're a good friend. You know that?"

"Thanks."

"I love seeing you two together. Just like me and Mahvash when we were younger."

"Yeah."

I loved being Sohrab's friend.

I loved who being Sohrab's friend made me.

"You're going to miss it here, aren't you?"

"Yeah." I played with my tassel. "I think I am."

Mom wrapped her arm around me and pulled my head down to kiss me on the temple.

"Did you have a good time tonight?"

"It was perfect," I said.

And it was perfect. But it was bittersweet too. Because I was running out of time.

I wished I could stay in Iran.

I wished I could go to school with Sohrab, and play soccer/non-American football every day, though I supposed I would have to start calling it regular football.

I wished I could have been born in Yazd. That I could have grown up with Sohrab and Asghar and even Ali-Reza and Hossein.

The thing is, I never had a friend like Sohrab before. One who understood me without even trying. Who knew what it was like to be stuck on the outside because of one little thing that set you apart.

Maybe Sohrab's place was empty before too.

Maybe it was.

I didn't want to go home.

I didn't know what I was going to do when I had to say good-bye.

"You have too much hair, Darioush."

"Um."

Babou had been hanging around Stephen Kellner too much.

He was trying to fit a white cap over my dark Persian curls, but it kept slipping off.

"Fariba-khanum!" He called down the hall for Mamou to bring him something, but I didn't recognize the word.

Mamou appeared in my bedroom doorway, smiling at the cap sitting crooked on my head.

"Here, maman." She stuck three hairpins in her mouth, bunched up my hair to stuff it under the cap, and pinned everything in place.

"Perfect."

"Merci," I said.

Mamou squeezed my cheeks—"You are so handsome!"—and left.

Babou took me by the shoulders and looked me up and down. I was wearing the white shirt he and Mamou had gotten me for Nowruz, and my one pair of khaki dress pants.

They were the same color as all the walls in Yazd. I wondered if I would blend into the buildings, and appear as nothing but a floating face.

Babou tugged on my collar to straighten it.

"You look very nice, Darioush-jan."

"Uh. Thank you."

I didn't feel nice.

I felt like I was on an away mission, disguised to infiltrate and observe another culture without violating the Prime Directive.

I felt like an actor, playing the role of the good Zoroastrian grandson.

I felt like a tourist.

But Babou fussed with my cap a little more, even though Mamou had already gotten it settled. He looked me in the eyes from time to time, like he was looking for something, and thought maybe—just maybe—I had it in me after all.

Babou hummed to himself as he smoothed out my shoulder seams and rested his hands on them.

"I am glad you are here to see this, Darioush-jan."

Maybe I wasn't such a tourist.

Maybe this was something Babou and I could share. Our very own *Star Trek*.

Maybe it was.

"Me too."

The Atashkadeh is Yazd's Zoroastrian Fire Temple.

It wasn't like a mosque or church, with services every week. It was only used for special celebrations.

But it had a fire burning inside all the time.

The fire inside the Atashkadeh had been burning for fifteen hundred years. According to Babou, it came from sixteen different kinds of fire—including lightning, which was pretty amazing if you thought about it.

We were all in light clothes: Mom, Laleh, and Mamou with

white headscarves and manteaux, and me, Dad, and Babou in our white caps.

Even Stephen Kellner, noted secular humanist, dressed up to go.

The Fire Temple wasn't as tall as the Jameh Mosque, or even the baad gir of Dowlatabad Garden. It was only two stories high, surrounded by trees. A still, perfectly circular pool mirrored the cloudless blue sky above us.

"Wow."

What the Atashkadeh lacked in height, it more than made up for in majesty: Five arches, held up by smooth white columns, fronted it, and a Faravahar was carved into the top. The winged man shone in unblemished stone stained blue and gold.

I wondered how it stayed so vibrant in the Yazd sun, which bleached everything else to blinding white.

When we parked the car, Mamou let me and Laleh out from behind her, but then she got back in.

"Um."

"You go ahead," she said. "Babou is not feeling very well."

I looked past her at Babou, who had gone pale, despite the golden sun pouring in the car windows.

It must have been bad, if he was going to stay behind.

He had been so excited to show us the Atashkadeh.

Mom led us up the wide stone steps to the temple, and showed us where to slip our shoes and socks off.

It was silent inside, a silence so intense, it squeezed my head like a too-small hat.

Even Laleh could tell this was the kind of place to keep quiet.

A tinted glass portal separated us from the inner sanctum, where a giant bronze chalice held the ancient fire.

I thought about Babou, waiting in the car. How many times had he come here to see the dancing flames?

How many times had his grandparents stared into the same fire?

And every other Bahrami. Going back generation after generation, through revolutions and regime changes, wars and invasions and pogroms. How many of them had stood where I was standing?

And how many would there be in years to come, if Babou was right and the Age of Bahramis was coming to an end?

Standing in that temple, staring into the fire that had been burning for hundreds of years, I felt the ghosts of my family all around me. Their soft presence raised the hair on my arms and tickled at my eyelashes.

I wiped my eyes and stood there, lost in the fire.

I knew that Babou was going to be one of those ghosts soon too.

No one had to say it out loud.

Babou went straight to bed when we got home. Mamou stayed with him. I heard their soft voices through the closed door.

I found Mom in the sunroom, with one photo album on her lap and three more on the couch next to her.

"Uh. Mom?"

"Come on in." She stacked the other albums to one side so I could sit next to her.

"You okay?"

"Yes," she said. Her voice was hoarse, like she had been crying. "Just looking at some old pictures."

She had the album open to photos of her in America: her college graduation, her bridal shower, her citizenship ceremony.

"Is that Dad?"

"Yeah."

At the bottom of the page was a photo of a young Stephen Kellner standing in front of a bright green door. Apparently, the Übermensch had once been an Überhippie, complete with a scruffy beard and hair that reached past his shoulders.

Imagine that:

Stephen Kellner with long hair. In a ponytail, even.

"Babou hated that hair. Your dad cut it to make him happy. He nearly had long hair in all our wedding pictures." Mom smirked. "God, can you imagine? Your dad would never be able to live it down."

There was a photo of Mom and (short-haired) Dad on their wedding day, with Mamou and Babou on either side of them; and one of them at a fancy restaurant overlooking the river; and Mom with a huge baby bump; and Dad lying on the couch with a little baby on his bare chest.

Dad's arms curled so gently around Laleh, who had her little legs tucked up under her stomach, and her face nestled in the hollow of his collarbone.

"She was so tiny back then," I said.

"That's you, sweetie."

"What?"

I looked closer. Mom was right.

It was hard to believe the little potato sack on Dad's chest could be me.

It was hard to believe how content Stephen Kellner looked, cradling me in his arms, his lips resting in a kiss on my fine baby hair. (It was not very dark and curly yet.)

I wished we could go back to that. To a time when we didn't have to worry about disappointments and arguments and carefully calibrated intermix ratios.

When we could be father and son full-time, instead of forty-seven minutes a day.

We couldn't even manage that anymore.

"This is my favorite photo of you two," she says.

"Um."

"He could always get you to sleep. No matter what. Even when you were teething, a few minutes on his chest and you were out like a light. You loved it when he held you."

Mom traced potato-me with her fingers.

"Look how much he loves being a dad."

Mom's voice quavered.

I wrapped my arm around her and laid my head against her shoulder.

"I'm sorry, Mom."

MAGNETIC CONTAINMENT

I wrapped Sohrab's cleats in the ads section of one of Mamou's Yazdi news magazines, covered with pictures of scruff-faced men in button-up shirts advertising real estate or plastic surgery or new cars.

It was our last game.

I was not okay with that.

I was not okay with saying good-bye to Sohrab.

And I kind of hated Mom and Dad for bringing me to Iran, knowing I'd have to say good-bye.

I left a few minutes early, so Sohrab could try on his cleats before we headed to the field. But when I got there, a strange vehicle was parked outside his house: a tiny grayish-brown hatchback that had been waxed to such a shine, I sneezed when I caught the sun's reflection off the front fender.

I knocked on Sohrab's door and then shifted the box of cleats. I wasn't sure what to do with it: whether I should hold it out in front of me, or hide it behind my back, or tuck it under my arm.

There was no answer. I knocked again, a little louder.

Sometimes Sohrab or his mom couldn't hear me knocking, if they were in the bathroom or on the phone or out in the backyard.

Maybe they were enjoying another Ping-Pong table full of romaine lettuce and Babou's sekanjabin.

I gave up on the front door and picked my way around the

side of the house, tiptoeing between the square stones that constituted the Rezaeis' landscaping.

But the backyard was empty—no Sohrab, no lettuce. Just the Ping-Pong table folded upright and pushed against the wall of the house. It rattled on its hinges, a rigid green sail tossed in the stiff Yazdi breeze.

I rubbed the flat of my thumbnail against my bottom lip. I wished I had some tassels.

I wondered if Sohrab and his mom had gone out. If they had forgotten I was coming by.

But then, through the little window in the door, I caught sight of Sohrab's amou Ashkan in the kitchen, pacing back and forth, in and out of my view.

I knocked on the back door.

"Hi. I mean, Alláh-u-Abhá, Agha Rezaei."

"Alláh-u-Abhá, Agha Darioush," he said. But there was a sadness in his voice, and he wasn't smiling.

Sohrab's uncle had the kind of face that looked wrong without a smile.

"It is good to see you."

He stood back to let me in. I slipped off my Vans and set them against the door. There was no sign of Sohrab.

"Um. Is everything okay?"

The other Mr. Rezaei sighed. Not an exasperated sigh, but a sad one. It made the hairs on the back of my neck stand up.

"Come in." He took my shoulder and led me into the living room.

Mrs. Rezaei sat slumped on the couch, looking like she had

just strode inside from a battlefield, leaving behind a trail of corpses in true Klingon fashion. Her hair was black flames licking the air around her. Her makeup, normally so careful, was wild and smeared. Her chest heaved.

She was sobbing.

I felt terrible for thinking of her like a Klingon.

I was a complete and utter D-Bag.

Sohrab had his arms wrapped around her, like he could keep her from flying apart if he squeezed tight enough. At first I thought he was shaking with the effort, but fat, sloppy tears were pouring down his cheeks too.

I didn't know what to do.

I didn't know what to say.

"Sohrab-jan. Mahvash. Darioush is here."

Mahvash Rezaei moaned. It was the worst sound I had ever heard in my life. It was the sound someone makes when they've been stabbed in the heart.

Sohrab took his mom's hand, gently uncurling her manicured fingers and weaving them with his own. He rested his chin on his mom's head and held her tighter.

"Um."

I felt so useless.

My palms were sweating on Sohrab's box, smudging the wrapping paper.

"Can I. Uh. Make some tea? Or something?"

I knew it was stupid as soon as I said it.

Sohrab's head snapped up.

"Go away, Darioush."

His voice was as sharp as a knife.

"Sorry. I just . . ."

"Get out!"

My stomach inverted itself.

"Sohrab," Agha Rezaei said softly. He spoke in Farsi, but Sohrab argued back, his voice rising in pitch and volume until it started cracking.

Sohrab's uncle shook his head and led me back to the kitchen. His hands shook as he filled the kettle.

"Here." I set Sohrab's cleats on the counter and grabbed the Rezaeis' tea out of the drawer to the right of the stove.

I swallowed and swallowed but I couldn't get rid of the pulsing lump in my throat.

"What's wrong?" I whispered.

I couldn't make my voice work properly.

Ashkan Rezaei opened his lips to speak, but then pressed them back together as they trembled.

He was crying too.

"It's my dad." Sohrab hovered in the doorway, radiating fury. His jaw clenched and unclenched. "He's dead."

I wished I could time travel.

I wished I could unravel everything and make it not true.

"Amou." Sohrab said something in Farsi to his uncle, who looked like his knees were about to buckle. He used that same knife-sharp voice he used on me.

Agha Rezaei shook his head and went back into the living room.

"What do you want, Darioush?"

"I'm sorry," I squeaked. That lump was still there. "What happened?"

Sohrab's face burned like a brand-new star. I could almost hear him grinding his teeth.

"They say he was stabbed. In prison."

"Oh my God," I said. "Oh my God."

Sohrab's eyes drilled into me. He jerked his chin at the countertop. "What is that?"

I swallowed and picked up the box.

"This—I got it. For you."

Sohrab stared at me like I was speaking Klingon.

"What is it?"

"Shoes. Cleats. For football."

"You came here to give me shoes?"

"Um." The lump had turned into sand. I was getting squeakier by the second. "Yeah. For our game today."

Sohrab's eyes flashed. He smacked the shoebox out of my hands and then shoved me.

He didn't push me hard, but I stumbled back, because I wasn't expecting it.

I wasn't expecting the look in his eyes.

"Get out. Go away. Leave!"

"But—"

Sohrab cut me off.

"You are so selfish. My father is dead and you come over to play football?"

Sohrab kicked the box of cleats across the kitchen.

"I'm sorry," I said.

"You're always sorry. God."

My heart felt like a warp core about to lose magnetic containment and breach.

"I . . ." The sand in my throat had spread to my eyes.

"Stop crying! You're always crying! Pedar sag. Nothing bad has ever happened to you. You do nothing but complain. You've never had anything to be sad about in your life."

I couldn't speak.

I just stood there, blinking and crying.

"Go away, Darioush," he said.

And then he said, "No one wants you here."

No one wants you here.

Sohrab turned and left, slamming the living room door behind him.

And then he screamed.

His voice shattered like glass.

Everything he said was true.

No one wants you here.

I knew it was true.

I stumbled out the back door.

No one wants you here.

I ran.

y socks crunched over gravel and concrete.

I had left my shoes at Sohrab's house.

I couldn't go back for them.

And I couldn't go back to Mamou's either.

I just kept running.

I was a coward.

Sohrab had left that off his list.

Clouds had rolled in off the mountains, casting the whole of Yazd in gauzy gray light. Without the sun, the old houses weren't blindingly khaki anymore. They were brown and dirty and sand-worn.

There was litter everywhere: white plastic lavoshak wrappers, and empty plastic bottles crusted yellow with dried-out doogh; scrunched up sun-faded newspapers and pictures of my new, unfortunate namesake, the real Ayatollah, frowning up at the gray sky.

I didn't like Iran anymore.

I wanted to go home. To Portland, not to Mamou's.

I kept thinking about Sohrab. About his father. How he would never see him ever again.

I thought about Stephen Kellner. How sometimes I wished I saw him less.

I thought about how selfish I was.

I really hated myself.

※ ※ ※

My foot was bleeding.

I had sliced my heel when I climbed the chain-link fence to our spot in the park. We were supposed to celebrate Sizdeh Bedar there.

I didn't think that was going to happen anymore.

From the Jameh Mosque, the azan sounded, piercing the quiet afternoon. All across Yazd, people faced the qibla to pray, a titanic multicellular entity focused on the same moment in space-time.

My throat clamped up, a compression wave that traveled down my chest and into my stomach.

Another containment failure.

I wiped my face against my Team Melli jersey, the one Sohrab got me for Nowruz.

No one had ever gotten me a gift like Sohrab had. One that showed he understood me perfectly. One that made me feel like I belonged.

No one had ever invited me to play soccer or hang around on rooftops or stand around a Ping-Pong table eating lettuce.

No one ever made me feel like it was okay to cry. Or bumped shoulders with me and made me smile.

I shook so hard, I thought the bathroom was going to lose molecular cohesion and collapse into a vibrating pile of dust.

I was never going to stop crying.

Sohrab was right about me.

Sohrab was right about everything.

I crossed my elbows over my knees and buried my face in the little hollow I had made.

I wished I had the One Ring, so I could have vanished.

I wished I had a cloaking device so no one would ever find me.

I wished I could just disappear forever.

"Darius?"

It was impossible.

How had Stephen Kellner located me?

The chain-link fence rattled as he hoisted himself up. "There you are."

"Hey." My throat didn't work right. I sounded like I had swallowed a pineapple with its skin still on.

Dad wiped his palms on his pants and sat down beside me, so close, our elbows bumped.

I scooted away so we weren't touching.

"We were worried about you."

"Sorry."

"Mr. Rezaei said you left Sohrab's house hours ago. Have you been up here the whole time?"

I shrugged.

Dad rested his hand on the back of my neck, but I shook him off.

"He told us what happened."

"About Sohrab's dad?"

"Yeah. And about you and Sohrab."

I felt another containment failure coming on.

I couldn't let Stephen Kellner see me cry.

So I said, "What made you look for me here?"

Dad nodded up at the Jameh Mosque. "This seemed like the kind of place you would like."

I bit my lip and blinked.

"Don't cry, Darius." Dad tried to wrap his arm around me, but I leaned away.

"I can't help it, okay?"

Dr. Howell likes to say that depression is anger turned inward.

I had so much anger turned inward, I could have powered a warp core.

But without the proper magnetic field strength, it exploded outward instead.

I couldn't sit down anymore, even though my foot hurt when I put weight on it.

"Sometimes I can't help crying. Okay? Sometimes bad shit happens. Sometimes people are mean to me and I cry. Sorry for being such a target. Sorry for disappointing you. Again."

"I'm not disappointed—"

I snorted.

"I just want to make sure you're healthy. Your illness can run away with you before you even know it."

"No, you just want me to be like you. You want me to ignore it when people are mean to me. When Trent bullies me. When Sohrab . . ."

I swallowed.

"You don't want me to feel anything at all. You just want me to be normal. Like you."

I picked up a jagged piece of roof and hurled it off into the empty park. My chest was about to explode, hurling matter and antimatter out until they annihilated everything nearby.

"You won't even watch *Star Trek* with me anymore," I whispered. "I'll never be good enough for you."

All my anger had fled, imploding back into my chest, slipping down the event horizon of the churning supermassive black hole inside me.

Slingshot Maneuver.

Dad's face had turned red and blotchy. "Darius." He sighed and uncrossed his long legs to stand up. "You've always been good enough for me. I loved you from the first moment I saw your little hands on the ultrasound. And felt your little feet kicking in your mom's belly. I loved you the first time I got to hold you and look into your beautiful brown eyes and know you felt safe in my arms."

Dad's hands twitched like he wished I was still a baby he could hold.

"And I've loved you more every day. Watching you grow up. Watching you grow into yourself. Watching you learn to cope with a world I can't always protect you from. But I wish I could."

He cleared his throat.

"Being your dad is my first, best destiny."

It wasn't true.

How could he say that?

"Remember those stories you used to tell me?"

I sniffled.

"Remember? When I was little?"

"Of course." He closed his eyes and smiled. "I loved putting you to bed."

"Then why did you stop, if you loved it so much?"

Dad bit his lip. "You remember that?"

"I remember."

Dad sighed and folded himself back down to sit on the ledge

of the roof. He glanced up at me but didn't hold my eyes—just patted the spot beside him.

I sat down, but farther away from him.

Dad looked up, like he was going to speak, but then looked at his hands and swallowed. His Adam's apple bobbed up and down, up and down.

"You're wrong. I want you to feel things, Darius. But I'm scared for you. You have no idea how scared. I take my eyes off you one moment and if it's the wrong moment, you could be drowning in depression, bad enough to . . . to do something. And I can't protect you from that. No matter how hard I try."

"I'm not going to hurt myself, Dad."

"I nearly did."

All the atmosphere on the rooftop fled, blown away by Dad's explosive admission.

"You . . . what?"

"When you were seven. My meds weren't doing their job. And I got to thinking about how you and your mother would be better off without me."

"Oh."

"I got so bad, I was thinking about it. All the time. Dr. Howell put me on a pretty strong tranquilizer."

"Um."

"It made me into a zombie. That's why I couldn't tell you stories. I could barely tell the time of day."

I didn't know.

"I lost myself for a long time, Darius. I didn't like who I became on those pills, but they saved my life. They kept me here. For you. And your mom. And by the time I was doing better and Dr. Howell tapered me off, your sister was born and I just . . . things were different. She was a baby, and she needed me. And I didn't know if you even wanted stories anymore. If you were ever going to forgive me."

"Dad . . ."

"Suicide isn't the only way you can lose someone to depression."

Dad looked up at me again. There were no walls between us.

"And it kills me that I gave it to you, Darius. It kills me."

There were tears in his eyes.

Actual human tears.

I had never seen my father cry before.

And due to some harmonic resonance, I started crying again too.

Dad scooted closer to me. And when I didn't scoot away, he wrapped his arms around me and pulled me down to rest his chin on top of my head.

When had I gotten taller than Stephen Kellner?

"I'm so sorry, son. I love you so much."

I let Dad hold me, like that tiny potato-sack version of myself, sleeping on his chest when I was a baby.

"You're okay," he murmured.

"No. I'm not."

"I know." He rubbed my back up and down. "It's okay not to be okay."

Dad and I stayed and watched the sun set, gilding the turquoise minarets of the Jameh Mosque for a few breathtaking moments before plunging Yazd into twilight.

Dad let me talk about Sohrab, and what he had said.

He let me be sad.

"You really love Sohrab. Huh?"

"He's the best friend I ever had."

Dad looked at me for a long moment. Like he knew there was more.

But he didn't ask.

Instead, he pushed the hair off my forehead, kissed me there, and rested his chin on top of my head again.

Maybe he knew, without me saying it out loud, that I wasn't ready to talk about more.

Maybe he did.

THROUGH A WORMHOLE

Sizdeh Bedar was pretty much cancelled.

Everyone was going over to the Rezaeis' house. They packed the food Mamou had made for the picnic.

"Happy birthday, sweetie. Have fun with your dad," Mom said, kissing my forehead before she grabbed a platter of dolmeh.

"Thanks."

Mom rested her palm on my cheek.

I thought about her dealing with Dad's depression for all these years.

I thought about her dealing with mine too, and how much harder it must be with two of us.

I thought about how painful it must have been, to want to help and not be able to.

Not really.

My mother was strong and enduring as the Towers of Silence.

So was Mamou. She kissed both my cheeks. "You are the sweetest boy I know, maman," she said.

"Darius?"

Laleh wrapped her arms around my waist.

"I'll always be your friend."

I knelt down and kissed Laleh on the cheek.

"I know you will, Laleh."

"I made you some tea. For your birthday. It's in the teapot. I didn't even put sugar in it."

"Thank you."

Laleh squeezed me again. She whispered in my ear, "You can add sugar if you want, though."

That made me smile.

"Okay."

It was weird walking down the streets of Yazd with my father instead of Sohrab.

Weird, but not bad.

Dad kept pointing out different doors that he liked, or baad girs he thought were particularly impressive. But he didn't stop to draw them. He had left his sketchpad at home.

"I want to spend time with you," he explained.

I didn't know how to handle all this attention from my father.

It seemed we had increased our intermix ratio by a substantial factor.

But it was nice.

The minarets of the Jameh Mosque were even taller than the baad gir of Dowlatabad Garden. I craned my neck and stared up at them.

"Wow."

"Wow," Dad agreed.

We crossed the fountained courtyard, staring up at the minarets and the huge, pointed archway that towered above us. It felt like being swallowed by an enormous celestial beast.

Dad was speechless.

I knew, without him saying it out loud, that he was in love with the place.

The halls and chambers were quiet. Morning prayers were done, so it was mostly empty, except for tourists like us. Our footsteps echoed endlessly. My dress shoes squeaked on the smooth tiles.

I had yet to recover my Vans from Sohrab's house, but Mom had promised to bring them back with her.

I studied my father as he stared at the tile work on the ceiling: endless geometric patterns that made me think of traveling through a wormhole. Dad's face was relaxed—no smile, no frown. All his walls had come down.

Dad had never hidden his depression from me. Not really.

But I never knew how close I had come to losing him.

How hard he fought to stay with us, even if it made him into a Borg drone.

I didn't want to lose him.

And he didn't want to lose me.

He just didn't know how to say it out loud.

I think I understood my father better than I ever had before.

Mamou made my favorite dish for dinner: zereshk polow, which is rice mixed with sweetened dried red barberries.

Red barberries are small berries that look like rubies, except they have little nipples on them.

It sounds weird, but they are delicious: tiny pouches of sweet, tart happiness.

In Iran, birthdays aren't that big a deal. There was no singing or cake. Mom and Dad said they were going to give me my gifts when we got home. But Mamou and Babou gave me a beautiful antique copper teapot—it was hand-beaten and everything—

and a pair of cleats. They were the same as Sohrab's, except blue, and sized for my Hobbit feet.

I still felt terrible about Sohrab, no matter what anyone said.

I hugged and kissed my grandparents, and Babou surprised me when he kissed me back on the cheek. He held me by my elbows and looked at me.

"Darioush," he said, so soft, only I could hear him. "Sohrab is hurting right now. But it's not your fault."

"Um."

"You are a good friend, baba. And he is lucky to know you."

He let me go and patted me on the cheek.

He almost smiled.

Almost.

After dinner—and tea and qottab—Mom helped me pack.

I didn't need the help, but I knew, without her saying, it was because she wanted to spend a little time with me.

The Dancing Fan was dancing harder than it had ever danced before. It knew this would be its last performance.

I had a basket full of clean laundry next to me, and I handed Mom shirts to fold. She had this cool trick where she got them into perfect squares, with the sleeves tucked into the center.

She pulled out the Team Melli jersey. It had cleaned up nicely, despite me depositing the entire contents of my sinuses on it, not to mention a gallon of stress hormones.

That jersey had been my talisman—my Persian camouflage—but now I was going home. I didn't need it anymore.

Maybe I had never needed it.

Maybe I never should have tried being something I wasn't.

I packed the jersey and covered it with my folded boxers to keep it safe. Just in case.

"Anything else?"

I shook my head.

"You sad to be going home?"

"Not really."

Mom looked at me.

"I'm going to miss Mamou." I swallowed. "And Babou."

Mom smiled when I added that.

I think I meant it too.

I think I really did.

"But . . ."

"I understand, sweetie."

"Thanks."

I sat in the kitchen, drinking tea with Babou and Laleh and reading *The Lord of the Rings*. I had finished the book but there were still the appendices.

I always read the appendices.

Babou was reading too, a green book with gilded pages. The sugar cube tucked in his cheek made his voice sound funny and his cheek puff out like a squirrel's. Laleh sat on his lap, listening to him read in Farsi, or occasionally slurp his tea. Her head kept nodding, but she refused to go to bed.

She did not want to go home.

She was much more Persian than I was.

"Darioush-jan," Mamou said. She smiled at us from the doorway.

She did not want us to go home either.

I wished I could take her with me.

"Sohrab is here. He wants to say good-bye."

Red Alert.

Sohrab waited for me in the doorway, staring at the welcome mat, with his hands behind his back. He hadn't set foot inside the house.

He looked smaller and flatter than I had ever seen him.

He had walls inside him now.

"Uh," I said.

He looked up.

"Hi," he said.

"Hi."

"You didn't come over today. I was worried."

"I wasn't sure if you wanted that."

He shuffled his feet. He was wearing the new cleats I had gotten him.

"They are perfect," he said. "My favorite color. You noticed?"

"Yeah."

Sohrab dug the toes of his cleats into the doormat and chewed the inside of his cheeks.

Things hadn't been this awkward between us since that day in the bathroom, when Ali-Reza and Hossein had compared my foreskin to religious headgear.

"Thank you," he said.

"You're welcome." My ears were on fire. If there had been any weary Hobbits around, looking for somewhere to melt the One Ring of Power, they wouldn't have needed a volcano. "I'm sorry about your dad," I said. "I'm so sorry."

I couldn't stand how sorry I was.

I wanted to reach out for him, to put my hand on his shoulder, to let him excrete stress hormones or scream or do whatever he needed to do.

But the walls weren't just inside him.

They were between us.

I didn't know how to breach them.

"It's not your fault," Sohrab said. "I'm sorry for what I said to you."

"Don't be."

"No." He shook his head. "I was hurting. And you were there. And I knew how to make you hurt as bad as me."

He still wouldn't look at me.

"I'm so ashamed," he said. "Friends don't do what I did."

"Friends forgive," I said.

"I didn't mean it, Darioush. What I said. I want you to know." He finally met my eyes. "I'm glad you came. You are my best friend. And I never should have treated you that way."

He chewed on his lip for a moment.

"Can you come out? For a little while?"

I glanced back at Dad, sitting on the couch watching soap operas with Laleh. He nodded at me.

"Sure."

THE CRACKS OF DOOM

I followed Sohrab down the silent street. He had something flat and rectangular clutched in his right hand, but I couldn't tell what it was.

I tried to swallow away the lump in my throat, but all that did was move the lump down to my heart.

Being around Sohrab had never made me so nervous before.

The park—our park—was dark and empty. The mercury lights around the restroom cast the whole thing in a dim orange glow, barely enough to see the links of the fence as we climbed. Sohrab did an awkward one-handed climb, careful not to drop whatever it was he was holding.

We sat with our legs over the edge of the roof, surveying our Khaki Kingdom one last time. Sohrab didn't say anything, and I didn't, either.

When had the silence between us crystallized?

I rubbed my palms on my pants to try and get the mesh marks off them.

When I couldn't take the quiet anymore, I said, "I'm so sorry about your dad."

Sohrab shook his head. "Thank you. But I don't really want to talk about it."

"Oh. Sorry."

I hated this new reality.

I didn't want to live in a world where Sohrab and I couldn't talk about things anymore.

"Don't be sorry. Maybe one day I will." Sohrab handed me the small package he was carrying. "I got you something. For your birthday." It was wrapped in Yazdi newspapers, same as his cleats had been. "Happy birthday, Darioush."

"Thank you. Should I open it now?"

"Yeah."

I pulled the paper off and crumpled it so it wouldn't blow off the roof. Inside was a framed photo of Sohrab and me.

It was from Nowruz, though I couldn't say for certain when it had been taken. Sohrab and I were leaning against the wall of Mamou's living room. Sohrab had his arm over my shoulder, and we were both laughing at something.

I wondered if Sohrab would ever laugh again.

"Is it okay?"

"It's perfect," I said. "Thank you. You're always giving me things. I feel bad."

"Don't feel bad. I want to."

I wiped my eye—a minor containment breach. "I never had a friend like you."

"Me neither," Sohrab said. He squeezed my shoulder. "You don't care what anyone thinks. You know?"

My ears burned. "I care what everyone thinks, Sohrab."

"No you don't. Not really. You don't try to change yourself. You know who you are." He bumped shoulders with me. "I wish I was like that. I always try to be what my mom needs. What my amou needs. What you need. But you are the opposite. You are happy with who you are."

I shook my head. "I don't think that's really me. You've never seen what it's like back home. How everyone treats me."

"They don't know you, Darioush." Sohrab grabbed my shoulder. "I wish you could see yourself the way I see you."

"I wish you could see yourself too." I swallowed. "You're the only person who never wanted me to change."

Sohrab blinked at me then, like he was fighting a containment breach himself.

"I'm going to miss you, Darioush."

"I'm going to miss you, Sohrab."

"I wish . . ."

But I didn't find out what Sohrab wished.

The azan rang out, piercing the still night.

Sohrab turned and listened, his eyes fixed on the Jameh Mosque in the distance.

I turned and watched Sohrab. The way his eyes lost their focus. The way his jaw finally unclenched.

I put my arm over his shoulder, and he linked his over mine.

And we sat like that, together.

And the silence was okay again.

The house was quiet when we got back, except for Dad and Babou in the kitchen playing Rook again.

"What time do you leave?"

"Early. Mom says we have to leave by five. Which means we'll probably leave by six."

"Probably," Sohrab agreed.

He looked at me, and I looked at him.

I didn't know how to say good-bye.

But then Sohrab pulled me in and hugged me.

He didn't kiss me on the cheeks like a Persian.

He didn't slap my back like a Soulless Minion of Orthodoxy either.

He held me. And I held him.

And then he sighed and pulled away.

He gave me this sad smile.

And that was it.

Maybe he didn't know how to say good-bye either.

I loved Sohrab.

I really did.

And I loved being Darioush to him.

But it was time to be Darius again.

Dayi Jamsheed came to drive us back to Tehran in the morning. I was showered and ready by five, so I waited out in the living room. I had finished the appendices of *The Lord of the Rings*, but I still had some econ reading left.

The truth was, I hadn't actually touched it since we'd arrived.

Laleh wormed her way next to me on the couch. Her silky headscarf was out of place, but it looked cute that way. She was soft and warm against my side as she laid her head on my chest and closed her eyes.

I loved my little sister. When I looked at her, I felt the same way as when I stared into the ancient flame of the Atashkadeh. Or when I heard the azan ring out across the city.

Dad found us like that, curled up against each other. He mussed my hair, but the joke was on him, because it was still wet from my shower. He dried his hand against his leg.

"Homework?"

"Just some reading for econ."

"I'm proud of you. For doing it."

I wasn't sure what to think of that—Stephen Kellner, expressing pride in me—but he was trying to make things better between us.

I wanted things to be better too.

"Thanks."

Laleh yawned and snuggled against my arm.

I could have stayed like that forever.

Mamou hugged me good-bye. She kept kissing me on one cheek and then the other, alternating back and forth until my face was hot enough to boil off the tears she left behind.

She took my cheeks between her palms. "I love you, maman."

"I love you too. I'll miss you."

"Thank you for coming to see us."

"I loved it," I said.

And I had. Really. I loved Mamou's hugs, and her cooking, and her laughter. I loved it when she let me help her with the dishes. I loved it when we sat together and drank tea.

I told myself I was going to call her every week on Skype. I told myself I'd always come say hi whenever Mom called.

But I knew deep down I was going to fail.

Because each time I talked to her, I'd have to say good-bye.

Now that we were part of each other's lives—our real lives, not our photonic ones—I didn't know if I could survive that.

I'd finally managed to open up the well inside me.

I didn't think I could block it again.

Mamou turned to wrap up Laleh in a Level Thirteen Hug.

I couldn't watch.

I slung my Kellner & Newton Messenger Bag over my shoulder and dragged my suitcase to the door, where Babou waited. The creases around his eyes were seismic in the morning light, but they were turned up.

"Darioush-jan," he said. "Thank you for coming."

He took me by the shoulders and kissed me on both cheeks.

"Take care of your dad. He needs you. Okay, baba?"

"Okay."

No one had ever told me Dad needed me.

But I wondered if maybe it was true.

Maybe Babou saw something I never had.

I wasn't sure if he really wanted it, but I reached out and hugged him. His face was scratchy against my cheek.

Babou surprised me when he wrapped his arms around me too.

"I love you, Babou."

"I love you, baba. I will miss you."

The worst was watching Mom say good-bye to Babou.

They knew they were never going to see each other again.

I thought about what Mom had said: how she wished I had known him before. Back when he was warmer. Stronger. Happier.

I knew she was saying good-bye to that Babou too. The one who carried her piggyback through the streets of Yazd. The one who tucked her in at night. The one who picked figs fresh from the tree for her every summer.

Babou kissed Mom on the forehead and then ran his fingers through her hair. The same way Mom always did to me.

I didn't think she would ever stop crying.

I watched Mamou and Babou wave to us, silhouetted in the front door, until Dayi Jamsheed's SUV turned the corner and they disappeared.

Laleh was already out again, drooling on my hoodie.

Dayi Jamsheed's SUV rode a lot smoother than the Smoke-mobile, even if he had learned how to drive from Babou, all evasive maneuvers and unsafe velocities.

With Laleh against me, and Mom talking to Dayi Jamsheed in soft Farsi, I started getting sleepy myself.

Dad looked back at me and Laleh. He caught my eyes, nodded toward Laleh, and smiled.

We were going home.

I thought I would feel different—transformed—by my trip to Iran. But when we got back home, I felt the same as always.

That's normal.

Right?

Laleh and I took two days off from school to get over our temporal displacement. Dad and I still watched *Star Trek: The Next Generation* every night, sometimes with Laleh and sometimes by ourselves.

When we watched "The Best of Both Worlds, Parts I and II"—Dad made a special exception to the one-a-night rule for cliff-hangers—Laleh got scared and ran up to her room.

I hoped she'd be back.

But maybe not right away.

"It's kind of nice when it's just us," Dad said.

"Yeah. But I don't mind if Laleh watches. Sometimes."

Maybe I did feel different after all.

Maybe something had changed.

Maybe it had.

Mom took me to get new wheels and a new seat for my bike while we were off, so I could ride to school on my own again. And on my first day back, I slung my Kellner & Newton Messenger Bag over my shoulder and headed out.

Even though I was still categorically opposed to messenger bags, it felt like the Kellner & Newton Messenger Bag had gone to Mordor and back with me. I couldn't cast it aside now, even though Mom did offer to get me a new backpack.

Javaneh Esfahani knew where I had gone, and so did my teachers, but I hadn't really told anyone else. So when I came back from spring break two weeks late, with a Yazdi tan, the rumors were already swirling.

"How was rehab?"

"Dude. I thought you died!"

"I heard you went to join ISIS."

Fatty Bolger had the Chapel Hill High School Rumor Mill in overdrive.

I spent the whole morning answering one question after another.

When I got to the lunch table, I dropped my messenger bag on the seat with a crash and rested my forehead on my hands.

"Hey," Javaneh said.

"Hey," I muttered into my hands. "Hey! I have some stuff for you."

I dug into my messenger bag for the plastic sack Mom had sent for Javaneh's mom. Dried shallots and pashmak and haji badum, which are these little baked almond candies, and a new tablecloth.

"Thanks. How was it?"

"It was . . ."

I didn't know what to say.

How could I explain Mamou and Babou and Sohrab and football and the rooftop to someone who had never experienced them?

How could I talk about them when I still felt the ache?

"It was?"

"It was," I said. "I don't know. It's hard to talk about."

Javaneh nodded.

"Maybe I'll get to go one day. We still have family there too."

"I hope you get to," I said. "I really do."

"We're on the South Field today," Coach Fortes said as we emerged from the locker room. "Let's go, gentlemen."

The South Field was a huge stretch of grass behind the Chapel Hill High School Library. It was not technically a field—it was more of a lawn, really, and there was a slight grade to it—but that was where Coach Fortes took us to play football/American soccer.

It felt very strange, wearing my red Chapel Hill Chargers T-shirt and black swishy shorts, instead of my Team Melli jersey.

It felt very strange wearing my own tennis shoes, instead of Sohrab's well-loved cleats, or even the new ones Mamou and Babou had gotten me for my birthday. (We weren't allowed to wear cleats in physical education. Supposedly it was for "safety reasons.")

It felt very strange playing on a full team, with my classmates calling out "Darius" or "Kellner" instead of "Darioush" or "Ayatollah."

I kind of missed that.

It was nice to discover I was actually one of the better players in our class. Better than Trent Bolger, at any rate, who was on the opposing team.

I kept blocking him, stealing the ball and passing it forward again, until he looked ready to burst into flame like an angry Balrog.

When we rotated positions, and I took a turn at goalie, I knew he would try to get even. He wove around our defenders, and tried to sneak a shot to my right, but I knew what he was going to do.

I dove for the ball, brushed the grass off my shins, and tossed it back out.

After dealing with the Iranian Soulless Minions of Orthodoxy, Trent Bolger and his American ones didn't seem so tough.

"Nice save, D-Breath," he said. "But you're used to balls flying at your face."

"Asshole," Chip said. He ran over to give me a fist bump. He had trimmed his hair over break, and pulled it back into a little topknot.

I kind of hated how cool it looked.

"Nice save, Darius."

"Oh. Thanks."

Trent glared at Chip, but Chip just shrugged him off and grinned at me.

I didn't know what to make of it.

Maybe Cyprian Cusumano wasn't as soulless as I thought.

Maybe.

Coach Fortes caught me on the way back to the locker room.

"You were pretty good out there, Kellner."

"Thanks," I said, but then I stepped in something.

It was squishy, and as soon as I smelled it I knew.

"Oh. Shit."

"Language!" Coach said, but then he turned back and saw me scraping my shoe on the grass.

People in the neighborhood let their dogs run through the South Field sometimes.

"Oh. You meant that literally."

"Sorry, Coach."

He snorted and shook his head. "Come on. We've got towels inside. I'll write you a tardy slip."

"Thanks."

I guess Coach Fortes was okay as far as coaches went at Chapel Hill High School, even if he was part of the Sportsball-Industrial Complex that allowed Fatty Bolger and his Soulless Minions of Orthodoxy to thrive.

(Go Chargers.)

Coach said, "Soccer is pretty big in Iran, huh?"

"Yeah. They call it football, though."

"You play a lot while you were there?"

"I guess."

"How come you never tried out for our team? I didn't even know you played."

I thought about Coach Henderson.

I thought about lack of discipline.

"I guess I didn't think I was that good."

"Well, you've got some skill. Why don't you try out in the fall?"

My ears burned. I almost told Coach no.

Almost.

But that's what Darius would have done.

Darioush would have tried out.

I thought about telling Sohrab that I had made the team. And sending him photos of me in my kit. And him squinting and congratulating me.

I thought about having fun on the field, like I did with him and Asghar and even Ali-Reza and Hossein.

"Maybe I will," I said. "Maybe I will."

kind of wished I could shower after physical education.

There was something to be said for getting clean and fresh again after a game of football.

But guys didn't do that at Chapel Hill High School.

Instead, I cleaned off my shoes with the towel Coach Fortes found me, got dressed, and headed to geometry.

My throat tightened when I saw Chip Cusumano sitting on the curb by the bike rack after school, twisting the end of his top knot around his index finger with one hand and fiddling with his phone with the other.

I checked my bike for any obvious signs of damage, but it seemed fine, and besides, Trent was nowhere to be seen.

"Chip?" I said.

"Oh. Hey. What happened to you after gym?"

"I had to clean my shoes off."

"Dog shit?"

"Yeah."

Chip shook his head.

"Did you need something?"

"No. Just wanted to make sure your bike was okay. I still feel bad about that."

"Oh. Yeah, it's okay now."

"Good."

"How was your trip? And your grandfather?"

"You knew about that?"

"Yeah."

"Um. It was good. Really good. Thanks."

We unlocked our bikes and walked toward the road. Chip kept glancing at me.

"Something wrong?"

"No. Not really." Chip grinned again. His eyes crinkled up, almost like a squint. "You just seem different somehow."

I shrugged.

"Maybe you brought some of your ancestor back with you."

"What?"

"Darius the Great. Or Darioush. You were named after him. Right?"

I was amazed that Cyprian Cusumano, Soulless Minion of Orthodoxy (maybe), had made that connection.

I was amazed he knew the proper pronunciation.

I was amazed he never once tried to make a joke about it.

"Yeah. I mean, I was named after him, but I'm pretty sure we're not related."

"Well, it's still cool." Chip adjusted the rubber band holding his hair in place. "Hey. Glad you're back, Darius."

"Um. Thanks."

"Cool. See you."

"Yeah. See you."

Chip followed me the first mile, laughing about the awkwardness of saying good-bye and then not actually parting ways, until he turned right at the Safeway and I kept going straight.

I didn't know what to make of his sudden and inexplicable change in attitude.

Maybe he was right, and I was different somehow.

Maybe I had brought a little bit of Darioush the Great back with me.

I would have to ask Sohrab what he thought.

He and I emailed every day.

Well, it was more like every other day, given the temporal differential involved in waiting for a reply. Sohrab lived half a day into the future.

This is why I hate time travel.

That night, we ate carry-out from the sushi restaurant around the corner from Dad's office. And then we watched "Family," which is the episode where Captain Picard goes home to France to visit his family and recover from being assimilated by the Borg.

It was his first time seeing his family in years.

"Is it just me, or is this really weird timing?"

Dad laughed.

"Not just you."

Mom sat down on my other side during the opening credits. Dad and I both turned to stare at her.

"What? I like this episode. It's all on the farm."

"Vineyard," Dad said.

Mom reached across me to swat at Dad's chest.

"Whatever."

Dad caught Mom's hand and kissed her on the palm, which made her laugh.

Mom spent the whole show running her fingers through my hair. It was nice, sitting there sandwiched between her and Dad.

(Laleh had gotten bored before the teaser was even over.)

Dad and I watched the ending credits all the way through, and then I got up to make some tea. Grandma and Oma had taken me to Rose City Teas when we got back, to celebrate my birthday, and I'd picked up some new Ceylon Nuwara Eliya to try.

While I steeped the tea, Dad pulled down a pair of cups for us and set them on the kitchen table. And then he sat down and waited for me.

We had started doing this, most nights, after *Star Trek*.

We sat together and I told him the story of my day. It was our new tradition.

I poured his cup, and then mine, and brought it up to my nose to smell it. Dad copied me.

"Hmm." He wrinkled his nose. "Lemons?"

"Yeah. And floral notes."

He sniffed again and took a sip.

"It's good."

"Yeah. Smooth."

We sipped and talked. I was a little nervous to tell Dad what Coach Fortes said, but he surprised me.

Stephen Kellner was full of surprises these days.

"Don't let him pressure you," Dad said. "But if you want to do it, we'll all come cheer for you."

"Okay. Maybe. I don't know if I'll have time. I was going to try for an internship at Rose City Teas next year."

"Paid or unpaid?"

My ears burned. "Unpaid."

"That's okay. It would be good for you."

I stared at my father—Stephen Kellner, the Übermensch—with his fingers wrapped around a teacup, drinking fine Ceylon tea, and telling me it was okay to take a job that didn't pay, in a field that was nothing like his own.

"Really?"

"Really. You love it. Right?"

"Yeah."

"Okay, then."

We finished off the pot, and while I pulled down our medications, Dad put the kettle on for another round.

"Something less caffeinated, though."

Mom and Laleh wandered back in as I set a pot of Dragon Pearl Jasmine on the table.

"This smells like sabzi," Laleh announced. She had elected not to use an ice cube, since it was steeped at 180° and not a full boil.

"It smells like Babou's garden," Mom said.

We sat around the table, drinking and laughing and smiling, but then we got kind of quiet.

It was a nice kind of quiet. The kind you could wrap yourself up in like a blanket.

Dad looked at me.

"You okay, son?"

"Yeah, Dad," I said.

I took a long, slow sip of my tea.

"I'm great."

AFTERWORD

In telling Darius's story, I wanted to show how depression can affect a life without ruling it—both as someone who lives with it, and as someone who loves people living with it.

I was twelve years old when I was diagnosed with major depressive disorder, and I spent four years working with my psychiatrist to find a medication (or, as it turned out, a combination of medications and counseling) to manage my symptoms. I count myself very fortunate: Because my family has a history of depression, my parents knew to get me treatment, and provided the support structure I needed. I was fortunate too that my depression never led me toward self-harm.

Depression takes different shapes for different people: For me, it took the shape of comfort eating (a lot). It took the shape of avoiding school for a month because I couldn't drag myself out of bed and face the morning. It took the shape of not doing my homework because I couldn't see the point in anything.

Even now, it sometimes takes the shape of staying at home, playing mindless video games, when I don't feel up to engaging with the outside world.

Living with depression can mean getting stuck in cycles of misunderstood motives, of always imagining the worst in people, or thinking they are imagining the worst in you.

It can mean pushing people away because you don't think you're worth their time.

It can mean taking medication to stay alive—to combat self-harm or suicidal ideation—even if it dulls parts of yourself you don't realize are there. (It's absolutely worth it.)

It can mean imagining that the people who love you will never love you enough.

But depression can be just as hard to witness as it can be to live with. It's frustrating to love someone and be unable to help them.

It's frustrating to repeat the same cycle of misunderstandings over and over again.

It's frustrating to constantly tell yourself that, if you could just figure out the secret, you could make everything better—but you can't.

No matter what, though, depression doesn't have to rule your life.

If you're living with depression, there is help out there.

If someone you love is living with depression, there is hope for them.

It takes patience, and kindness, and forgiveness.

I'm still learning how to take care of myself, and learning how to take care of those I love.

If you're learning, too, there are resources available.

National Alliance on Mental Illness: nami.org

Anxiety and Depression Association of America: adaa.org

Depression and Bipolar Support Alliance: dbsalliance.org

Crisis Text Line: www.crisistextline.org or text HOME to 741741

National Suicide Prevention Lifeline: suicidepreventionlifeline.org
    or call 1-800-273-8255

The Trevor Project (LGBTQ Lifeline): www.thetrevorproject.org or
    call 1-866-488-7386

Trans Lifeline: www.translifeline.org or call 1-877-565-8860

ACKNOWLEDGEMENTS

There are so many people who had a hand in bringing this book into the world, but if I taarofed as much as each and every one of you deserve, the acknowledgements would be longer than the book.

Thank you to my agent, Molly O'Neill, for being a tireless champion, a wise counselor, and the best partner in this endeavor I could have asked for. Thank you for your generous advice, your excellent phone calls, and an amazing cake.

Thank you to the entire team at Root Literary: Holly Root, Taylor Haggerty, and Chelsee Glover-Odom, for all your support.

Thank you to my editor, Dana Chidiac, who understood the secret heart of my book, and helped me bring the best possible version into the world. Thank you for your patience, your passion, your keen eye, and your endless good humor.

At every stage of this process, I've counted myself lucky to be part of the Penguin family. Thank you to the entire Dial team, who have invested so much in Darius: Lauri Hornik, Namrata Tripathi, Nancy Mercado, and Kristen Tozzo.

Thank you to my copyeditor, Regina Castillo, for a fantastic copyedit, and for including my first ever en-dash.

Thank you to my cover designer, Samira Iravani, for a gorgeous, unforgettable cover. I still get goosebumps every time I look at it. Thank you to Adams Carvalho for a stunning illustration. And thank you to Theresa Evangelista, jacket art director, for making it all happen.

Thank you to Mina Chung for making the book's interior as beautiful as the exterior.

Thank you to my rockstar publicist, Kaitlin Kneafsey, and to the entire publicity team, especially Shanta Newlin and Elyse Marshall.

Thank you to the marketing team, including Emily Romero, Erin Berger, Caitlin Whalen, and especially Hannah Nesbat. Persian Penguins Unite!

Thank you to the school & library team, headed up by Carmela Iaria, and to the sales team, led by Debra Polansky.

Thank you to the team at Listening Library, especially Aaron Blank, Emily Parliman, Rebecca Waugh, and the fantastic narrator, Michael Levi Harris, for bringing Darius to life in audiobook form.

Thank you to the entire production team. Holding this book in my hands has been a dream come true.

Thank you to Laila Iravani, Parimah Mehrrostami, and Iraj Imani, for filling gaps in my knowledge.

Thank you to Janet Reid, the most famous of fishes, for telling me to go forth and conquer.

Thank you to Brooks Sherman, for insight and inspiration.

Thank you to all the booksellers, librarians, teachers, and bloggers who have spread the word about Darius.

Thank you to my Northwest Tea Family: James Norwood Pratt, Valerie Pratt, Emeric Harney, Rob Russotti, Tiffany Talbott, and the late Steven Smith. Tea is love.

Thank you to Andrew Smith, Christa Desir, and Carrie Mesrobian, for encouragement, friendship, and advice.

Thank you to Arvin Ahmadi, Becky Albertalli, Laurie Halse Anderson, Sara Farizan, Nic Stone, Jasmine Warga, and John Corey Whaley for loving Darius as much as I do.

Thank you to Lana Wood Johnson, for keeping me sane. Thank you to Kosoko Jackson, for keeping me honest. Thank you to Lucie Witt, for keeping me laughing. Thank you to Mark Thurber, for keeping me grounded. Thank you to Ronni Davis, for keeping me going.

Thank you to Nae Kurth, who has been with Darius since the very beginning. (And what a draft that was!) Without you, this book would not be what it is.

Thank you to the Awesome Community, for always having my back; to Josh and Sheila, for all the Star Trek love; to Marcie, for tea and quiet conversation; to Alan and Pam, for mastering the art of chelo kabob; to Jeff, JoAnn, and Ava for fellowship and loin-girding; to Kristina, Rachel, and Q, for Sunday brunches and Taco Tuesdays.

Thank you to my parents, Kay and Zabi, for giving me the space to become who I am.

Thank you to my sister, Afsoneh, for always supporting me.

Thank you to my family. This one's for you.

And finally, thank you to you, the reader. May your place never be empty.